FINDERS KEEPERS

AN ABSOLUTELY GRIPPING PSYCHOLOGICAL
THRILLER

NATALIE BARELLI

Furphies Press
NSW Australia
v1b
Paperback ISBN: 978-0-6487312-5-2
eBook ISBN: 978-0-6487312-4-5

Cover design by Deranged Doctor Design

PART I

CHAPTER 1

I checked my horoscope this morning (Aquarius), like I do every day. I learned that Pluto is in exact conjunction with the sun and that I'll be reunited with something or someone that I thought was lost forever. It could be a friend, a piece of jewelry, or even a dream I thought was out of my reach. Whatever it was, it would be momentous.

Incredibly, I felt nothing. No impending sense of doom, no foreboding warning bells, not even the tiniest lurch in my stomach. I'd recently lost a pendant in the shape of a star my boyfriend Ben had given me—I don't usually accept gifts from boyfriends because I'd hate for them to think we might get serious—but I liked that necklace, so I was pleased with my horoscope because I thought it was about that.

Which meant that when my worst nightmare came to pass, I was completely unprepared.

It happens as I'm walking on Seventeenth Street, my tote bag swinging against my shins, Taylor Swift's "Begin Again" in my AirPods. It's early spring, the skies are blue, the air is clear, and the hem of my dress floats a little with every step. I'm on my way back from work—returns desk at a department store, seventeen-fifty an hour, two days a week—to meet Ben for a drink before we start our shifts at the restaurant. Would it have made a difference if I'd turned left instead of right and walked down another street? Unlikely. The book was already a bestseller, or at least well on its way. I would have found out about it sooner or later.

I glance at the window of Barnes & Noble, and I guess my body registers it before I do because from nowhere, a wave of nausea hits me.

It's the window display. It's taken up with dozens of copies of the one book. They hang from the ceiling at various heights, bright yellow covers flapping faintly like giant butterflies.

Diary of an Octopus.

An ocean rushes in my ears. *Don't be stupid, Rose. It's a coincidence, that's all.* It's just that I hadn't expected to see it, that stupid title that makes me want to punch my own face whenever I think of it, which is never. I push air down in my lungs as I tell myself I'm getting worked up over nothing. It's just a funny book, the autobiography of a famous person, someone who writes sketches for late-night TV shows. Whatever it is, it's nothing to do with me.

But I'm inside anyway, elbowing my way past people who grunt at me while I stumble through, aiming for a pyramid of that same book with its loud, yellow cover and its stupid title. I take one, my mouth dry. I'm already opening it, only vaguely aware I've sent a column of books toppling.

Dear Diary,

The day I turned thirteen, my dad told me and my mom that he was moving in with Mrs. L, his secretary at the meatpacking plant. The one with the two little boys and the husband who died last year in that accident.

I want to keep reading, I really do, but the words are flying all over the page, zooming in and out of focus and coming back together in the wrong order so it's gibberish now. I drop the book, and it lands on the floor, cover open, like a dead bird. I bend down to pick it up, but someone is already doing it. A woman's hand with short, buffed nails and a silver ring on her index finger.

"Well, somebody is a little overwhelmed!"

I look up. She has short, dark hair, a flat nose, and a plastic card hanging from her neck that reads, *Hi, I'm Sally.*

"Sorry," I mumble. I gather the books from the floor and stack them on the table, try to restore the pile to its original shape, but she shoos me away.

"Don't worry. We're used to it. Emily has a lot of fans."

"Emily?"

"God, don't you love her?" she breathes, eyes wide. Her eyes flick up, and I follow her gaze to a tall poster hanging from the ceiling, where a woman with long blond hair reads a copy of her own book. I only say *her own book* because it's her name on the cover, but by now I already know it isn't remotely *her own book.* I stare at the name until it comes into focus.

Emily Harper.

"Have you bought your copy yet?"

Sally points at the book I'm holding. I'm still struggling to breathe. I shake my head.

She checks her watch. "Well, she's here for another ten minutes, although there's a bit of a crowd at the cash register and a line waiting at the signing desk…"

"Signing desk?"

"You go and get your book signed and then come and see me. I'll get you fixed up at the cash register. You'll be okay. Just get in there before she leaves."

And finally, it dawns on me. That's why there are so many copies of the same book displayed in elaborate pyramids everywhere you look.

It's a book signing.

I glance at the line of people holding their copy of *my diary* against their chests.

Whatever it is, it will be momentous.

This is it. It's happening. The moment I've been dreading.

They're going to know what I did.

They're going to hang me.

CHAPTER 2

I walk like a drunk to take my place at the end of the line. I open the book to a random place, but before reading, I close my eyes for a second. *Don't go crazy. Don't be Scary Crazy Rose again, imagining things that aren't true. It's just a title, for Christ's sake. You're seeing what you expect to see, but it's not real. You can open your eyes now and read that page and laugh at yourself.*

I open my eyes.

Dear Diary,

Mr. B. took me and Toby home in his Corvette after school today, because it was raining and it was late. I sat in the front and Toby in the back and we dropped Toby off first because he lived closer.

Afterwards we stopped at the railroad tracks to wait for the train to pass. I pointed to my house. I told Mr. B. about the fish tank in our living room, about how when the train rolls past the water will quiver for a full minute. "To a goldfish, it must be like a tsunami," I said, and he smiled at me, like I'd just said something sweet but also clever, and I felt a gliding sensation in my chest.

He turned back to wait for the crossing, and I studied the side of his face, his jaw, strong and masculine, his lips the color of ripe plums, the little coarse hair growing over his Adam's apple. He turned to look at me again, and my heart exploded as the gap between us closed. He caressed the corner of my mouth with his thumb. "I love the way you think," he whispered.

I love him so much!!!

Love, Emily.

I slam the book shut. I'm going to be sick. Someone behind me nudges me forward and I look up. The line has moved on, and I'm holding it up. I walk a few steps and open the book again. I have to know if she included the last entries. I mean, everything else I can live with—maybe, just—but not the last entries.

"I've told her everything," he said, his arms around her shoulders. "I'm sorry, Emily. I love my wife. You and I, it was all a terrible mistake. You must see that, don't you?"

I cried for days, but I never spoke to him again, not the way we used to, I mean. Only in class. And not even then. But then I understood the betrayal, how I'd been used and discarded like a piece of trash...

I scan all the way to the end, and for a moment I think I really am crazy, and that's absolutely fine with me. I don't care if I've lost my mind, if I've become the kind of person who blows their nose in their socks and puts coffee mugs on their head, as long as *this is not my diary.*

Except it is, but not quite.

It's not just the last entry that's different. She's taken every one of my cringe-worthy little fantasies and wrote them like *they actually happened.* Mr. Bellamy never caressed the corner of my mouth with his thumb. I just imagined what it would be like if he did because I saw it in a movie.

I flick back more pages like a crazy woman. My phone

buzzes in my bag. I ignore it. It's probably Ben wondering where I am.

"Hello! What's your name?"

I look up, startled. I didn't realize it was my turn, and I'm completely unprepared. Although how I could have prepared for this moment—other than bring a gun—is unclear.

Emily Harper is waiting for me, a big sunny smile on her face, her hand outstretched. I study her face. *Do I know you? Do you know me?* I hand her the book, but my hand is shaking. She smiles a reassuring smile at me. "What's your name, honey?"

"This is my book," I stammer. I hadn't meant to, obviously. Otherwise, I may as well turn myself in to the authorities and be done with it. But Emily misinterprets what I said because she replies, "And thank you for buying it. I really appreciate it. Who do you want me to sign it to?"

I've tried to remember how often I named myself in the tens of thousands of words I wrote, and I can't think of a single time. I didn't like my name back then. I had planned to change my name to Amelie when I was older, after *Amelie*, the romantic comedy my mother and I watched fifty times, and also because I thought I looked like her. I didn't. I had the right hair, sort of, but that was about it. But in my mind, we could have been twins. So I would sign my entries with *A*.

Love, A.

Did I write *Rose* anywhere at all? Ever?

Someone clears their throat behind me. Screw it. I'm not taking any chances. I glance at the arrangement of purple flowers on the corner of the table.

"Iris," I say.

"Like the flower!"

I watch her closely while she writes, "To Iris" in big loopy letters, light-blue ink. I study her face, her impossibly long silky eyelashes, her soft blond wavy hair. She has a yellow butterfly above her right ear and a barrette above her left that spells out in rhinestones, *Let It Go*.

She signs her name below my dedication. Her signature takes up two-thirds of the flyleaf. *Emily Harper*, with some kind of blob at the end that takes me a moment to identify as a butterfly.

She hands it back to me. "Enjoy!" she sings then looks over my shoulder, ready for the next devotee.

I haven't moved. I've learned nothing about her, or why she is pretending to be the author of my diary, or how she got her hands on it, although I have a pretty good idea about that one.

"Thank you so much," she says, trying to move me on. I feel the line behind me swelling up like a blowfish, puffing its collective cheeks with impatience.

"But how—" Someone jostles me out of the way.

"There you are. You made it! Well done, you." Sally takes my elbow. "Come this way." I let myself be guided in a daze. When we reach the bank of cash registers, she takes the book from me and rings it up. I fumble for my wallet and pull out my Visa card.

How did she do it?

Except I know exactly how she did it.

"There you go!" Sally hands me my book in a paper bag. "Receipt's in there. Have a nice day!"

And now I'm outside. My phone buzzes again. I rummage through my bag with shaking hands. "I'll be right there," I tell Ben, and then I hang up.

CHAPTER 3

It's been two years since I left the laptop on the counter of a coffee cart at LaGuardia Airport. The only thing on that laptop was the diary I kept as a thirteen-year-old girl. One interminably long document in which I poured my heart out about my great, tortured, and unrequited love for my high school teacher. I say unrequited because while I was brimming with hope, I knew it was all in my head. Sort of. I did get confused sometimes, especially at the end. I should really say, *obviously* at the end. But that was the kind of girl I was back then. Weird, overly emotional, imagination on steroids. When I think of my thirteen-year-old self—which I never do —it doesn't feel like me, more like some weird distant cousin you spent time with on vacations because your parents said you had to, but who you never liked and laughed at with your real friends behind her back.

Until I lost the laptop, I carried it with me everywhere. So after the initial few weeks of horror, it slowly dawned on me that it might really be gone forever. That knowledge turned out to be unexpectedly liberating. Weeks turned into months, and I started to forget about the laptop altogether, and especially about what it contained. Fast-forward to today, and I can say that I never think about Mr. Bellamy anymore. I never think about his wife, or Miss Amy, or my old junior high school, or Pike Creek, Kansas. And if a memory from that time does pop into my head, I will put my palm out, metaphorically as well as physically, and say, *Go away*. To be fair, I'd been doing that successfully even before I lost the laptop, but losing it had brought it all back in a rush of emotion that was so brutal, it made me feel like I'd been holding the tide back with a piece of balsa wood. It was only a matter of time.

Months went by, nothing happened, and the tide receded. I felt freer than I'd ever felt. Like I'd sawed through my own foot and escaped the dungeon.

I was twenty-two years old with two part-time jobs and a boyfriend, Ben. I was happy—happy enough, anyway—and right there was my first mistake. Because let's face it, I have no right to be happy.

That's the part I always forget.

I'm frozen in place, standing outside Barnes & Noble. I can't just leave. Should I wait for Emily Harper? And then what? Punch her in the face? Tell her that I know she didn't write *Diary of an Octopus* because *I* did? She'll have me arrested before I have time to say, *About the murder… I can explain.*

I'm trying to figure out my next move when a compact SUV double-parks outside the front door of Barnes & Noble, blocking the right lane. A woman with masses of curly red hair steps out, leaving the hazard lights blinking. She has a long neck and long, skinny legs, and she's wearing a pink top and a pink bouffant skirt, the overall effect not unlike a pink flamingo. She's carrying her phone in one hand and a large take-out cup in the other, her bag looped around her elbow.

I wait a few minutes, wondering what to do now. I check my watch. When I look up, the same woman is coming out, this time carrying a cardboard box with both arms and using her chin to keep the top flap closed. Emily Harper follows closely behind, slurping from the straw in the smoothie cup. She adjusts a pair of gold mirrored Ray-Bans over her nose and stares down at her phone.

I follow right behind them.

"Hey, Tiff, sweetie, did you remember to get the flowers from Figs?" Emily says.

Tiff shifts the cardboard box so it's wedged between her body and the car.

"No. Sorry. I didn't have the time. I'll do it later."

"That's okay, I don't have to have them. It was just a thought."

Emily gets in the passenger seat while Tiff pushes the boxes into the back before walking around to the driver side. And then they're gone.

I'm meeting Ben at Tavern On Green. I was supposed to be there at four thirty, but I'm thirty-five minutes late. Ben and his business partner Liam own a French-slash-American bistro nearby where Ben is the chef and Liam does the front of house. I get an evening waitressing shift on Thursdays and Saturdays, which is how we met. And today is Saturday. And there's no way on earth I'm going to work today.

"Hi." I sit quickly opposite Ben at the far table, dropping my bag on the floor.

"Where were you? I was getting worried!"

"I got held up at work."

"Bad day?"

"Yes. Bad day. Really bad."

"What happened?"

"No, nothing, it's fine," I say, thereby contradicting myself. He shoots me a confused look. I'd sooner hammer nails in my kneecaps than tell Ben what just happened. What would I say anyway? *I did something very, very bad once. Wanna know what it is? Don't worry. You're about to find out. Everybody is.*

"Truly. I just got held up."

He waits for me to tell him the story. An angry customer at the returns desk, a stain on a dress that very likely wasn't there before. Someone wants a discount because they chose a size too small. The color of the shoes wasn't the same online. He knows these stories. I tell them often.

But I don't have it in me to make anything up right now, even though I'm usually very apt at it. I make things up often, little white lies, like telling Ben I can play the guitar when what I really mean is that I learned the chords to "The House of the Rising Sun" but I can't remember them, or that my parents died in a car accident.

"I was trapped in the back seat," I said. "I had to chew through my seat belt to free myself, crawl through a broken window, and walk two miles to the closest gas station. I was three years old."

All I'm doing is applying an Instagram filter to my life. Everybody does it. I do it because there's nothing remotely interesting about me. Unless you count the fact that I'm a psychopath, which I guess could be interesting. Although I haven't killed anyone in over nine years, so I like to think of myself as a *recovering* psychopath. Still, the urge to strike could come at any moment. And I suspect it's like riding a bicycle. Once you know how…

"I got you a G&T, but it went flat so I drank it." He grins. I love his grin. It's one of the things I love most about Ben, that he finds everything funny, and when he grins it makes

me want to laugh. Plus he's very hot. He has a nice mouth—
thin lips, but in a nice, precise way.

He turns away and signals the bartender, making a loop
with his index finger. The waitress brings a fresh G&T and I
knock it back immediately.

"You okay?" Ben asks.

"I'm fine." I wipe my mouth with the back of my hand.
The last thing I want is for Ben to think anything is wrong.
He'll be asking questions all night otherwise. *What is it? Talk
to me. Let me help.*

He glances down at the floor. "You dropped something."
He bends down, and I realize too late what it is. I dropped
my tote bag on the floor earlier, and the book slipped out.

He picks up the brown paper bag. The Barnes & Noble
logo is clearly visible on the outside. "You got a book," he
says, already sliding a fingernail under the corner of the
sticky tape.

My hand is already on his. "Don't."

"What?" He chuckles. "You don't want me to see what
you bought?"

"It's a surprise," I say.

He tilts his head at me. "You bought me a book?"

"Yes. But it's a surprise."

"You're sure you're okay, Rose? You look pale."

"I don't feel well. I'm sorry but I can't work tonight. I
have to go home. I'm really sick. But you go. You don't want
to be late."

He studies me for a moment. I look around the bar,
pretend to yawn, then remember too late how hard it is to
fake a yawn.

He frowns, checks his watch. "You can't do your shift?"

"I'm really sorry. I feel like hell."

"That's really late notice, Rose."

"I know. Sorry. It came over me just now."

He nods. "Okay. I'll make a call and figure it out." He stands, taps his pocket for his wallet.

"Don't worry, I'll get it."

"No, you won't," he says, but not unkindly—quite the opposite. I never have much money. I work as much as I need to pay my bills and that's about it. My only ambition in life is to make it through the day with minimum hassle.

I live in Brooklyn, the far-away part, in a small apartment that I share with a couple called Ryan and Ashley, both post-grad students at NYU. Actually, it's their apartment, as in they have the lease on it and I rent a room from them. As far as the authorities are concerned, I reside with my not-dead mother in New Jersey. Any mail I get goes to her house, which gives her an excuse to have lunch with me once in a blue moon, so she can give me the odd letter about some overdue library book or whatever. Let's just say I find those encounters excruciating, and I avoid them at all costs.

Meanwhile I live on Ryan and Ashley's furniture. I don't even have my own bed, and even though we have very specific rules about where we store our food, somehow mine always gets mixed up with theirs. Like the packet of macarons Ben gave me which I found opened and half empty. *Oh, was that yours? I thought Ryan bought it. You're sure it was yours? Okay, sorry, I'll replace it.* She never does, but that's probably because Ryan is really weird around me. He never speaks to me, ever, but I often catch him staring at me. Sometimes when I'm in my room, if I haven't closed the door completely, I'll see him, or one eye of him, through the gap in the door. I know that Ashley thinks I want to fuck Ryan, and frankly, if she could get further from the truth, she'd be on Mars.

Sometimes Ben stays over, but rarely. Ryan will be sprawled on the sofa watching reruns of *Big Bang Theory* and Ashley will be massaging his feet. Ben and I will end up bunking down in my bedroom, which is tiny, and we'll make out like a couple of teenagers because there is literally nothing else to do. The third time he stayed over, Ashley told me I'd have to pay extra for the hot water he uses when he showers in the morning, which made no sense considering I already pay half the bills even though I'm only a third of the occupants.

"You want to stay at my place?" Ben asks. He keeps a key slipped between the wall and the skirting in the hallway. When I stay over, I can let myself in before he comes home from work.

"No. Whatever I've got, I don't want to give it to you."

Just go, I think. *Let me go home.*

I have to read the book. I have to know what she left in. I have to know how much time I have before they come for me.

"I'll check in with you later," he says, bending to kiss my lips. "Go and curl up with a good book," he adds, tapping the paper bag.

My stomach lurches.

"I will," I say.

CHAPTER 4

I grab a cream cheese bagel on the way home. On the Q train, I unwrap the greasy paper, ball it up, and push it in the space between the seats. A tired-looking woman sitting opposite me gives a sideways, slightly disgusted look when I shove the bagel in my mouth in one go, using my fingers to push it all in. What she doesn't understand is if I don't eat now, I won't eat at all. Not once I open that book.

I've got forty minutes to go before I get home. I wipe my mouth with a tissue I find crumpled in the bottom of my bag. I was going to crack open the book and start from the beginning, read about my own life, in my own words, but when I tear open the paper bag, I find I can't do it. Not yet, and not in front of a carriage full of people. I need to be alone for this. In case I scream.

So instead, I get out my cell and google Emily Harper.

I've never heard about Emily Harper until today. I don't have any social media accounts because I prefer the handful of people who knew me in my past to forget I ever existed.

But to learn about Emily, I have no choice but to create an Instagram account since that's where she lives.

Emily has 112,947 followers, which makes me slide down my seat and groan into my phone. Are they all going to read *Diary of an Octopus*? Have they read it already?

Her Instagram bio states that *You Are Not Defined By The Mistakes Of Your Past*, and that you should *Forgive Others as You Forgive Yourself*, which, I have to say, as a philosophy to live by, I don't mind one bit. Under different circumstances, I might have learned a lot from Emily Harper. Also, I can see why it makes my diary absolutely on brand.

Emily writes long, confessional captions with titles like, *Why good people sometimes do bad things*, and *Forgiving yourself is the first step to making positive change in the world*. If only. I wonder if she has turned my "past mistakes" into a tale of redemption and forgiveness. Somehow, I doubt it.

I skip through the rest of her posts and study her photos. She looks so pretty, so warm and kind, it's hard to believe she's a liar and a thief, but here we are. And always with an arrangement of butterflies in her hair. Sometimes just one above her left ear, sometimes an entire crown of them, like a halo of wings. It's her trademark, because the butterfly is what emerges from the chrysalis, and sometimes your spirit has to be ugly before it can be beautiful.

I find more posts and videos of her on TikTok (I had to sign up to that too), where she'll sit with a girlfriend drinking Prosecco in gold flutes and talk about what it takes to become your better, happier self. Emily talks a lot about her past mistakes, the ones that made her semi-famous even before she became an influencer. I find an older interview she gave for *Darling* magazine where she explained why she fell in with the wrong crowd.

"I don't want to blame my parents," she said, "but I was left alone a lot."

Emily is the only child of John and Marjorie Harper. Her father is an attorney, and her mother is an interior designer. Emily grew up on the Upper East Side, attended the best schools, got the best education. But she was lonely, and the wrong crowd came along, made up of other very rich kids who also were left alone a lot. She was sixteen when one Saturday afternoon, one of her friends, a young girl named Violet, told their little gang about her parents' vacation house in some bucolic enclave of the Hamptons where they could have a party without telling the parents. They went there—on the train and on foot, which took some doing— and smoked joints and emptied her parents' liquor cabinets. Things got out of control, and someone threw up in Violet's mother's fifteen-thousand-dollar Birkin bag that had been left in her walk-in closet, while someone else used a Sharpie to draw a mustache on a painting by Jean-Michel Basquiat. A few hours later, when the haze had cleared, fearful that they'd be grounded for, like, a week, they decided to stage a robbery. It worked. They got away with it. The little gang got a taste for the life of crime, and after that, they would go to each other's houses when the parents were away and drink the bar dry, smoke joints, and take things that they had no use for and would have been theirs for the asking anyway, like a small Caravaggio or their father's entire collection of luxury watches.

Eventually, they got caught and paraded in the press as rich bling kids with too much money and zero sense of their own privilege. Also, they were called stupid since they were stealing from themselves.

They were sent to counseling and ordered to perform a few hours of community service, which in Emily's case consisted of volunteering with a Hot Meals program for the homeless.

"It was so humbling," Emily says in that interview. "It

was the life-changing experience of my life. For the first time ever, I realized the suffering that is out there, and that I could help, and that, you know, it's not even that hard. Most of the time, just a positive attitude is enough to change people's lives. I wish my parents had made me do things like that before. It opened the door to my better self."

Emily goes on to discuss the book deal she scored two years earlier: twenty thousand dollars to write about those past mistakes and how self-forgiveness changed her life. Then the deal fell through, although she doesn't mention if she had to repay the money.

"It felt repetitive to write about myself," she says, "since I've written so much already about my experiences. I didn't think writing my life story would bring anything new to my journey of self-forgiveness. But I'd promised my fans a book and I didn't want to disappoint them. So, I decided to turn my attention to writing fiction. I got the idea to write the imaginary diary of a young girl who doesn't realize until it's too late that she's being preyed upon. I decided to self-publish it. It was a better fit for me at the time. I'm very proud of what I've achieved."

And she should be, the interview tells us. Because *Diary of an Octopus* did so well on Amazon that Ms. Harper was able to score a publishing deal.

"I am a living testament of what hard work and self-belief can do for you. I say this to my fans every day: never, *ever* stop believing in yourself!"

I press my fingers against my temples and take a deep breath, then resume reading.

Interviewer: "You called your main character Emily, but it's not about you?"

Emily: "That's a very good question, thank you. You see, my fans are used to my confessionals. That's what they love about me. I write about myself all the time. I thought if I named the character anything else, it would be confusing to my fans."

I had to read that line a couple of times because I found it completely confusing, and I imagine the fans, all 112,947 of them, will absolutely assume whatever she describes in her book really *did* happen to Emily.

One reviewer called it bold and brave and incredibly original. A work for its time. A heart-wrenching fictional insight into the mind of a thirteen-year-old girl as she is being groomed by her English teacher, written in captions and journal entries. By the end, you'll want to reach inside those pages and grab her abuser by the throat.

I'm holding my phone in both hands, my elbows on my thighs. My right leg is shaking, and it won't stop. I sit up. Other passengers are glancing at me with suspicion from above their phones and Kindles and free newspapers. I have a sudden urge to roar at them. *You're scared of me? Good! I'm Scary Crazy Rose, don't you know?*

I put my phone facedown and rest my elbow against the window, put my hand over my eyes. When I wrote all these stupid diary entries, I never thought for one moment they might be interpreted as tales of abuse. To me, it was a love story. One day we would marry. I would be the next Mrs. Bellamy. We would live in the prettiest house in Pike Creek. He was in my mind every waking moment. He was the reason I got up in the morning and the reason I couldn't wait to go to bed at night, just so I could dream about him, about how his breath might feel against my neck, about how much he wanted me, about the torture he endured by not being able to have me. Those fantasies were vague, indistinct. I was only thirteen years old, and a naïve thirteen-year-old at that. There wasn't a whiff of sex in my diary. Nothing beyond the touch of his lips on the side of my neck.

Now I wonder what Mr. Bellamy will think if he ever

reads it. *When* he reads it. Because he will. And I'm not even thinking, *what will he think when he finds out what I did to his wife*, I'm thinking, *what will he think when he finds out everybody thinks he's an abuser?*

I want to bring my phone to my face and scream into it. *You know nothing!* I read on and come across a passage where Emily describes herself in the book as a "waif-child, summer-kissed hair, freckled-nosed…"

God. Really? I mean, heck, at this point maybe things will be okay. My hair is black and my skin, always pale, doesn't have a freckle in sight, just a vague bluish tinge. To be fair, I never described myself in *Diary of an Octopus*, but I find it interesting Emily Harper fashioned her main character (me) into some kind of Mary Ingalls replica from *Little House on the Prairie*, with big blue eyes and long blond hair and purity oozing from every pore.

"Even though this is a novel, I wanted my main character, Emily, to be true to who I am. That's why she *had* to be painfully innocent and naïve."

I'm trying to be grateful for these lies since they'll make it harder to link the book to me, but right now I can't summon anything other than a will to die. I am swaddled in a thick fog of horror at what Emily Harper has done, and I can barely breathe.

CHAPTER 5

My parents sold our house. Dad went to live with Mrs. L and acquired an instant family. This Kool-Aid family flavor has two boys, six and eight, with cute haircuts and dimpled cheeks. Maybe he always wanted a son, I don't know. I've been trying to remember but I don't think he ever said.

My mother and I moved into our new crappy house. It's smaller than our old one, far away from my school, no grass in the backyard, and on the other side of the railroad tracks. I hate my bedroom. I asked my mother why we had to move, and she says it's because she doesn't want to run into them in our old neighborhood. She says "them" like she's trying to get rid of a bit of phlegm in her throat. Where would you run into them? I said. It's not like we ever go anywhere.

I'm going to be sick. I'm in my room, the door firmly shut, sitting on the edge of my bed, and I'm only on the first chapter.

It's even worse than I remember. I mean, I stopped reading my own diary a long time ago. What was the point? I knew what was in it. But seeing it printed on the page is like an out-of-body experience. I have a sudden, visceral memory of being thirteen and spending Sundays with my dad, telling him tales of how horrible my mother was, even though she wasn't, but I figured that was a narrative he could relate to, a point of common interest between us. I'd invented so many stories about how *horrible* my mother was, I could have kept him on the hook for days. But instead of joining in, my dad would sigh and say, "Just try to make it work, honey, okay?"

"But she's so *horrible!*" I would cry, undeterred. I spun increasingly far-fetched tales of my mother's horribleness. (*She locked me in the cupboard under the stairs because I refused to take her side. She made me eat cockroaches for dinner. I had to scrub the kitchen floor with a toothbrush just to get breakfast which was a cold slop of porridge anyway, and you know how much I hate porridge.*) I lied so much and so often it became second nature. Then I lied some more, and eventually, I forgot I was lying.

Every Sunday turned into every second Sunday, then the occasional Sunday where I got to experience my dad being a dad to other kids who were happy and wore braces, which would set off a geyser of resentment in me. I longed for braces, the way some people long for freckles or curly hair. I fantasized that I would move in with my dad and take my rightful place in the Kool-Aid family, my teeth full of braces, but he said it was best if I stayed with my mother for now. So she'd have someone. We could revisit the arrangement later, he said.

It should go without saying we never revisited anything.

At one point I find myself biting the book just to stifle my screams, and when I pull it away, there's a clear crescent shape on both sides. I grab my pillow and scream into it.

And I haven't even started on the good parts yet.

· · ·

That year I fell in love with a man old enough to be my father. Now who could have seen that coming? Mr. Chet Bellamy—English teacher, seventh to twelfth grades—was so far removed from any other teacher we'd ever had, he may as well have come from Mars. My school was pretty ordinary, and our teachers were good, solid, well-intentioned people who believed in what they did but could only achieve so much with the resources at their disposal. Let's just say the going look at my school was "worn-out."

Then Mr. Bellamy showed up. Everyone wore casual clothes, but when he did it, he looked like he'd been plucked out of a mail-order catalog. He was the most handsome man I'd ever met in the flesh, with his full head of hair and his green eyes and his crooked smile. He was like a movie star in our midst, and it's fair to say all the girls had a crush on him, and some of the boys too. To top it off, he'd played baseball in college, so he volunteered to help coach the school team in his spare time. Everybody loved Mr. Bellamy.

He asked me to stay back after class once. This was not long after my father left, and my grades had fallen dramatically. I was distracted in class; I'd been late turning homework in, if I turned it in at all. He wanted to know why. We were sitting at one of the desks like we were both pupils, and that felt strangely intimate that he'd come down to my level. He was telling me that he didn't see how I could pass unless I did extra work to catch up, but I was only half listening. I kept looking at his long, dark eyelashes, at the five o'clock shadow on his jaw, at the way his mouth moved when he spoke. His top lip was swollen, like he'd been stung by a bee, and I had an urge to press down on it with my finger. He told me I had real talent, and it would be a damn shame if I failed. I felt myself grow hot at the compliment. He said I should consider doing the Creative Writing elective unit, that the extra credit would bring me back up. I said yes, obviously.

No one had ever told me I was good at anything before. It made my face hot.

That day, our knees briefly brushed against each other, and it made my skin tingle. I explained that my computer was dead and I had to use the ones at the library, as my mother refused to buy me a new laptop—which was a lie, obviously. I mean, there was nothing wrong with my computer, but I felt the need to explain why I'd been a disappointment, and while I was at it, cast myself as a kind of forgotten and neglected child, entirely dependent on the kindness of others.

The next day as I left the class, he held me back.

"Have this one," he said and handed me a silver rectangle, cool to the touch and heavier than it looked. "I upgraded. I don't use it anymore." It was important I had the right tools, he said. Because I had so much talent.

I took his laptop home and handled it like it was a precious treasure. He'd wiped everything from the drive, so it was like new. It felt too pristine to use for mundane things like my assignments, and anyway, I still had my own laptop for that, so I just kept it as it was. A shiny, unspoiled treasure.

I got to study poetry, which I'd never done before, and since I was going through my dramatic phase, I turned out to be uniquely well-suited for it. I wrote short stories that he encouraged me to submit to a writing competition for high schoolers. One day he kept me back after class to go over poems together, show me how I could have found a better, more "elegant turn of phrase." No one had ever used words like that in my presence before. It gave me a glimpse of what it must be like to be grown up, and for some absurd reason— or maybe because that week my mother and I had been watching *Little Women* and *Pride and Prejudice* on rotation—I pictured a teapot with an elaborate gold-and-red leafy pattern and matching cups and saucers. I imagined myself pouring tea for Mr. Bellamy while he frowned at the pages I'd written and occasionally gave a little nod. "Here," he'd say, tapping the spot with his pipe. "Now that's an elegant turn of phrase."

"You should write a journal," Mr. Bellamy suggested one day. "It's an excellent way to practice your writing skills."

It had only been a month since my dad had left, and it had happened so fast, I was still finding it hard to believe it had happened at all. The previous summer we'd spent a week-long family vacation in Pensacola, staying in a small cabin on the beach. I kept thinking about that vacation, about the three of us in the car, my father driving, laughing at my mother singing along—very badly—to The Carpenters or Diana Ross on the radio, and me in the back seat surrounded by snorkels and tennis rackets and beach towels and umbrellas, sometimes singing along too, mostly admiring the seashells I'd been collecting.

And then he left us.

I kept going back to that one moment when he walked out the door of our house and through a different door in another house in a different part of town. I'd ruminate on it like a cow regurgitating a ball of grass. Whenever I felt like I'd digested it, it came right back up again. I felt there must have been something I could have done to stop him, but that I'd missed my cue, so I replayed the scene in my mind over and over, desperately trying to catch the moment when I could have turned it all around.

I opened Mr. Bellamy's laptop, created a new document, and began typing.

The day I turned thirteen my dad told me and my mom that he was moving in with Mrs. L, his secretary at the meatpacking plant.

So I guess that's how it started.

CHAPTER 6

My mother would sit in my dad's old armchair and knit furiously while we watched old romantic movies from her collection of DVDs. Knitting was a skill she took up after my father left, and you got the impression she did it to keep her hands busy so she wouldn't go over to my father's new house and strangle the entire family. The first thing she knitted was a scarf. She knitted that scarf for a long time until one day, she looked down and noticed the pools of multicolored wool that were snaking around her feet and the bits of yarn that had deposited themselves everywhere on the carpet. By that stage, the scarf was fourteen feet long. She stared at it like she had no idea how it got there or what to do with it, so she tore off the yarn with her teeth, handed it to me, and asked me to put it somewhere she'd never see it again.

The next day, I wrapped it around the oak tree outside Mr. Bellamy's house. It was still there that last time I went there, soiled and tattered by the rain. I was so happy that he'd kept it. I was sure he knew it was me who'd done it, and that he left it there so he could think of me every time he went in or out of the house. The fact that he'd never taken it down was, to me, a clear and unassailable declaration of love.

Much later, after it was all over, after I'd done the terrible thing, begged to be sent away, and settled into my new school, my mother sent me a Christmas sweater. She'd improved immeasurably by then, as evidenced by the intricate snowflake and deer shapes scattered throughout. It should go without saying that I would have sooner stuck pins in my eyeballs than wear the sweater, so it lived at the bottom of my trunk under my bed. I did find a use for it though—I wrapped the laptop inside it and never pulled it out again.

In the early days at my new school, I'd lie in the dark and fantasize that I hadn't actually done the terrible thing, that it really was those men, those drifters who'd done it, just like the police said. Then I would imagine Mr. Bellamy appearing at my door, his green eyes glassy with tears, a deep crease between his eyebrows. I imagined him dropping to his knees and pressing my hands against his mouth. *I'm sorry. It's you. It's always been you. I can't live without you. I tried. God knows I tried.* He would then produce a small box (dark-red velvet) and open it to reveal a ring (a single diamond on a gold band, not too big, but still substantial). *Marry me.* These fantasies were like a drug. I was still an addict, even if I knew somewhere deep down it would never, ever happen. Some nights I wished it so hard, scrunching my eyes so tight that I'd wake up with red welts between my eyebrows and my eyeballs hurting like someone had punched them all night.

But mostly, I was terrified. *What did you do, Rose? Did you do something, Rose? Something bad?*

I was terrified he knew that it was me. He'd guessed because he knew me better than anyone else. I was terrified he would tell someone, and I'd be sent to prison for the rest of my life.

I'd long fallen out with my best friend Lola because of all

the weird, scary things I'd been doing in the lead-up to the *very bad thing*, but I was desperate to know if Mr. Bellamy had told anyone of his suspicions about me, so I called her anyway.

Lola and I used to be inseparable. When I think about Lola and me, before all the bad stuff, I picture us running. We used to run all the time. We used to say we could run faster than the wind. We'd run with the rain on our faces, we'd run down the hill, down the road, we'd run to the lake… we'd just run. And when we weren't running, we were laughing. There was a joke going around about a goat called Kevin—I've long forgotten the joke—but we could bring the other one completely undone with one raised eyebrow and one word. *Kevin*.

And when we weren't laughing or running, we were riding our bikes, jumping into creeks, climbing trees, fishing... We'd sit on thick branches up in the oak tree near her house and talk about who we'd marry—a hot fireman for Lola, a lion tamer for me—and if either of us felt particularly aggrieved that day, we'd catalog all the ways people misunderstood our genius. Sometimes she'd talk about the horrible things her sister Kimberlee had done, or I'd complain about my mom, my dad's new wife, our classmates, whatever. To be fair, Lola's grievances were way worse. Kimberlee was very pretty and a couple years older than Lola and nasty as hell. She'd cut her own favorite dress with her mother's sharp scissors and say Lola did it. Or she'd smash her own money box, hide the money she'd supposedly saved (which she'd stolen from Lola anyway), and accuse Lola of doing it. Their mother always believed Kimberlee. "It's because she's the pretty one," Lola would say. Lola had one eye that kept drifting inward, so it was quite hard to concentrate on what she was saying, but you got used to it eventually. Also, Lola wore glasses with thick black frames that made it look like you were staring deep into the eyes of a goldfish, which is how she got her nickname: Fish-eyed Lola. I always thought she was pretty and the nickname was mean, but we were at the age where children are at their most unforgiving. Nobody wants to hang out with the runt of the litter, and we two misfits naturally found each other. Crazy Rose and Fish-eyed Lola.

When she came on the phone, she sounded cold. "What do you want?" She probably thought I was going to apologize for my behavior toward her, maybe even tell her I was normal again, but instead I asked about Mr. Bellamy. Had he said anything about me?

She misunderstood why I was asking, which was understandable. I'd been following him around like a love-sick puppy for the best part of a year.

"What's wrong with you? His wife just died! He barely comes to class, and when he's there he cries all the time."

"But does he ever ask about me?" I said.

There was a pause. "You're sick," she said. Then she hung up.

Then about four months after I did the terrible thing, Lola called to tell me that Mr. Bellamy and Miss Amy had gotten engaged and would be leaving the school. I was so shocked I couldn't reply.

"Did you hear what I just said, Rose? Mr. Bellamy and Miss Amy! Can you believe it? She's like, twenty-three, and he's like a hundred years older than her."

He's thirty-seven, I wanted to shout. *And thirty-seven isn't old, not when you're a man, not when you're Mr. Bellamy.*

I knew she only rang because she thought the news would upset me. And she was right.

"I have to go." I hung up and chewed on a thumbnail, picturing Mr. Bellamy and Miss Amy in the teachers' lounge.

I imagined him on one knee. *Marry me.* Miss Amy tearing up, then nodding violently. *Yes!*

I ran to the bathroom and threw up.

Time went by, I resolved to move on. I became tougher, harder, more like the true me. I joined the drama club, I got a boyfriend, a romance that lasted a little over a year and ended without fuss or tears. My mother moved on with her life, which was the one good thing I achieved by leaving Pike Creek. A couple years after I left, my mother, who had never gone farther than Florida, went on a cruise to Mexico. She returned with a tan, a perm, and Albert. Six months later she sold up, left Pike Creek, and moved to a small town in New Jersey where she and Albert married.

Mr. Bellamy receded from my mind. I never opened the laptop anymore. By the time I got to senior year, I'd stopped charging it altogether. When I moved out of the dorm, I lost the charger.

I still held on to it, just in case I ever got the knock on the door. *We're investigating a cold case. The death of a Mrs. Charlene Bellamy. Your name came up. Do you have a minute?* I held on to it because still, somehow, in my screwed-up brain, if I could explain, maybe they'd understand. Maybe they'd let me go.

The day I moved to New York, I lost the laptop at LaGuardia Airport. I remember very clearly packing my things and coming across it. I hadn't touched it in years. I considered getting rid of it altogether, but first I'd have had to get a charger, charge it up, delete the document, wipe the drive. I didn't have time for that, so I decided to take it with me, for now. Ironically, I packed it in my carry-on because I kept hearing stories of lost luggage, and I didn't want to take any chances. Then on arrival, my mother was late picking me up. I was standing next to an unattended coffee counter, searching for my phone, and without thinking I pulled out the laptop, which was still wrapped in the Christmas sweater, and put it on the counter. Then I heard my name. I looked up to see my mom, her hand high in the air. It was only when we were in the car that I realized with a lurch of horror that I no longer had the laptop with me. I made Albert stop the car and I searched through the trunk, but I knew I'd left it behind. I made them drive back to the airport while I chewed on my fingernails, my heart thumping in my chest like someone punching me from within. I ran inside to the same unattended coffee cart, but it was gone.

Days went by. I called the airport four times a day, every day. *Have you found a laptop?* And every time the same reply. *No. Have you tried lost and found?* And I'd scream into the phone, *Yes! Obviously!* and throw the phone against the wall.

That was almost two years ago, and I never got it back. Eventually I forgot about it.

Kind of.

At least Emily Harper changed the ending—not that mine was much of an ending anyway. She kept the second last entry more or less the same. The one where I truly lost my mind.

Dear Diary. Today I'm going to see her.

I try to think. In my version did I write, *see her?* Or did I write, *kill her?* I can never remember. Anyway, then it goes,

I'm going to do it! I'm so excited, Mr. B. and I will finally be together! He loves me! OMG!!! HE LOVES ME!!! I've never been so happy in my life. He will be at the school baseball game tonight. (He's one of the assistant coaches because he's so PERFECT!) I'm going to go to see her and tell her about us because I know that's what he wants. He really really loves me and I'm the only one who can make her understand. After tonight, we're going to be together!!!!

Love, Emily.

Emily's version finishes with Emily going to see her teacher's wife, just like I did, to tell her they were in love. So far so good.

And that's where the similarities end.

In Emily's version, when she knocks on the door of his house, it's him who opens the door. She's shocked. He's supposed to be at the game, that was the plan. He goes to stand in the middle of the living room and puts his arm around his wife's shoulders. She's very pretty, his wife, but not as pretty as Emily. And of course, a lot older.

"I've told her everything," he says. And Emily is confused. She thinks he means that he told her about him and Emily, so why the arm around his wife's shoulders? And why does *she* look triumphant?

"I'm sorry, Emily," he says. "I've realized I'm still in love with my wife. You and me, it's over."

So Emily goes home, flings herself on her bed, and sobs into her pillow. She decides she's going to forget about Mr. B. She's going to banish him from her mind and show Mr. B. that she can live without him, which I could have told her is harder than it looks. But as she dries her tears, she realizes that if she lets her pride get the better of her, Mr. B. will do it again to other girls, and she can't, in good conscience, let that happen. Brave Emily emerges from the ashes of naïve/innocent Emily. Brave Emily understands now that the relationship was abusive, and that it's not her fault. So she sits at her little desk in the corner and writes a letter to the school principal.

The day I turned thirteen my dad told me and my mom that he was moving in with Mrs. L...

Full circle. Beautiful, soaring, hopeful, very sad and yet uplifting and so different from my own ending to be unrecognizable. *Yes!* Of course, my version didn't have an ending per se, although Mrs. Bellamy might have argued otherwise.

My final entry? The one I wrote the next day, shaking with shock and fear? It didn't make the cut. Maybe it was too short.

I did it again. I'm a monster. I'm going to hell.

Emily Harper doesn't know these people in my journal. There are no clues, no mention of Pike Creek, Kansas, not the name of my old school, nothing. It was my journal, a place where I poured my heart out. I had no need to spell out where I lived or where I went to school. Chet Bellamy is just Mr. B., Miss Amy is Miss A., and his wife is just that, his wife.

But there are other things. There's the description of my father leaving us for Mrs. L and her two boys. The fact they both worked together at the meatpacking plant. Then there's Fish-eyed Lola who has become someone called Laura and who was jealous of Emily. There's the heart I carved on top of my desk, now with *Emily* and *Mr. B.* intertwined within.

And that's nothing.

I did it again. I'm a monster. I'm going to hell.

The worst thing, the thing I can't stop thinking about, the thing that is making my stomach curl with dread, is that Emily Harper has my laptop.

I hit my forehead with my fists and bite my knuckles until they are rimmed with bruised indentations. I do that for a long time until I stop, panting.

There's only one thing I can possibly do right now.

I have to get that laptop back.

CHAPTER 7

My mother used to say if you want to make friends, make yourself useful. I stay up all night trying to figure out how to make myself useful enough to get inside her apartment and take my laptop back. That's if she still has it, obviously. Maybe she's destroyed it. I mean, that's what I would have done in her shoes. And heck, if that's the case then that's a fine thing because that means there's no *hard evidence* tying me to the murder.

But I have to be sure. Because if Emily turns the laptop over to the police? I'm savvy enough to know they can identify when the document was created and by whom, and of course Mr. Bellamy will tell them he lent me that laptop. The police will be able to ascertain, beyond a shadow of a doubt, that the second last entry was written a few hours before Mrs. Bellamy was murdered, and the last entry was written the following morning. They'll talk to my mother who will tell them all sorts of incriminating things about me (she always struggled to tell the difference between fantasy and reality—also, she had a black heart). And they'll talk to Lola who will regale them with stories of how much I'd changed that year, how I'd started to wear tons of makeup and I'd show up to school with inches of black kohl around my eyes and blush on my cheeks and bright shades of lipstick on my lips, how I'd stopped playing the games we used to play because I suddenly declared them childish and Lola would say to me, "What's wrong with you? You're so up yourself, Rose!" And I'd smile benignly, and in a thoughtful tone I'd say, "When you're older, you'll understand." Which, it should go without saying, used to annoy her no end. But back then I was gifted with all the immaturity of childhood and none of its charms.

If Emily still has my laptop, then I will find it. And then I'll destroy it. I'll take it apart and burn it. I'll stick it in the microwave. Then there'll be nothing tying the book to me.

I wrack my brain trying to remember why I didn't destroy the laptop before, and all I can think is that I had some kind of twisted logic. There was a reason in keeping it once, one that made sense to me, which went something along the lines of: when the police came for me—and they would, it was just a matter of time—breaking the door down in the middle of the night with their bright flashlights on their helmets and their weapons pointed at my head, I would be on my knees holding up the laptop like a white flag, because I thought if I could show them, if I could explain, I could make them understand.

Which is, by far, the stupidest belief I've ever held, and that's saying something.

But I can't think about that right now. I need to stay focused on getting the laptop back. Then at least I'll have a chance. They'll have nothing more tying me to Mrs. Bellamy's death than they've had so far. Which is nothing.

· · ·

It's Sunday morning. I stayed up all night, alternating between checking what Emily put in the book with my fingers splayed over my face and reading about her online. Then I saw she has another book signing today at an independent bookstore called *Next Page* on Broadway.

And that's where I will be, and I'm going to make myself useful.

My plan goes like this:

I assume Tiff will come and pick her up the way she did yesterday. So I'll catch her before she has a chance to go inside and send her away on an errand. I'll say Emily sent me, and she wants her to buy flowers from... Figs, was it? Yes, that's it. Figs. I'll tell her that Emily will make her own way home, and then when she comes out, I'll be there, waiting. I'll tell her how much I enjoyed her book. Emily will be looking for Tiff, and I'll say something like, is everything okay? Is something wrong? And I'll offer to get her an Uber because I'm such a fan, and that way I'll get her address. That's all I want. Her address. Then I'll show up with some story or other and get in and get my laptop.

Oh my God, this is so bad. Apparently I can kill people at the drop of a hat, but coming up with a strategy to retrieve my own laptop is beyond me.

Think, Rose. Focus. Of course, Tiff will call Emily wanting to know about this change of plan. So when I get my book signed, I'll find a way to hide Emily's phone. She had it on the table next to her yesterday. She'll probably do the same today. I'll put it on silent and hide it under a book or something.

I can do this. All I want is to make friends and get her address. It's fine. I can do this. *Icandothisicandothisicandothis...*

Then I see that Ben texted me this morning.

You feeling better? Wanna come over? I'll cook you some eggs.

I stare at the text. Once upon a time, if the guy I was

seeing texted me something like that, I would have replied, *Dude, I hate eggs. Don't contact me again.* I don't hate eggs. But I don't let anyone get close to me. I have no intention of entering into a serious relationship. I prefer my own company. Also I might kill them. You never know.

But with Ben, it's different. I get little butterflies in my stomach when Ben texts. He's the nicest guy I've ever met. He and Liam are generous with the staff. They pay well, make sure the tips are shared equally, and even pay for an Uber to take us home because a girl at night in this city... And that's not even the point. Whenever I set eyes on him, my first impulse is to take his clothes off. Also, he cooks great eggs.

So yeah, it's kind of a red flag. Psychopaths don't play house and have babies. Actually they probably do, but not this one. I'm not stupid. I know I have to pay for what I did, one way or another. I must never be truly happy. Someone like me settling down with someone as truly good as Ben would create a really bad fault line in the universe. There'd be earthquakes and floods and locust plagues for days. I should really end the relationship. I tell myself this often. But then I think, what the heck. What's another day?

Anyway, not today. I have work to do today.

I type back. *Still sick.*

Ok. Take care x

I respond with a thumbs-up emoji and turn off my phone.

An hour later I come out of my bedroom dressed and ready to go out as Ashley emerges from hers. She leans against the doorjamb, her bare foot on top of the other, bright-red toenails. She has a sarong loosely tied around her chest, the knot between her breasts. Behind her, Ryan's naked foot is sticking out from under the bed covers. Throw in the tousled hair, the flushed cheeks, the smudged eyeliner… They've just had sex. I get it.

"We have to put your rent up," she says. "It's because of inflation."

"Inflation?"

"We can't keep up with the costs of running this place."

I bite the inside of my cheek. In every photograph taken of me, my mouth is puckered and twisted to the side, making me look like I smoke a hundred packs a day and chew tobacco in between. I've tried to stop doing it, but I haven't had any success so far.

"But I pay half the bills," I say. "What other costs do you have?"

"Don't you watch the news, Rose? Everything is going up. The cost of living is going up. Heating is going up. Electricity is going up. Food. Everything."

"I know that, but—"

"Three twenty a week. Starting next month."

Behind her, Ryan snorts a breath in, the way people do when they've forgotten to breathe in their sleep.

"Coming, babe!" Ashley calls over her shoulder. She smiles coyly, lightly touching the base of her throat. "So impatient…"

"I think it was a snore," I say.

"I'm sorry?"

"I don't think he was calling for you. I think he just snored."

"Oh, so you've got ultrasonic hearing all of a sudden?"

"No, I just meant—"

"Three thirty. It was going to be three twenty, but now it's gone up."

"Three thirty?" I blurt.

"That's right. I charge extra for ultrasonic hearing."

"How am I supposed to get that much money every week?"

"Sell your ass, Rose. I'm sure you'll be very good at it."

She doesn't slam the door exactly, but she sure shuts it firmly.

At the bookshop on Broadway, I buy another copy of my own book. I smile confidently at the cashier.

"You're getting it signed?" he asks, holding up a paper bag in one hand and the book in the other.

"I certainly am," I chirp. "I can't wait."

I take my place at the end of the line, holding my own journal against my chest, but this time I copy the way the other women do it, hugging it like it's a precious baby rather than a dead cat. I almost falter when I reach the front of the line. I remind myself that she knows nothing, that she's a liar and a thief, and that she doesn't care who she hurts.

"Hi," I say when it's my turn then watch for a reaction, an indication that she recognizes me, but I get nothing. Emily beams her lovely, warm smile at me.

"Hello," she says sweetly. "Thank you so much for waiting."

It's the same setup as yesterday, although the table is more flimsy. A trestle table someone put there for the occasion. She has her little pile of books, her pens, her glass of water, same vase with the purple irises. As I hand her the book, I bump my hip hard against the table. I meant to make it look like I'd tripped, but somehow I forgot that part, so I just ended up shoving my hip against it like I was practicing my Latin moves. The table shudders enough to send the vase toppling.

"Oh no!" Emily cries. She's stood up quickly to get away from the water dripping to the floor.

"I'm so sorry." I hadn't counted on the vase toppling over, but in a way, it's even better. I rummage through my bag for something to mop it up with but I have nothing, not even a tissue, so on impulse I take off my cardigan and use that. It's one of my favorites, pale-green cotton with a scoop neck bordered by little green-and-white-striped bows. I wore it today because I thought it made me look painfully naïve and innocent.

"Hey! That's okay, sweetie," Emily says, crouching to pick up her wet pens.

"No, really. I'm such a klutz," I say. Lots of people are helping now. They've come out of the line and are picking up books, which they air-dry by flapping them in the air.

"Are you okay?" they ask Emily, their hands hovering, their eyes scanning her body for signs of damage as if I'd kicked her in the ribs and then stomped on her head.

"I'm okay," Emily assures them. She looks at me. "What about you? You okay, honey? You sure? You didn't faint, did you?"

"I don't know, maybe," I say.

"Oh, sweetie. Do you want to sit down? Can we get a chair, please? Hello?"

"No, I'm fine now. I don't know what happened. I'm just so nervous!" I stand, my sodden cardigan in my hands, and I realize I haven't done the one thing I set out to do, which was to put Emily's cell phone to silent. I see it now on the table. I pick it up and pat it dry with the hem of my cardigan so I can surreptitiously flick it to vibrate, although by this stage nothing I do can be called surreptitious. Emily is frowning at the phone and then at me. I gaze down at what I'm wearing. I wouldn't have worn it if I'd known I'd be taking off my cardigan. It's just cheap nylon and it's not even white anymore, more like gray, and there are faded yellow rings under the armpits so I look like I've just crawled out of a donation bin.

"Sorry about the mess," I say, putting the phone back face down on the table.

Everything is more or less back to normal now. Store staff have retreated to whatever they were doing, and the women behind me have gone back to an orderly line.

"So, where were we?" Emily breathes. She's smiling again, like she wants me to know everything is fine, it's no big deal. She blows a lock of hair out of the way and opens the book to the fly page. "Who should I make it out to?"

"It's Iris. And I'm so sorry. Really, really sorry."

"That's okay, honey. Happens to the best of us."

She signs the same way as yesterday, with her nice pen and a flourish and a butterfly blob at the end. She hands me back my book. I press it against my chest and leave, delivering one last heartfelt apology.

Outside, I don't know what to do with my sodden cardigan, so I shove it in the trash then sit on the bench at the bus stop and wait. The signing is due to end at three, and it's 2:45. At 2:55 precisely, the same compact SUV arrives, double-parks, flicks on its hazard lights, and the same woman as yesterday gets out of the car, keys in hand, a large paper cup in the other.

"Tiff?"

Tiff stops. She pushes her gold sunglasses to the top of her head with a beautifully manicured hand and studies me. "It's not Tiff."

What? Oh God. I've got the wrong person. There are so many rich, beautiful, upper-class women driving SUVs around here, I can't tell one from the other. "I'm sorry. I thought you were someone else."

I'm about to move away when she says, "It's *Tiffany*."

Of course it is. "Oh, right. Sorry about that. Emily sent me."

"I figured that. She's the only one who calls me Tiff, and just so you know, I prefer Tiffany. So what can I do for you?"

I take a breath. "Well, Emily wants you to go to…" The name of the flower store has vanished from my mind. I stand there, one finger on my chin, eyes skyward, and I'm thinking, *Oh, well done, Rose. Heck, this is going to be over before it starts.* But then it comes to me.

"Figs Florist. That's it. She wants you to go there and buy flowers. Like you did last time. But lots of them. I mean, even more of them than last time."

"Now?"

"Yes, please. It's important."

"Why? She wanted them for the signing, and it's almost over."

I shrug. "I don't know. I mean, that's what she said."

I don't know what I was thinking when I came up with this harebrained idea, but I think we can all agree I need my head examined. Obviously, this was never going to work. Maybe I should turn around and go home while there's still time, before Tiffany signals a passing police car.

She frowns at the entrance to the bookshop. People are walking out holding their paper bag under their arm. Tiffany reaches into her bag, and I just know she's going to pull out her phone, and sure, I set Emily's to silent, but what if it's face up? She'll see Tiffany is calling. I'm so stupid, I should just shoot myself in the head and be done with it.

I put my hand on her arm. She looks at me in shock, flicks her arm away from my touch. "What are you doing?"

"She's in a meeting with her publisher," I say.

"Her publisher? You mean Jerome?"

I nod. "Yes, Jerome. She doesn't want to be disturbed.

She was very clear about that. She really needs the flowers, and she absolutely doesn't want to be interrupted."

Tiffany narrows her eyes at me. "Sorry...who are you again?"

"Iris. I'm Emily's friend." I glance at the door again. My heart is racing. In my mind, it was going to be over in seconds. Ask Tiffany to go get the flowers so I can be there when Emily needs a ride, so I can be *useful* to Emily. I stand there for what feels like a decade while Tiffany stares at me, brow furrowed.

"Anyway," I say, fake relaxed, brushing my hair out of my face. "The flowers. Emily said it was urgent."

Tiffany hesitates, then she puts her phone back in her bag and hands me the paper cup. "Okay, well... Please tell her I'll drop them off at her place."

I nod, try not to skip with joy all the way to the trash can where I drop what turns out to be a very green smoothie into it. It runs all over my cardigan.

CHAPTER 8

A decade passes. Or that's what it feels like. I'm beginning to think she's left via a back door or something, but finally she comes out. She looks like a movie star with her gold mirrored sunglasses and her enormous leather handbag looped around her forearm, effortlessly elegant in her white shirt and ripped jeans, a butterfly farm in her hair.

There are a few stragglers with her, and she chats amiably, but her eyes dart around. I wait until the women move on with a cheery goodbye, a cheery thank-you, even a kiss on the cheek, and only then do I take a step forward.

Except there's another young woman now. She has come out behind her, and she is carrying the cardboard box. My heart sinks. Of course Emily would have an endless supply of helpers. I will be of no use to her, which means that my plan, flimsy and riddled with holes as it is, is about to fall in a heap. I plaster on a smile anyway and walk up to them, then recognize the second young woman as one of the store staff who helped put the signing table back together.

"Emily? Hi! I'm so sorry about before."

Emily stares at me over her sunglasses.

"The klutz," I say.

She smiles. "Ah, yes. The nervous mouse."

I laugh. It comes out high-pitched and weird, just like a mouse. I turn to the young woman. "You look like you've got a lot to carry. Can I help?" I smile broadly, the smile of the needy, but it doesn't matter—she can't wait to get rid of the box. She immediately hands it to me and says a quick goodbye to Emily before going back inside.

Emily tilts her head at me. "Iris."

"That's me. Good memory." I put my book on top of the box and hoist it against my chest. It's heavier and bulkier than I'd expected. "I'll take this to your car if you like. It's the least I can do."

She sighs, looks around. "The thing is, my PA was supposed to pick me up, but she's not here."

"Oh, really? That's too bad." With some difficulty, I wedge the box under my arm so I can use my phone with my free hand. "Let me help. Where are you going?"

"Why?"

"I'll get you an Uber. It's the least I can do. Where to?"

"You want to pay for an Uber to take me home?"

"Yes, absolutely. It's the least I can do," I repeat for the third time, and I'm thinking, God, I hope she lives not far from here. I so cannot afford anything right now, especially not an Uber ride to Connecticut or New Jersey or even the Upper East side.

"Iris! That's so sweet of you! But there's no need. I'll get it. But thank you."

No. She can't get it. I need her address. I need to put it in my phone. I need to order her an Uber.

But it's too late. She's already tapping on her own phone.

"But thank you, Iris," she says, moving to take the box from me. "You're very sweet."

"No!" I snap, pulling the box away from her grasp like

48

it's mine. I remind myself of my plan. I am a fan, a big fan. A stan fan. I want to tell her how much I loved her book, and how I would do anything for her because I'm such a super fan, but I find that I can't. I'm trying—I've got the words ready to go, *I loved your book so much!* But my mouth refuses to play along.

"I'm so sorry about before," I say instead. "The water, all that. I feel terrible. Was anything damaged? I can pay for it. Did you lose any books?"

She flaps a hand. "It was fine, just a bit of water, that's all. No lasting damage."

How disappointing. "Well that's a relief. Can I at least pay for your Uber? I'll feel terrible forever otherwise. I won't be able to ever sleep again from the embarrassment." I smile to show I mean it, but in a nice way. Definitely not in a I'm-going-to-kill-myself-if-you-don't-let-me way.

She shakes her fingers through her hair as she looks around, for Tiffany, presumably. Then she taps something on her screen and drops the phone back in her bag. "Well. That's very kind of you, Iris. If you're sure…"

My heart does a little dance. "Yes, absolutely. I'm very sure." I balance the box on my thigh and order the Uber at the same time.

"Why don't I take that off you," she says.

"No, no, really, I've got it."

She laughs as I stumble, my thumb hovering over my screen. "Where to?" I don't look at her in case she catches the eagerness on my face.

She tells me an address in Hudson Yards, and I do a mental air punch. *Yes! I've got it!* Emboldened by my success, I tell her how much I *loved* her book.

"Really?"

I swallow the bile that's rising up my throat. "Really," I say. I almost add, *I loved it so much I could eat it, see?* Then picture myself tearing off the paper bag with my teeth and eating the pages one by one. *That's how much I loved it!*

"You read it already?"

Oh, well done, Rose! Caught out at the first hurdle. "On my Kindle. I couldn't put it down. I'm a massive fan."

She laughs and pushes her glasses to the top of her head. "You can't be. I'm nobody! I mean, I've got a book…" She does a funny little sideways shake of the head, like *okay, maybe that's a big deal.* "But I'm no one, really." Then she adds, "Compared to others, I've only got a very small social media presence."

"That's not true. I mean, you've got a massive presence, and you're growing every day. There are tens of thousands of people who are finding out about you. You help so many people."

"You think so?"

"Absolutely!"

"Thank you. I appreciate it."

I sure hope so. I'm giving myself heartburn here. "Not at all," I say. "I truly mean it." But I'm on a roll now. I can't stop talking. I tell her that she's helped me so much, that I think she's so brave—it's a word that comes up often in her posts—and that after everything that happened to her, the way she turned her life around, she makes people like me believe in themselves (another winner). She nods gravely as I speak, makes quiet little comments throughout like, *Good, that's what I'm hoping for… It's so important for young girls… Yes, self-forgiveness, so critical.* I explain that I, too, have done bad things in the past, and her advice has been the catalyst to my journey of self-love.

"What did you do?" she asks, curious.

Dear Diary,

Today I'm going to kill her.

Love, A.

"Nothing," I say. "Just kids' stuff."

"Like what?"

I shrug. "Nothing much."

Thankfully, the Uber arrives before she asks again. She opens the back door and turns to me, extending her arms to take the box.

"Would you like me to come with you?" I ask, trying to keep the note of desperation out of my voice. "I could bring this upstairs to your apartment. It's quite heavy."

"There's no need, Iris. You've been very sweet, thank you."

"It's right near where I live," I say quickly. "I was going this way anyway."

"Oh? Where do you live?"

I glance at the screen on my phone that still shows the map with her address. "Thirty-fourth Street?"

As we ride toward her place, me with the box on my lap, I wrack my brain for something to say, but there's no need. Emily is focused on her phone. "I wonder where Tiff disappeared to," she muses.

"I'm sure there's a simple explanation," I say.

"Maybe, but it's not like her at all."

I try to think of ways I can stop her from calling Tiffany. I'm considering taking the phone from her, telling her she spends too much time on the screen and do you know what that does to your retinas? But Emily isn't calling anyone. She's scrolling through her status updates. So far Tiffany hasn't called Emily either, as far as I can tell, which means she's on her way to Figs Flowers or whatever. I remind myself that I'm actually a very good liar. Everything is going according to plan.

We ride in silence all the way to her building. When I get

out of the car, she doesn't try to take the box from me. She doesn't ask if I want to come up. She stops outside her door and punches numbers on the keypad. The door clicks open and I follow her inside, my heart bursting with joy. In fact, I'm so happy right now, I could kiss her.

Just kidding.

For a moment I'm tempted to tell her she should be careful who she lets in her apartment, that there's such a thing as a wolf in sheep's clothing, and that she doesn't know what some people are capable of.

But I don't.

CHAPTER 9

I've seen photos of Emily's apartment on Instagram, and she often will film a video in her living room. I know the basic layout. It's two stories—living-dining-kitchen downstairs, bedrooms and bathrooms upstairs. It's not very big, but it's a gorgeous space, airy and light, with pale timber floors and walls of exposed bricks and lots of green plants in pots that hang from the very high ceiling, a couple of small palm trees in clay pots, and lots and lots and lots of butterflies in impossible colors pinned to the wall like they're in flight or preserved in glass boxes. They're fake, of course, but still.

Then there's the enormous terrace which you access via french doors framed by two large windows, and more plants out there too. It's beautiful, no doubt about it. Like an oasis.

"You're okay, Iris?"

I smile. "Yes. It's amazing. I love it." My eyes scan the room (Emily Harper is surprisingly messy), taking in the coffee table (a dirty paper cup, piles of magazines...), the sofa (cream-colored, plush, with piles of colorful cushions on top). A half dozen shopping bags from Bergdorf Goodman are on the floor, all empty as far as I can see. My eyes move to the dining room table. It's crammed with things: jars of face creams, bottles of lotion, a half-empty bottle of vodka, lipsticks, mascara, palettes of eyeshadow, a full bottle of Xanax which I'm sorely tempted to swipe but don't, a magnifying round mirror, a video camera on a miniature tripod, a lamp in the shape of a donut, more magazines, stacks of unopened bills, more potted green plants in various states of neglect, and then I see it.

My laptop. It's partly hidden by a yellow manila envelope and whatever other crap she seems to collect, but it's definitely my laptop.

I feel my chest rise and fall with excitement, and I have to will myself to calm down. I put the box on a corner of the table, pushing a camera out of the way.

"Can I use the bathroom?"

Emily has a finger hooked in the back strap of her sandal, using the table for support. "Sure, it's that way." She jerks her chin toward the corridor we came from. Her sandal lands on the floor with a delicate plopping sound. "On the left. Last door."

"Thank you." I lock the door and sit on the toilet lid. I tell myself to breathe. Remember the plan: distract her, grab the laptop, get out of there.

I glance around the tiny room for something to use as a distraction. There isn't much, but I don't need much. I pick up a ceramic soap dish shaped like a seashell, hold it up high, then let it drop. It smashes on the tiled floor.

I open the door. "Oh, no!"

Emily arrives. "Oh, sweetie." She clicks her tongue at the mess. "What is it with you?"

"I have very poor hand-eye coordination."

She sighs. "Clearly."

"Was it expensive?"

"I don't know. I don't think so."

"Oh, good. Well…" We both stare at the fine little shards of ceramic. I bite on a fingernail. Neither of us says anything, and I hear the beat of my heart in my ears.

"I'll clean it up," I say finally. "Do you have a dustpan?"

"That's okay. I'll do it."

My heart leaves my ear canals and returns to my chest where it does a little jig. I follow her back to the kitchen where she retrieves a small dustpan from under the sink. I don't dare speak in case she changes her mind and makes me do it. The moment she has her back turned, I am at the dining room table, my arm shooting out, my hand shoving the envelope aside, inadvertently sending it flying to the floor.

But I've got the laptop! I'm already swinging on my heels, about to run to the front door, except…it's not my laptop. It's not even that close. It's just silver, that's all.

"There. No harm done," Emily says behind me. I've put the laptop back where it was, and I'm picking up the manila envelope from the floor. "Don't worry about that," she says. "My cleaner will be here tomorrow."

I put it back on the table anyway. Emily empties the contents of the pan into the overflowing trash can. I lean back against the table.

"I'm so sorry."

"That's okay, Iris. Don't worry about it." She opens the fridge and gazes at its contents. "You want something to drink before you go?"

Before you go. "I'd love some water."

She pulls a bottle out of the fridge and frowns at it. "Have a glass of wine instead."

"Sure, okay."

Glass of wine is great. You can sip a glass of wine. You can take your time and then you can ask for another one. I perk right up. The laptop is in this house. I feel it calling out to me. I'll find it, one way or the other.

Emily pours us two generous glasses. I sit on the couch, check my fingernails, and find that they're filthy. If I were still wearing my cardigan, I'd pull the sleeves over my knuckles. Instead I sit on my hands.

"How old are you?" she asks.

"Twenty-two."

"Such a baby."

"I'm an old soul. What about you? How old are you?"

She sighs. "Just old."

"You can't be that old. You look amazing."

She glances up. "Thank you. That's a really sweet thing to say. I'm twenty-nine."

"You don't look twenty-nine. You look, like, twenty."

She smiles as she hands me my glass. "Thank you, Iris. That's really sweet. Now I'm just going upstairs to get changed. I won't be long."

"Okay, sure. Take your time."

I watch her go up the stairs, carrying her glass of wine. The stairs are of the floating kind, timber treads that lead up to a hole in the ceiling with seemingly no supporting structure and no railing on either side. I take a sip of my wine and glance around the room, willing my laptop to materialize. I get up and examine bookshelves that have very few books but a substantial collection of vinyl records and a record player. I check behind the records, behind the couch, behind the cane chairs. I quietly open kitchen cupboards and look behind doors. All the time I hear Emily moving upstairs. At one point she talks on the phone, but I can't make out the words.

Eventually I run out of places to look and sit back on the couch. I take a sip of wine, then clock the smart speaker on the kitchen counter, a round meshy thing with a blue orb at the top. I know what this is. Ashley has one. She uses it to ask about the weather and order food in bulk for the cat.

I get up, bend down to it. "Alexa?" I whisper, trying to match the pitch of Emily's voice. "Where's the *other* laptop?"

Nothing.

"Alexa? It's me, Emily. Where do I keep the *other* laptop?"

"Why are you talking to my oil diffuser?"

I jump and turn around. Emily is walking down the stairs, wearing what looks like a pair of silk pajamas. "Is that what it is?"

"Nah. Just kidding. What did you need?"

"Ha! That's funny. Oil diffuser. Good one." Emily has pulled her hair in a high ponytail. She reminds me of Miss Amy, except Miss Amy was never as sophisticated as Emily.

"Iris?"

"I was wondering if there was a computer store around here."

"Ah. No idea. I don't think Alexa knows either, to be honest."

Alexa lights up. "Mhmm?"

"That's funny," I say. I don't know why. A loud buzzer rings, and for a moment I think it's Alexa, but Emily presses an intercom button on the wall. A small screen lights up, and all I see when I peer over her shoulder are masses of flowers.

CHAPTER 10

I was supposed to be gone by the time Tiffany showed up. That was the plan, but it's all happening in the wrong order. I don't have the laptop, I'm in Emily's apartment, and now Tiffany is here too. Or I assume it's Tiffany. It's hard to tell behind the masses of flowers she's carrying. It could be anyone delivering a funeral wreath, really.

"Where have you been?" Emily says, chin raised, hands on waist.

"Excuse me?" Tiffany replies.

"I have to be able to count on you, Tiff. That's what I'm paying you for, okay? And for Christ's sake, can you put these down? They're giving me a headache."

I am shocked at Emily's reaction. I crab-walk toward the potted palm, vaguely thinking I could hide behind it while Tiffany explains in an increasingly high-pitched voice that *some girl* passed on the message, and was Emily in a meeting with Jerome? Because Emily never told her about that, and Tiffany left a message, and why didn't Emily call her back?

And then she spots me. "It's her!"

"I don't know what you're talking about," I say, chewing on a fingernail.

"Yes, you do. You're the one who told me to go and get the flowers, same as last time, you said."

"No I didn't."

Emily turns to me. "I don't understand." Then her eyes grow wide. "I remember you! You were at B&N yesterday."

I shrug. "So?"

"You bought the book twice?"

"I might have."

"Why?"

They both look at me, Emily with a raised eyebrow, Tiffany with barely suppressed anger.

I shrug again. "Hey, I'm sure lots of people bought the book twice. It's a collectible item. You're very popular."

"Oh my God. Are you stalking Emily?" Tiffany asks.

"Of course not!"

"Yes, you are! You just said you went to Barnes & Noble yesterday and again at Next Page today. That's stalking!"

"No it's not."

"Then you told me to go and get the flowers. You said that was what Emily wanted! That's what you said!"

"No, I didn't. You're dreaming."

Tiffany's eyes grow like saucers. "You're lying!"

"That's enough, Tiff!" Emily snaps.

"What?"

"How can I trust anything you say?"

"What are you talking about?" Tiffany says.

Emily brings her face right up to hers and her index finger no more than an inch from Tiffany's nose. Then with a slow, deliberate poking of her finger in that narrow space between them, she says, "I. Know."

Tiffany tucks her chin in, and from my vantage point, with her little head atop her flamingo neck, she looks like a question mark. She blinks a few times. "What are you saying?"

"You know exactly what I'm saying."

"No, I don't! Are you firing me?"

"Yes." Emily walks past Tiffany to the door and holds it open.

"After everything I've done for you?" Tiffany says.

"Oh, for Christ's sake, Tiff. Don't be so dramatic. Just go."

Tiffany leaves without looking at me. Then Emily closes the door and leans against it.

"Oh, wow. I mean, it's none of my business, but what just happened?" I ask.

"You're not a stalker, are you?"

"Cross my heart," I say.

She nods. "I didn't think so." And I'm thinking, *you probably shouldn't take your stalker's word for it*, but whatever.

Emily takes the flowers and throws them into the trash. They don't fit. Half of them end up on the floor. "Tiff is screwing my boyfriend."

"Oh, wow."

She goes to sit on the couch and rests her forehead in her hand. Is she … crying? I come to sit next to her, slowly so as not to startle her. "There, there," I murmur, my hand hovering over her back without making contact. I lean forward a little to look at her face. "How did you find out?" I ask.

"The usual way. I found messages between the two of them on his phone."

"Oh, wow. And does *he* know you know?"

"Not about Tiffany. But I ended things with him when I

saw the photos and I blocked his number. I just hadn't told Tiff yet."

"I see," I say gravely.

She pats the area under the eyes with the tips of her fingers. "I bet you thought my life was perfect." She lets out a bitter laugh. I don't mind it. "I bet you can't believe any man would cheat on someone like me." She raises a hand. "You don't need to say it. I know that's what you think." She takes a slug of wine. "Well, take a peek behind the curtain and meet the real Emily Harper. Pathetic, single, crying loser."

"I'm so sorry," I say. Obviously I'm not. I'm thrilled. If circumstances were different and we knew each other better, I'd gently pat her shoulder and ask, "Do you think, maybe, this is karma?"

Instead, I shake my head. "Men have such primitive urges."

Emily nods. She doesn't say anything else, just sits there, staring into the middle distance.

"What was his name?" I ask softly, unable to stop myself from poking at her tender wound.

"Matt."

I nod. "That's a nice name. And how did you meet him?"

"At a film screening—at the after-party, I mean. He's a filmmaker. Or he says he is, but he hasn't made a real film yet. Just shorts. Crappy arthouse shorts. Student shit."

I nod gravely. "You know, long before *Titanic*, James Cameron did short arthouse student films that were very disparaged at the time, and look where he is now."

"Really?"

"Matt could well turn out to be the next Quentin Tarantino. Just saying." She frowns at me, and I think maybe I took it too far. "And that's why you're better off without him. You could do so much better than Quentin Tarantino. Do you have a picture?"

She looks around, for her phone I suspect. I see it on the kitchen counter and grab it for her. Her bottom lip quivers as she flicks through her photos. Then she shows it to me.

The man in the photograph is sitting on a bar stool, wearing a beret. He's got one elbow on the bar behind him and is smirking at the camera. I have no idea what she ever saw in him.

"Wow. You could do a lot better than Matt," I say. I bring the phone closer and squint at it. "What is he wearing?"

She looks over my shoulder. "Tweed jacket. That's his whole look. The French beret…all that. He thinks it makes him look intellectual or French New Wave or something."

"God…" I whisper. "I take it all back. This guy will never amount to anything. Are those…elbow patches?"

She half nods, half shrugs.

I scoff. "Never date a guy who wears elbow patches. It's like holding up a neon sign saying 'I'm the laziest person in the world. All I ever do is sit there and nurse my beer, or at my desk, my chin in my hand.' Because how else do you use your elbows so much that you need to protect them from a possible rash?" I bring the phone close to my face, like I'm talking into it. "Somebody has to do the work, Matt. Somebody has to make the world turn, clean the vomit on the street, care for the wounded, and I guess that's not you. Good riddance, Matt, you and your elbow patches."

I toss the phone into her lap. "We should have called him. Told him to his face."

Emily's mouth slowly breaks into a smile, and then she laughs. And I do, too, only because she is, and it feels like we're friends, girlfriends, sitting on a couch, sipping white wine and making each other feel better about *boys*.

"You're ruining my mascara!" she squeals, running her fingers under her eyes.

"Next time get the waterproof one," I say, pleased with myself. I was going to add, *because we're going to do a lot more laughing, you and I*, but I didn't. Mostly because I don't think we will, not if I have anything to say about it. Also, who knows? I might kill her. She won't be laughing then.

CHAPTER 11

Just kidding. I actually have to tell myself this sometimes. *Come on, Rose, cut it out. You're just kidding.* It's good to be reminded, in case I forget. You can't be too careful.

"Okay, random question here, but why didn't you fire Tiffany when you found out?"

She sighs. "Because I thought I could handle it until I found another PA. She's really good at her job, and I don't know what I'd do without her. Also I'm not one hundred percent sure it's her. Her name isn't on the messages. They're just pictures of her tits."

"I see. And have you seen her tits in real life?"

"Of course not. Why would I?"

"No reason. Just trying to connect the dots here."

She takes a sip of her drink. "Let's talk about something else."

"Sure. So how did you get the idea for your book?" I ask, spreading one arm over the back of the chair, fake nonchalant.

She rearranges herself on the couch, her mood lifting right up. "Well, I had been offered a substantial book deal by a prestigious publisher for my autobiography—" She flaps a hand. "I won't say who it is, so don't ask me. Anyway, long story short, I decided to write fiction instead, and just like that, I had an idea for a coming-of-age story, told from the perspective of a young girl as she navigates her nascent sexuality and discovers there's always somebody out there who wants something from you. Always. And you have to learn to fend for yourself. It's very inspiring. Everyone says so."

I'm staring at her, wondering how she does it. How does she lie so convincingly like that? Did she practice? Does it come naturally? I wish I knew. I think I could learn a lot from Emily Harper.

I must have been silent for a long time because suddenly she says, "Am I boring you?"

"No!" I exclaim. "Of course not."

"Anyway, enough about me. Tell me about yourself, Iris."

"Sure. What would you like to know?"

"Well, let's start with…do you have a boyfriend?"

"No, no boyfriend." There's no way I'm telling her about Ben. Why would I? I'm Iris, her biggest fan. I have no hobbies, no friends, no boyfriend. My life revolves around Emily Harper and that's it.

"You could be quite pretty, you know. If you tried. You wouldn't stay single for long." She moves a lock of my hair out of the way, and it takes all my willpower not to grab her wrist and snap it off. Instead I sit there, smiling benignly. Honestly, Emily Harper doesn't know how lucky she is that I have exceptional self-control.

She studies my face. "I don't think this is the right cut for you. And you should wear eyeshadow. Bring out your eyes."

"I've never put on eyeshadow. I'd probably look like a panda," I say, remembering how I used to slap on eyeshadow and eyeliner and kohl until I absolutely looked like a panda.

"I'll show you," she replies.

My heart does a little jig. That sounds like we're going to see each other again. "I'd love that," I say, smiling broadly.

She pours herself another glass of wine. I've barely touched mine, but I let her top me up anyway. "So you live nearby. Do you like the area?"

"Actually…" We're getting along so well, I decide to tell the truth. "I kind of lied about that."

She recoils slightly. "Why?"

"So I'd have an excuse to get in the car with you. I'm really sorry. I'm not a stalker, I swear. Or maybe just a small one." I bring my index finger and thumb together. "Tiny stalker."

"So where do you live?"

"Brooklyn. The far end."

"Oh! But that's miles away. How do you get home?"

"Train."

"Well, not tonight you won't. It's my turn to get you an Uber."

"Oh, no, that's okay. I'm used to it."

"Don't argue, Iris. It's already dark, and we're having a nice time, and I'm not ready for you to go home yet. I'm glad you got Tiff away from me. I feel like I'm having a vacation. And if you go home on the train, I'll end up worrying about you all night."

I blink at her, the words lingering in my brain. *I'll end up worrying about you.* I am itching to tell her, *Give me my laptop back then, you thief. You'll have to worry about me a whole lot more if you don't give me my laptop back.*

"Why do you live out there anyway? What's out there?" she asks.

And right there is everything I ever need to know about Emily Harper. "Because it's cheaper?"

"Oh."

The conversation moves on to her parents. "I used to

hate my parents. I was a very neglected child. But I did a lot of therapy, and I'm okay now," she says, sounding doubtful. "And they've been good to me." She nods to herself. "They gave me this apartment. I mean, obviously because they feel guilty, but so what?"

"So what, indeed," I repeat, gazing around the gorgeous apartment.

"They own thirty million dollars' worth of real estate, so it wasn't a big deal to them, but it's better than nothing."

"So you're an heiress," I say.

She smiles coyly. "Just a small one. But enough about my parents. Tell me about yours."

"Still together," I chirp. "And still madly in love after all these years."

"Just like mine." She smiles. "That's so rare."

She wants to know where I grew up (Wisconsin). But where in Wisconsin? she asks. And because I am unprepared, I say, "You wouldn't know it. Small town. Tiny town. One-horse town."

I invent a childhood of ordinary tranquility, how I came to New York because my parents thought I should extend myself, discover the world, meet new people. She nods throughout. We talk about self-forgiveness, her pet projects. She wants to know what "kids' stuff" I was referring to before in answer to why I need self-forgiveness. I shrug and tell her I have no idea what she's talking about. She doesn't press. She tells me she's afraid of getting old, that she wants to meet a man and start a family. "Does that sound weird?"

"Hardly," I say.

She drinks the rest of the bottle while I sip my glass slowly. I tell her about my job—although I pretend it's a different store—and what I do there. I don't know why. It's phenomenally boring, after all, but I'm on a roll. I tell her how most female customers return designer items that have been clearly worn, sometimes even slightly soiled like they've dripped caviar on the front or whatever, and the tags are gone, of course, and still, they want the full refund, and I have to go, no, it doesn't work like that. Nobody else is going to buy it in that state, are they. And anyway, there's a very clear return policy for special-occasion garments and you know that, because you would have gotten the card, the one that explains the return policy and that clearly states the tags have to be on the garment. It's not up to me. I don't make the rules, but I am paid very poorly to enforce them.

Emily doesn't respond, and her head rolls sideways onto my shoulder. Her glass is on its side on her lap, and a single drop of wine drips onto her thigh.

She's fast asleep.

I gently slide out from under her, careful not to wake her, and put a cushion under her head. I bend down to check for any movement behind her eyelids (none) and listen to her breathing (deadly quiet).

I stand and tiptoe up the stairs.

There are two bedrooms upstairs. I start with Emily's. It's just as messy as downstairs, but the room itself is beautiful. Large windows, a small deck, green plants. The walls continue the exposed-brick theme, but they're painted white and covered with colorful artwork. Above her bed hangs a large photo of herself on a beach somewhere, wearing multi-colored sunglasses made of butterflies and a red scarf that floats in the wind.

I don't have much time. I check under the bed first and find nothing but old socks and a beaded necklace, which I leave in place. I open her closets and check shelves, run my hands through her clothes. I go through her drawers, check the cupboard under the vanity in her (gorgeous, but messy) bathroom.

And then I hear a phone ping.

It's coming from downstairs, and I quickly run back to the landing, but on the way, I notice another door. It doesn't have a door handle and is painted the same color at the walls (beige). I can see the gap though, between the door pane and the wall. I run my fingers along it, my heart quickening. It's like a secret door, and there must be a trick to open it. I am dying to know what it is.

Ping! I push it with the tips of my fingers, and it springs outward.

It's a storeroom. And it's packed with boxes.

It's here. I know it. I can feel it pulsating. *Come and get me...* But I can't. Emily's phone has pinged again. I press the door closed gently and peek from the top of the stairs. She's in the same position on the couch, still asleep. I run quietly down the stairs and see her phone on the floor next to her, the screen lit up.

Ping!

I run to the bathroom, wash my hands, my heart thumping. When I come out again, Emily is sitting up, her arms stretched over her head. She startles when she sees me.

"Iris! You're still here! I think I fell asleep."

"Just for a couple of minutes," I say. "Do you want another glass of wine?" I move toward the fridge.

"God, no." She rubs her eyes and yawns. "You should go home."

She gets up, rubbing her arms. My bag is on the floor near her foot, and she hands it to me. I take it reluctantly then loop it over my shoulder. "If you wanted to talk some more about Matt..."

"No, that's okay. Well, bye, Iris."

"Okay, well..." I walk toward the front door. I have my

hand on the door handle. I open it then close it again and step back.

"Maybe I could—" I was going to say, *leave you my number in case you wanted to hang out sometime*, but she puts her hands on my shoulders, turns me around, and walks me toward the door.

"Go home, Iris. It's late."

She makes no mention of getting me an Uber.

I'm still holding my phone when I get outside. It's been off all day. When I turn it on, I have a couple missed calls and a couple texts from Ben. I call him back.

"Hey, babe, I was wondering where you'd disappeared to."

"I know. I forgot my phone was off." A wave of absolute doom crashes on my chest. I was supposed to get the laptop. I had one chance, one chance only, and I blew it. I wonder how long it will be before it all explodes in my face, before somebody out there recognizes that *Diary of an Octopus* is all about me. Lola would, if she read it. Mr. Bellamy definitely would. My mother would.

Someone will.

And then they'll hang me.

"Have you had dinner?" Ben asks.

"No."

"Want to come over?"

Of course. It's Sunday. The restaurant is closed on Sundays.

I hesitate. I shouldn't, really. What's the point? We have no future anyway. I should just end it.

But I don't.

I tell him I'll be right there, and then I hang up.

CHAPTER 12

Ben makes spaghetti with mushrooms in a creamy white wine sauce that he serves in blue bowls with shaved parmesan on top.

"I may have to go away for a while," I say, playing with my food.

"Oh? Where?"

I shrug. "I don't know yet."

"Home?" he asks.

I shudder. I'd be insane to go back to Pike Creek.

"But why?"

I stare at him. He hasn't shaved today, and there's a tiny bit of chive caught on the stubble of his chin. If I were closer, I'd lick it off. "Ashley is putting up the rent to three fifty a week."

"Three fifty?" He was about to take a swig of his beer; now he holds the bottle in the air, an inch from his mouth. "For that dump?"

"Exactly." I resume playing with my food. "I don't make enough at the store. Even if I could work more hours, it's just minimum wage. I should really get another better-paid job, but I've got no skills. My mother always said I should go to secretarial school. Maybe that's what I'll do. Go to secretarial school."

He looks at me, his mouth in a half smile.

"I'm not joking, Ben."

"You could probably get more shifts at the restaurant. Did you ask Liam?"

"It's mostly tips at the restaurant."

"That's not true. And anyway, if you were nicer to the customers..."

I look up. "I am nice to the customers."

"I mean more chatty. Engage them in conversation. The way Pip does. She makes loads of tips."

I wince. Everyone gets the tips equally, so I know I'm riding on Pip's coattails, and I wonder if that's why he brings it up. Also Pip is cute and sweet, and while I've never stood close enough to check, I suspect her hair smells of bubblegum.

"You seem sad," he says.

"You think?" I snort.

He looks down at his food, frowning, and twirls spaghetti around his fork.

I'm angry now, mostly because he brought up Pip. I push my chair back theatrically. "I should go home."

"Come on, Rose. Don't go. Stay the night." And a part of me is glad that he's asking me to stay, but it would have been a lot nicer if he'd said that when I announced my imminent—and permanent—departure.

"Hey, it's up to you," he says, taking another swig of beer.

I stay over.

· · ·

When I get up, the sun is just poking through the curtains. Ben is still asleep. I search for my signed book still in its paper bag, then remember I left it behind. Great. That's great. I've gone overnight from super-fan-stan to someone who couldn't give a shit.

There's a notepad on the fridge door with a pen attached where Ben jots his shopping list. I have the urge to write something. *In Case I Never See You Again...*

I read his list.

Cereal; Pick up laundry; Dentist Friday 2:15; phone charger; coffee

I try to imagine what that list would look like if I lived here, too, my to-do items mingled with his to-do items. *Cereal; Steal back laptop; Pick up laundry; Burn laptop; Dentist Friday 2:15. Check what can be traced back to me in book; phone charger; Refrain from strangling anybody; Coffee; Refrain from killing anybody, in any manner.*

Unless it's Emily. That should go without saying.

Outside I call work and leave a message that I'm sick. It's important that Emily and I stay friends, and I've spent all night thinking about how much she dislikes Tiffany. There's an opportunity for me right there, surely. I will be an outlet for her dislike of Tiffany. A wedge to be driven between them.

I go to Emily's place, find a bakery that's open, and buy croissants. I stand outside her building and ring her apartment.

It's eight thirty in the morning, and she takes so long that for a moment I think she's gone out, but finally the door buzzes open.

"Hi!" I show her the bag in my hand. "I bought croissants. Do you like croissants?"

She laughs. "If it isn't my tiny stalker. Come on in. I love croissants."

I follow her in. She looks like she just got up, with her hair on top of her head, held up by three or four butterflies, and her silk pajamas. Also, she's smiling, so that's *great*. She doesn't look like she's about to have me arrested.

"Actually I'm here to pick up my book. I think I must have left it here."

"Ah, yes." She reaches for it on the table. "I found it yesterday under a manila envelope." She does a half-shrug. "No idea how it got there."

"Thank you. I was devastated when I couldn't find it."

"That's okay." She smiles. "Look, I'm glad you came by. I wanted to say, I'm sorry about last night."

"You are? Why?"

"You were very sweet to keep me company while I poured my heart out about Matt."

"Oh, that." I wave a hand. "What a loser."

"Do you want some coffee?" she asks.

"Yes, please."

"After you left," she says, busying herself with the coffee machine, "I went to bed, and I was thinking about Tiff and everything…"

I flap a hand in the air. "Don't think about Tiffany. She's bad news. Get rid of her. That's my advice."

"I need her too much."

"No, you don't. You're Emily Harper. You can do anything."

She smiles. "I need more friends like you."

"And I'm right here. Also, I'm short on friends, so…"

She stands at the espresso machine, one naked foot on top of the other. She makes herself a cup of coffee, then one for me. A decade passes. She takes a sharp breath. "Maybe we could help each other out. Since your living situation is, you know, difficult... Would you consider coming to stay here for a couple months while you find a place to live? In exchange, if you're okay to do some work for free—just part time, that's all—then I wouldn't rely on Tiff so much. I could find another PA, and you'd save money... What do you say?"

She looks at me, her eyebrows raised, but in a sad way. Like she's afraid I might say no.

I'm just trying not to jump up and do air punches. "I'd love that!" I say.

"Oh, really?" She looks relieved. Then serious. "You don't have furniture or anything, do you? I can't possibly take in any furniture..."

"No, nothing like that. Just my clothes."

"And you're not going to murder me in the night, are you?" She smiles.

"Haha. That's funny. So when can I move in?"

"Um...when do you want to move in?"

"I could move in today!"

"Why not?" She checks her watch. "I have some work to do... Five o'clock this afternoon okay with you?"

"Absolutely!"

"Great. Oh, and would you mind..." She rummages through her things on the table until she finds what she's looking for. "It's my dry cleaning. Would you mind picking it up on your way over?"

I take the white docket. "I'd be happy to."

"Great. I'll see you back here around five. Let me give you some keys."

I was so focused on my *get in/get the laptop/get out* plan, I wasn't thinking of anything else. When I look back at the past week, I feel a sting of disbelief at how naïve I was. That's the problem with knowing you're scary and crazy—

and most people don't, but I've been told so many times, it's impossible not to blot up that fact—you forget some other people are too. It never occurred to me I was about to move in with an even bigger nut job than me, and that's saying something.

But in that moment, when I'm so happy I could have done somersaults all the way down the stairs, I still think I'm the smartest person in the room.

CHAPTER 13

I go from Emily's place to work at the store for the rest of the morning. Before I leave, I tell my supervisor, Mr. Flynn, that I need a couple of days off.

"You look pale, Rose," he says, frowning. "I saw you called in sick this morning. You all right?"

I don't mind Mr. Flynn. He's a kind man, you can tell. He furrows his brow and asks if I'm pregnant. Honestly, most people would have balked at the question, but not me. He could have enquired about my favorite sexual position, and I would have answered as earnestly as a girl scout describing the overhand knot. That's how happy I am. I'm about to reply, *Pregnant? No, just a stomach bug,* but then I change my mind. I just need some time, but I don't know how much yet. And while I feel reasonably confident my mission will be quick and successful, you never know. I don't want to lose this job if it's more than a couple of days.

I put my right hand over my left and with a shy smile I say, "We don't know yet. We're going to see the doctor this afternoon." He smiles kindly, nods, then tells me that parenthood is the most gratifying job of all, and for a moment I wish I hadn't said I was pregnant.

But then the moment passes.

Everything I own fits into a duffel bag and a backpack. I leave a note for Ashley on the coffee table.

Hey Ash, I've found cheaper accom. I'm paid-up until the end of the month under the old rate—the pre-subatomic hearing rate—*so you can consider that my notice.*

The dry cleaner's is on the corner of Tenth and Fortieth, three blocks away from Emily's apartment. I walk out with a suit, four shirts, and two pairs of pants, all wrapped individually in light plastic. I carry them over my shoulder, the metal coat hangers digging into the inside of my knuckles while I drag my duffel bag with my other hand.

I'm in the lift at Emily's place by quarter to five. I picture the storage room. I only saw the inside for a few seconds, but I can recall it like it's imprinted on my retinas. Vacuum cleaner on the left near the door (Dyson), toilet paper rolls packed by the dozen on the top shelf, cardboard packing boxes (Fragile, This Way Up) that look like they've never been opened, an ironing board against the back shelf, linen, towels, all nicely folded. I could do it in thirty minutes. I'd just need Emily to go out for an hour and I'm out of there.

"Hi," Emily mouths. She's on the phone. "Listen, babe, I have to go. Yes. I know. I'll call you back. Just try to think positive, okay? Love you!" She turns to me. "Iris! Welcome. Come in, sweetie!"

There's soft, soothing music playing on the smart speaker, the kind of music you could fall asleep to. A candle is burning on the coffee table. "Is that all you have? You do travel light! I like it! Let me show you to your room."

"Thank you! And can I say I'm so happy to be here. And your candle smells wonderful! What is it?" I was laying Emily's dry cleaning on top of the couch, but she stops me. "That's going upstairs," she says.

"Oh sure, okay."

I follow her up the stairs, and there's something about those floating steps that feels like you're taking your life into your own hands. By the sixth step I'm already dizzy with possibilities. It would be so easy—you wouldn't even have to dive. You could just slowly lean to the side with the weight of your body and let yourself fall. You'd break your neck, for sure. If you wanted. And, I imagine, sometimes I would.

"I'm so glad you're here," she says over her shoulder. "I think it's going to be fun, don't you?"

"Me too. Absolutely. Lots of fun," I say, struggling under the weight of my load.

Upstairs, she takes the clothes from me and puts them on her bed. "And this is you…"

We enter the spare bedroom. I put my bag at the foot of the bed and clap my hands, exclaim how beautiful everything is. I'm not lying. It's certainly the most beautiful room I've ever slept in. I even have my own en suite bathroom and french doors that open on the terrace, an ample closet, and a white dresser against the wall with a large circular mirror above it. The luxurious atmosphere of this room makes me think maybe I should take my time, stretch out the adventure for as long as I can. Maybe when I find the laptop I could hide it somewhere, and then stay for another month just to enjoy the one-million-thread-count Egyptian cotton sheets and the ultra-plush towels and the pristine white bathrobe hanging behind the door.

"Why don't you unpack later? I've got a nice bottle of wine in the fridge, and there's a fabulous sushi place down the street that delivers. And of course we need to talk about work. I thought I'd start with my goals for this year, so you get the big picture. She counts on her fingers— "Half a million followers on Insta, one million on TikTok, an interview about my book with The Cut—"

I'm going to be sick. She rattles on about all the things we're going to do, and all I can think is, I know I'm a recovering psychopath, but what's one more? I could kill her now, just to shut her up. Quick twist of the neck. She wouldn't even know.

Just kidding. Sort of.

That night, I work hard to come across super enthusiastic about everything she throws at me, which takes some doing, because I find that I hate her a little more every minute. I'm smiling on the outside, but on the inside, I'm stuck on a radio station that's playing "Who The Hell Does She Think She Is" on rotation. I mean, who steals someone else's diary and publishes it as her own? What kind of self-entitled, megalomaniac thinks that's okay? And that they'll get away with it?

But, on the outside, I am a picture of self-control. Emily talks a lot. I get the impression that she's lonely, and that's why she wants me here. She needs an audience, and what the heck, I'll clap in all the right places. What do I care? I'll be out of here by tomorrow anyway.

"I'm sorry about Tiffany, by the way," I say. I'm the new best friend. I say all the right things.

She frowns. "Why?"

"You know, with Matt and all that."

"Oh, that!" She flaps her hand. "It wasn't Tiff. I made a mistake. It was another girl."

I hold my breath. Suddenly I'm thinking, *So where does that leave me?* "So, wrong tits?"

"Wrong tits."

"Wow, okay. That's good news. How did you find out?"

She flaps her hand again. "I don't want to talk about it right now."

"Sure. Fine with me. Does that mean she's still your PA?"

"Yes, but I told her since you're here she can take the week off."

"So does that mean I can stay?" I ask, my hands together between my knees. I bite my bottom lip, waiting for her answer.

She frowns. "Of course. Stay another week or two, and we'll see what happens then. What do you say?"

I jump, punch the air. "I say, yes!"

She laughs.

"So everybody's happy," I say. "That's good."

She clicks her tongue, shakes her head. "You're really the sweetest thing, you know that?"

Around eleven, we go to our respective bedrooms. I lie on the bed fully clothed, staring at the ceiling, and wonder how long it will take Emily to fall asleep. I feel good about this. In fact, I would call my plan *flawless*. I'm in her house, she thinks my name is Iris, she doesn't know where I live or where I work. By the time I leave this place, she won't even know she's been burgled. I'll simply leave a note saying I changed my mind about moving in.

An hour later, I tiptoe to the door and put my head out. Silence. The door to her room is ajar, and I very quietly walk up to it and stick my eye against the gap. It's too dark to see anything, but I'll take my chances. I tiptoe back to the little storeroom, feel in the dark with my fingers, and gently press the edge of the door. It opens with a click. I wait to see if the sound has stirred Emily. It wouldn't matter if she woke up now—I'd just tell her I lost my way—but once I'm in there going through her stuff...

Nothing. I slip inside the room, pull the door closed as much as I can—you can't close it from inside—and turn on the light.

CHAPTER 14

How long was I in there, I wonder? Two, three hours? A significant amount of time considering it's not a big room, but that's how long it took to painstakingly go through every box, every shelf, every corner. I know more about Emily Harper's intimate habits and personal taste than I ever wanted to, but that's where we are. What did I find in Emily's precious boxes? Shoes, mostly. Hundreds of pairs of luxury shoes, not even in their original boxes but shoved together every which way. I mean, who writes *Fragile - This Side Up* on a cardboard box full of old shoes? Emily Harper, that's who.

To be fair, it wasn't just shoes; it was also clothes, dresses, coats, shirts, pants, all of which I had to take out individually and shake loose because, hey, I've been there. I used to keep my laptop wrapped in the sweater my mother made for me, the one that made me look like I was auditioning for some Christmas horror movie. I also found boxes of decade-old, caked makeup, half-empty jars of face lotions, old magazines, tins of paint in various shades of white and gray, old posters. Then there was the linen—sheets, pillowcases, towels

—but by that point I figured it was enough to run my hands through it and feel for the laptop.

It wasn't there.

It wasn't in this room.

I close the door to the storeroom and return to my bedroom. I am unbelievably disappointed. I have to resist the urge to barge into her room, unhook her pretty picture from the wall and slam it on her head. Would that wake her up? Or would I need to scream into her face as well? *Where is it, you thief? Where's my laptop, you fraud?* I want to grab my pillow and tear it apart with my teeth. *Calm down, Rose. Don't go crazy. Think logically. Where can it be? Proceed by elimination.*

I bet it's in her bedroom.

Still, I search this room too—my so-called bedroom—because it would be just my luck to tear the place down and all the time it was under my bed. Except it's not. But still, I search every inch of the built-in closet. I slide my hands everywhere under the mattress. I search the bed and comb the bathroom like I'm a forensic scientist looking for a single fiber. I search behind the toilet because I've seen the movies and I know all the tricks. I check for any loose tiles in the ceiling, but it's not that kind of ceiling.

In the end, I give up. It's not in the storeroom, and it's not in this room. I get into bed and pick up the paperback, and as much as it repulses me, I start reading again. It's crucial that I know how much detail she has left in that would give me away. It's a matter of survival.

Dear Diary,

I can't stop thinking about us getting married. I think about it all the time. I was in his office today, and I couldn't help it. I told him.

Oh great. That's great. Obviously, I didn't *tell* Mr. Bellamy I wanted to marry him. If I had, he would have sent me to the nearest asylum.

I read on, cringing with every word. All I can think about is Mr. Bellamy reading this book the way Emily wrote it—like it all *actually happened*—and I just want to die.

"I want you to meet my dad."

I was trailing his desk with my fingertips. I looked up at him. His eyes were wide with shock, like I'd just asked him to cut his wedding finger off. "You cannot be serious."

"Why?"

"You know why." He wasn't angry, just puzzled. He went back to marking papers. Conversation over.

"You ashamed of me?"

He didn't answer right away. "Are you being deliberately obtuse?"

Obtuse. Later I would look up that word, but I already had an inkling of what it meant. Context is everything.

"Why not? You'd like him. And he would like you."

He would be impressed by you, I wanted to say. He would be impressed that a man like you loves me. Maybe he would see me in a new light. I pictured us having dinner at my dad's new house with his new wife and his new kids. I pictured Mr. B. smiling at something I said, squeezing my hand. Me meeting my dad's eyes. Maybe he'd wink at me. (You did good, kid.) I imagined feeling grown up in that house, my dad's new wife stealing glances at Mr. B. Maybe flirting with him even. He wouldn't notice. He would only have eyes for me.

"I don't think your dad would like me."

"You could ask for my hand in marriage. He'd like you then."

I'd imagined that scene so many times, all I had to do was rewind and press play.

Me waiting outside, sitting on the low wall that borders my dad's new front yard. When Mr. B. and I move in together, we would have a front yard too. I would grow daffodils. I would wear a red apron with needlework in the shape of a cute house. I would make cherry pies and greet him at the door with a cold beer. I would sit on his lap and he'd tell me about his day, about how stupid the students were, not talented like me. He'd tell me how Miss A. still refused to speak to him, which she started to do when she heard we were getting married. My dad would come for Sunday roast dinner. Sometimes I'd let him bring his new wife, only because I know she's a lousy cook. I mean, I don't know know, *but let's say she's a lousy cook. Because I will be an excellent cook. I will be like Meg from Little Women, determined to create a perfect home. No matter what happens during the day, Mr. B. will always come home to find a happy, smiling wife. I'll make strawberry jam—my mom never made jam, and you have to wonder, would my dad have strayed if she had?—in cute little jars with red-and-white-checked tops. Mr. B. will bring friends home whenever he feels like it, and he won't have to ask. I'll always be prepared, unlike Meg who fell over at the first hurdle. I picture Mr. B. coming out with my dad, lots of backslapping, me hopping off the little wall, my dad holding me at arm's length. Congrat-ulations, sweetheart. You got yourself a good man. I'm proud of you.*

"What's going on in that pretty little head of yours?"

I pulled myself out of my dream. I loved the way he looked at me, like he found me amusing, but also he wanted me.

"I love you," I said. "And I'm sad."

Mr. B. put down his papers and drew me to him. I sat on his lap. He took my chin between his index finger and thumb. His fingers smelled of tobacco.

"You're too young to be sad, and you're too young to get married. It wouldn't even be legal. They'd put me in jail."

"I bet it's legal in other countries, like France."

"It's not legal here."

"But you'll marry me one day?"

He brushed my lips with his thumb. "One day," he breathed into my mouth.

. . .

I sit up abruptly, my heart pounding. *Congratulations, sweetheart.* It stopped me for just a second because my father never called me *sweetheart.* But I recognize the cadence. And just like that, I can see the words on the page, just the way I typed them.

Congratulations, Rosie.

CHAPTER 15

I lie in the dark curled up on my side, my heart thumping. She knows me as Iris, so why does it matter if I wrote "Rosie"? So what if she knows the author of the diary is Rose or Rosie?

It doesn't change anything. *Don't overthink it, Rose. Find the laptop and get out of here and everything will be fine. You got away with it, remember?*

That's right. I got away with it. It's been nine years since Mrs. Bellamy died, and nobody has ever knocked on my door.

Except that's not strictly true. A black-and-white police car drove up to my house three days after they found her. *To Serve and Protect*, it said on the side panel. I was in my bedroom, peering from behind the curtain. A uniformed officer knocked on the front door, and I crouched under the window, my back against the wall and my arms around my legs, like I was trying to take up as little space as possible. I remember hitting the back of my head against the wall over and over, my hand pressed hard over my mouth so no one would hear me scream. I heard voices—the male officer's, my mother's. They were both calm, polite. I couldn't hear what they were saying, and I scrambled to my bedroom door and opened it, but by no more than a hair.

They talked about the murder—shocking, you don't think it could happen in this town, not like this. I could picture my mother wringing her hands together, the way she did with her face all scrunched up. She invited him to sit down and offered him a cup of coffee. He said no, politely, then he went straight to the point.

"I'll get straight to the point, Mrs. Dunmore. It's Rose I came to talk to. Is she home?"

I started to get up, my eyes darting for an escape. I was already crab-walking back to the window when I heard my mother say, after a moment's hesitation, "Rose isn't here. She's out with her friends. What did you want to ask her?"

I stopped in my tracks. I'd never heard my mother tell a lie, and I didn't know if that shocked me more than the fact the police wanted to talk to me. I took my position by the door again.

"Then maybe you can help me, Mrs. Dunmore."

"I'll sure try, Officer Craine."

"What time did Rose finish school last Thursday?"

"Three thirty, just like every other school day."

"Did she come home right after school?"

"She certainly did."

"And did she go out again?"

"No, sir. She stayed right here, with me."

"She didn't go to the game?"

"No, sir."

"Everybody at the school went to the game, but Rose didn't?"

"She's not a very athletic girl. She doesn't care for sports much."

"And she didn't go out at all after she came home from school?"

"No, sir."

"How can you be so sure?"

"I came home from work at four—I work at the hospital —and I asked her to help me take the washing in. I do the washing on Thursdays. We ate early—"

"What did you have?"

"Baked beans." Then she added, "With bacon. And ground beef." Like she was afraid he might think all she did was plonk of tin of beans in sauce on a plate and call it dinner.

"And you say Rose stayed home after that?"

"Yes, sir. We watched an episode of *Glee* on TV, because that's one of Rose's favorites, and then … let me think, it was *The Goldbergs*, I think. Thursday night. Yes. Then Rose went to bed about nine; I stayed up for another hour or so, then I went to bed. I saw the light under her door, and I went in. She was reading a book. I told her to turn it off because it was late."

There was silence except for the faint scratching of a pen on paper. "I understand Rose had a bit of trouble at school."

"What kind of trouble?" my mother asked stiffly, as if she didn't know.

"Something about the class pet?"

I groaned silently. My mother of course knew all about the incident with the class pet. She'd been called to the school to discuss it.

"What does this have to do with anything, Officer?"

"I'm just getting context here."

"Well, sir, the context is that my daughter has gone through a difficult time after … my husband and I separated. She didn't take it well. And who could blame her? She's thirteen years old."

"I understand. Children are always the ones to suffer, aren't they?"

I was listening so hard I could hear the click of a pen, the slap of hands on thighs, the rubbing of fabric. "That sums it all up nicely for me, Mrs. Dunmore. Thank you for your time."

"She's a good girl, my Rose, and I won't let anybody say otherwise," my mother said through gritted teeth.

"I understand. No one's suggesting anything here, Mrs. Dunmore."

"So why are you asking these questions about my Rose?"

"Well, I'm sure it's nothing, but her name came up in our investigation…"

"Excuse me?" my mother shrieked.

"I understand Rose had developed a certain…attachment toward Mr. Bellamy."

"Who said that?"

"I don't think it's a secret, Mrs. Dunmore. I mean, I understand everyone at school is aware of Rose's feelings toward Mr. Bellamy."

"What are you saying?" my mother shrieked.

"Like I said, her name came up. But you've cleared that up for me, so we're all good."

"Is the Kansas Bureau of Investigation on the case?" my mother asked coldly.

The policeman gave a small laugh. "We may be simple folk down here, Mrs. Dunmore, but we don't need the KBI to tell us how to run our business. I was a detective before I retired out here. I know how to conduct an investigation. There's nothing to worry about, Mrs. Dunmore. About Rose, I mean. Like I said to Mr. Bellamy, we have a lead. We have a witness who saw two men who looked like they weren't from around here get away in a car with out-of-town plates.

They didn't get the tags, but we're looking into it. Like I said, I just wanted to clear it up about Rose."

"You have to stop this," my mother said sternly after he left. "You have to stop this nonsense, Rose."

I wiped my nose with the back of my hand and studied my dirty fingernails.

"You have to stop living in your fantasy world. You're too old for that now. People will get the wrong idea, and it'll get you into trouble. A lot of trouble."

We never spoke of it again. The police never returned. Nobody ever doubted my mother. She was active in our church. She was an administrator at the hospital. She volunteered in the homeless kitchen on weekends… She had given me an alibi, and that was that. It shocked me, that she'd lied. It worried me, too, because I hadn't known she was capable of it, and it made me uneasy. Like I wasn't sure who she was anymore.

The next day I went to my favorite place, under the mulberry tree. I sat with my arms around my legs and my forehead on my knees. I tried to figure out how I could fix things, even though deep down I knew things were beyond fixing.

And that's when he said my name.

"Rose."

I looked up. He was crouched next to me. He looked so sad, like he'd cried rivers of tears that had etched grooves into his hollowed cheeks. Without thinking, I reached for him, just to touch his face with my fingers, something I'd never done before, and he jerked back, a mix of fear and pity in his eyes.

Then, softly, gently, like I was a wild, damaged animal, he said, "Did you do something, Rose? Something bad?"

And I looked into his eyes and whispered, "I didn't get to tell her."

"What?"

I saw him recoil then. I saw myself reflected in the horror on his face. Like he was looking at a monster. At something dark and evil. That, more than anything that happened before or after, was the moment I realized how sick I was.

"That you love me. I didn't get to tell her."

"That never happened! Oh God, Rose…" His voice cracked. "If you did something, you have to tell the police."

"You said you loved me," I whispered, desperate. And there were no words to describe how shocked and terrified he looked.

"Oh God, Rose," he said again, his mouth distorted with pain, his eyes swimming in tears. "It's all in your head!"

I scrambled to stand, my back scraping against the bark. He kept talking, faster and faster, his words sounding like they came to me over the roar of an ocean.

"Tell the police, tell your mother, tell somebody, Rose! Tell them what you did!" And then more softly he said, "There's something wrong with you. Something very wrong. You have to get help."

I put my hands over my ears and ran back to my house.

I barely got out of bed after that. I refused to eat, I refused to speak. After a week of unsuccessful coaxing, my mother stood in the doorway, wringing her hands together.

I was lying on my stomach. She came to sit on the edge next to me. "There's nothing to be scared of, Rose. These bad men are long gone. You know what the chief said.

They'll find them one day, and in the meantime, nothing is going to happen to you."

I knew the police had their suspects in their sights but at that stage hadn't found them. This I'd first heard from Lola, who told me the principal gathered everyone in the hall a few days after the murder. They had a moment of silence for Mrs. Bellamy, then Mrs. Morales told the school assembly that the police had said it was a robbery gone wrong. Someone had seen two men, drifters, in the area. The police were certain it was them, that they thought the house was empty. Wrong place, wrong time.

I read the same in the paper my mother left on the kitchen table the next morning. The men were long gone, and the authorities were on the hunt. Poor Mrs. Bellamy was in the wrong place at the wrong time. Although you might say that it wasn't just Mrs. Bellamy who was in the wrong place at the wrong time. It was me too.

"Is it because of Daddy?" she asked next. I nodded. I figured I may as well blame him for it. She sighed. "What do you want to do, Rose?"

I begged to be sent to boarding school, like my friend Clara's parents did to her, and eventually my mother relented. There was some chatter about my father. Visitation rights, they called it, as opposed to my father wishing to spend time with me. "We can take her for a day here and there when she's on a break," I overheard him say wearily, thereby dispelling any fantasy that the only reason I hadn't moved in with my father and the Kool-Aid family was because my mother needed me.

One week later I was sent to Sacred Heart High School for Girls in Arkansas.

"They'll eat you alive," my mother murmured.

I never returned to Pike Creek.

CHAPTER 16

I wake up to the melodious sounds of flutes and violins drifting from downstairs. I sit up abruptly, my heart thumping. The book is still open on my lap, and it slides to the floor. And that's when I remember. I'm in Emily's apartment. I check the time on my phone—6:05 a.m. I've been asleep a grand total of three hours.

I shower and go downstairs to find Emily making herbal tea in a glass pot.

"Did you sleep well, sweetie? Were you comfortable? You must let me know if you need anything, like fresh towels or whatever."

I mumble something about sleeping really well. I'm so tired my mouth can barely form the words. I point to the coffee machine on the counter. "May I?"

"Yes, of course. Just pop a capsule in. It's ready to go."

"Thank you."

"We have lots to do today, you and me," she says when I've poured myself a cup.

"That's what I'm here for!" I chirp. We sit down at the computer. This is my first day on the job and, I'm very much hoping, my last. Emily is walking me through her social media process and I'm nodding along, like I totally know what she's talking about. I am to monitor the many comments she gets on her socials, delete the horrible ones—of which there are very few, she assures me—and post nice enthusiastic replies to the positive ones.

"So which one are you?" she asks, scrolling through her Instagram.

"Which one am I what?" I reply, swallowing a yawn.

"Which profile is you? I searched for you last night, but I couldn't find you." She smiles. "I know you're one of my biggest fans, and I thought I had an inkling, but I'm stumped." She swivels the computer toward me. "Where's Iris, my biggest fan?"

She's smiling in a nice, warm way, but my heart sounds like someone slam-dunking basketballs inside my chest. *Don't be silly, Rose. You can do this.*

"I'm very shy," I say. "I'm more of a lurker."

"Oh come on. You can't lurk on Insta. You know that."

I nod. I don't know that.

"Come on, sweetie. Don't be shy."

I bring the computer closer—like sure, okay, whatever, I'll show you—but I am kicking myself in the shins for being so stupid. I should have thought of this, and I didn't. Why? Because I didn't think it would come to that. I thought I'd find the laptop in the storeroom and get the heck out.

Emily is logged in, and I scroll through her followers, acting bored, one cheek resting in the palm of my hand. I find one with a broken window as their avatar with the user-name @smashbang. You just know instinctively that person isn't right in the head and I like them already. I load up their page. There're hardly any posts, just the odd car crash. I swivel the screen back to Emily.

"Like I said. I'm kinda shy. Also I lie a lot. In case you're wondering why it says I'm from Venice Beach, California."

"I see." She makes little shakes of her head while I resist the urge to gnaw on my fingernail. "Well," she says finally. "Not exactly what I had in mind for my biggest fan, but you know what? That's okay. We can work on that."

"We can?"

"Yes. I'm going to make you all better. Also I can see that you do like a lot of my posts."

Emily leaves me with instructions to review today's comments while she chats with her friend Anastasia on the phone. The first post I check is a photo from the book signing at Barnes & Noble. And that person standing in line, so absorbed in her book that she hasn't noticed she's holding up the line behind her, is me.

I stare at the photograph. I look deranged, my eyes wild, my mouth distorted.

"How you doing, Iris?"

Emily is standing over my shoulder suddenly. I turn to face her. She's rubbing cream into her face. I can feel little beads of sweat prickling along my hairline. "Really well, Emily. Really well."

"Good, let me know when you're done. We need to do TikTok next."

She picks up her magnifying mirror and sits on the couch. I go back to the post. I can't have a photo of me associated with that book. If someone I know sees it—I mean someone I knew way back when—I'm dead. It's that simple.

I click around frantically trying to figure out how to delete it. At one point I accidentally delete her entire account. *Are you sure?* Instagram helpfully prompts me. I click around like a crazy person. *No. Stop. Go back.* Finally, I figure out how to upload another photo from that day, this one taken outside the store.

I take a deep breath. I have to relax. I have to calm down.

I scan the comments on her posts, which are all surprisingly similar. *Love your post! ... Great content! ... So good! ...* Hundreds and hundreds of those same comments. I bombard them with heart emojis in reply. Along the way I am also scouring for any other photos that include me, but so far I haven't found any.

It takes me a while to figure out how to check her direct messages, but I get there. I find four messages from friends, all of which tell her how much they loved the book. I send them to the trash and unfollow them. I'm about to close the window when I notice that the requests tab has an unread message. I click on it.

Hi Emily. My name is Lola. I messaged you a few times, but I haven't heard back. I was wondering if you knew Rose Dunmore? Because I read your book, and there was a lot of things that made me think of Rose. If you could reply, I would really appreciate it. Thank you. Lola Johnson.

"You okay, sweetie?"

I turn around. "What?"

"You made a funny noise."

"Right. I do that sometimes." Emily is standing over me. I don't know whether to raise my hand to cover Lola's message or close the browser or snap the laptop shut, because whatever I do, it will look like I'm hiding something.

She narrows her eyes at the message. "Oh, no..." she whispers.

"I guess she's mistaken you for someone else," I say, biting the inside of my cheek.

Emily is very still. She bites her bottom lip as she speaks, which is quite the challenge, and I speak from experience. "Just delete it."

"You sure?" I ask, not because I want to keep it—I sure don't—but because I have suddenly become aware of her discomfort. It's like for a moment I'd forgotten that Emily *knows* she stole the book. For the first time I wonder if it keeps her up at night. If she's like me, wondering whether she'll get caught. But I guess I'm too slow because she snatches the mouse from me and deletes it.

"Who is it?" I ask.

"I don't know. She keeps messaging me. I don't know anyone called... by that name. She's a freak. I get them sometimes."

And just like that she's back to her normal self. But my heart is in my throat. So Lola is on to Emily already. It won't be long now, then.

Later, for lunch, Emily pulls a concoction from the fridge and calls it lunch. It's some kind of herb and seaweed salad. "I know it's only leftovers..." she says. I glance at the green-gray mush and wonder, leftover from when? When we were plankton?

"What do you want to do this afternoon?" I ask. I am praying that she has to go out somewhere. I don't think I can handle this much longer. I really have to find that laptop and get the hell out.

"We're going out to sell my book," she says, daintily dabbing at her tooth to dislodge a bit of seaweed.

"Oh? Do you have a book signing?" God, that would be perfect. I could go there with her, then come back here, get my laptop, and disappear. I check my watch. "If that's the case I better get ready, order an Uber."

"No, not a book signing," she says. "I don't have another one of those for weeks."

Emily tells me we're going to get this book on the New York Times bestseller list even if it kills us. We're going to do our own little marketing campaign because every bit counts. The plan is to go from bookstore to bookstore and ask whether they have the book in stock. If they do, we buy a couple of copies—show them it's a hot ticket item—and if they don't, we order it.

Our first venue is a small independent bookstore on Tenth Avenue.

"Go and ask about it," Emily urges. She looks toward the front desk. "Go on. And if they don't have it, order it," she reminds me, as if I could have possibly forgotten.

I walk over and ask the young man. "Do you have a copy of—" I drop my voice. "*It Starts With Us* by Colleen Hoover?"

"Yes. There's a wall of them over there."

"Oh, right. What about, *The Notebook?* By Nicholas Sparks?"

"Erm…" He types on his keyboard. "No, we don't. We ran out."

I order a copy. It costs me twelve bucks I don't really have, but I have no choice. When I come out, Emily is at me. "What did he say?"

"He'd sold out, like an hour ago."

She claps once. "Of course! I should have known."

"I ordered four copies. He'll call me when they get in."

"Great. Good job, Iris."

After that, we go to more bookstores. Some of them—many of them—do stock the book, and Emily gets me to distract the attendant so she can stick it on *This week's top sellers* or *Staff recommendations* display shelves. We develop a routine. I go and ask about books like *A History of Hand Knitting* or *Where Does Grass Come From? All Your Questions Answered*

and More! I have to take up as much of their time as I can—
Are you sure? Look again. Maybe it's finger knitting—while Emily
does her juggling trick. Then she'll give me a signal—pull at
her earlobe—meaning it's time to go. What she doesn't know
is that before I leave, I will lean into the counter and say, "By
the way, my friend back there, she's not very well. She thinks
she's a librarian, so when she goes into bookstores, she gets
this urge to move books around. Yes, it's very sad. Anyway,
best check your display shelves. Just in case."

Emily Harper is a clinger. For the next two days, she doesn't
leave my side. She is like glue. Emily Harper has this need
bordering on desperation for constant company and constant
reassurance (Yes, I'm sure you'll make it to the top fifty any
day now. Yes, the New York Times bestseller list people are
idiots and don't know what they're doing. Yes, this dress looks
amazing on you). It's so important that the book sells well,
she says, touching her hair, so she can help as many people as
possible. I have no idea why she thinks *Diary of an Octopus*
would help anyone, but here we are.

Meanwhile, every time she leaves the room, I search for
my laptop in case I missed it the first time around, which I'm
pretty sure is the definition of insanity: doing the same things
over and over and expecting a different outcome.

I run my hands under the furniture and come back with
nothing but dust bunnies. I shift the couch, find lighters,
pens, a ring with a blue stone which I pocket, an old parking
ticket. Between the side of the couch and the wall I find a
glass pyramid about as tall as my hand. There's a brass
plaque on the bottom: *Award for Best Emerging Wellness Influencer.* I hide it under a cushion. I'll steal it later, only because
she doesn't deserve an award. She's a fraud.

When I hear the floorboards creak above me, I shift it

back and sit with my hands between my thighs, twisting my mouth like I always do. I steal things, too, because screw her. She's making a killing from my book. I swipe a small wooden box with mother-of-pearl inlay I found under the shelves, a pair of gold dangling earrings that I don't even like but I know she does, a small brass candle holder. These things I collect like a crow collects shiny things, and I hide them in my duffel bag.

During the day we traipse around town from bookstore to bookstore to perform the same routine. Also we take photographs of Emily. Lots of photographs of Emily. On benches, at bus stops, in parks. She poses with butterflies on her head, standing on a bench with her arms wide like she's Rose DeWitt Bukater in Titanic, or she'll hold up my book in front of a tree while looking painfully naïve and innocent, or make goofy faces, butterfly sunglasses on, having so much fun. Then we post these photos on Instagram, where I surreptitiously check if Lola has messaged again.

She hasn't. But I scroll through her life anyway. Lola is not an over-sharer, but there are a few pictures. There's a photo of her at a school prom where I recognize a few faces. I focus on Lola. She's laughing at the camera, raising a glass of something. She's got glitter on her eyelids, she's not wearing glasses, and her eyes look nice, normal. I wonder if she'd had corrective surgery. She looks pretty, happy, and I find I miss her so much, it's like a stitch in my heart.

I remind myself that if Lola is looking for me, it's not to wish me happy birthday. There's no point in missing her. If I ever see her again, it will be at my trial for murder.

Finally, it's Thursday, which means a small reprieve. I'm working at the restaurant tonight, and not a moment too soon because I am slowly going insane, trapped in this place with this woman.

CHAPTER 17

Emily pours a glass of wine. "We haven't discussed my podcast yet," she says. "I'm so excited! I can't wait to tell you all about it."

Oh my God. This will never end, I can tell. She will never leave me alone. Ever.

I take a breath and plaster on a smile. "Your podcast? Wow! I love podcasts. Can we talk about that tomorrow? It's just that I have to go soon. I waitress at this restaurant and…"

"What, now?"

"Soon, yes."

"Oh!" She blinks a few times. "But I was really looking forward to us spending time together."

She's insane. Truly. We have done *nothing* but spend time together. "I know, me too… But unfortunately, I have to work." I pout sadly.

She bites her bottom lip. "Which restaurant is it?"

"A burger joint on Broadway," I lie. There's no way on earth I would tell her I work at Brasserie Murray. She'll know it, for sure. She'll want to come with me. So we can spend more time together.

"A burger joint?"

"Yes."

"What is it called?"

"Best Burgers In Town," I lie again.

"Oh. And do you work there often?"

"Only when they need me. Which is hardly ever."

"All right, I suppose…" she says with a sigh, as if I was asking for permission. "That's too bad, but…oh well, never mind. I'll see you tomorrow, I guess."

My heart soars when I get outside. After spending two days cooped up with this nut job, I feel like I have wings. I arrive at the restaurant half an hour later with a spring in my step.

"Hey, Rosie, how you doing?" Bernie says.

Bernie lives on the street, his possessions stored snuggly in a shopping cart. He likes to watch people come and go. In a few days he'll move on to another one of his favorite spots. He has a story, but it's not mine to tell. Suffice to say he's not unhappy—quite the opposite. Some nights after work I'll sit with Bernie for a chat. He doesn't say much about himself and I don't say much about myself so we get along just fine. I'll tell him about my favorite romantic comedies from the eighties—many of which he knows well—and he'll tell me about his favorite movies and put on his best Jimmy Stewart voice and ask me if I want him to put a lasso around the moon. We talk for hours.

We chat briefly before I go inside. I put on my apron—we wear those little black aprons with pockets like they do in French cafés—and go to say hi to Ben in the kitchen. When he sees me, he quickly checks that no one is watching and pulls me to him.

"I've got something for you," he says.

"What?"

He has his back against the wall and fumbles with his pocket. He presses something small and cold into the palm of my hand. "Move in with me."

"What?" I pull back, study his face. His skin has that sheen he gets when he cooks, and a lock of hair is stuck on his forehead, just above his left eyebrow.

"Get out of that horrible place. Those people are toxic."

"Who?"

He blinks. "Ashley and Ryan. Your roommates. What's wrong with you?" He takes my face in his hands. "Move in with me, Rose."

"Move in with you?"

"Yes!" He laughs.

"Why?"

A pause. "Why do you think people move in together?"

"Because they want to cut the rent?"

"I'm not asking you to pay for anything! I own my apartment. I mean, I have a mortgage, sure, and maybe one day we can—"

"For how long?"

"For as long as you want."

"As long as I want what?"

He raises his hands. "Am I missing something? Because this is not the response I expected."

I put my hands flat on his chest. "Okay, I get it. It's a joke, and it's a super funny one. Absolutely. Hahaha, now I have to go to work." I move away.

He grabs my elbow. "It's not a joke, Rose."

"Okay, you've had your fun. Come on."

"I'm being serious. Move in with me! Please?"

"Ben, there is absolutely no way I'm moving in with you. Now let me get to work."

He doesn't say anything, and I turn around to look at him. I am taken aback by the look on his face. He looks… is it sad? Is that it? And angry, too, I think. What is wrong with him today?

"Oh my God." I look at him square in the face. "You actually mean it?"

"I thought I was being clear. I don't know what went wrong," he adds with a hint of sarcasm.

I stare at him. For a very short and very delicious second, I wonder if I could move in with him. Pretend I'm normal, everything is great, and let's have babies. But then I shake the thought away. Ben doesn't know who I am. He doesn't know the things I did. If he did, he'd never want to lay eyes on me again.

"I'm not moving in with you," I say.

"Why not?"

"Well, for one thing, I'm staying with a friend of mine. I moved in two days ago."

"And you're telling me this now?"

"Yes, I am."

"Who is it?"

"No one you know." I give a half shrug, like I have so many friends he couldn't possibly expect me to talk about them all. "Her name is Emily."

He presses his lips together. "How come you never mentioned her before?"

"I don't know. It didn't come up, I guess."

He frowns. "Can't you move out? I'm asking you to move in, Rose, with me! Don't you want to move in with me?"

"Not really." I brush a crease down the front of my apron. "She needs me."

He nods slowly. "Right."

"She's going through a really hard time. She just broke up with her boyfriend. And she lost her PA. I mean, she found her again, but for a moment there it was really rough on her."

"Right."

I hadn't realized my hand was still closed over his key. He uncurls my fingers and takes it back. "Never mind."

"I'm sorry?" I blurt. But he's already gone.

He barely speaks to me after that, just the minimum exchanges to get by. I'm in a bad mood now, and the people at table sixteen are getting on my nerves. It's three guys in suits that keep sniggering like schoolchildren. They try the wine and declare it corked, like they'd know a corked wine from a mint julep.

I bring out their orders and set the plates on the table. I hold up my giant pepper grinder. "Ground pepper?"

One of them, the ringleader, the jerk-in-chief in a pink-striped shirt, wriggles his nose at his lobster Mornay, hovers the flat of his hand over it, and says, "It's cold. Send it back and get me a fresh lobster Mornay. And don't reheat this one. I'll know." Then he sits back in his chair, hooks his arm over the back of it, and sniggers at his companions.

I point at the steaming plate. "You'll find it's exactly the temperature the chef wants it to be." I turn away.

"Hey!" He snaps his fingers, loud enough for diners nearby to stop and listen. "Am I dreaming?" He turns to his companions. "Am I dreaming? Did I not ask her to get me a fresh lobster?" He turns back to me. "Are you deaf or just stupid? Send it back."

I return to his table. "If you'd just try it…"

"Don't make me ask again, lady."

Now, normally, the thing to do would be to let Liam deal

with it, but I'm over this. I'm over everything, really. I just want to curl up somewhere and die.

I sigh, pick up the plate of lobster Mornay. For a second I'm sorely tempted to drop on it on his head. The man in the pink-striped shirt shoots me a self-satisfied grin.

"What's going on here?" Liam asks as I walk past with the plate. I don't reply. For all I know I'm about to get fired and I don't care. I grab a set of cutlery and a linen napkin from an empty table and walk out of the restaurant with the steaming lobster.

"Hey Bernie, I brought you dinner."

"You didn't have to do that, Rose." He licks his lips and rubs his hands together. I've done this before—bought him dinner using my discount—but never lobster Mornay. This is going to set me back a hundred dollars, at least, even with the discount. Bernie tucks the linen napkin in the collar of his sweater. He grins at me. "Thank you, Rosie."

"You're welcome. You want cracked pepper with that?"

When I go back inside, the boys are putting their jackets on. Liam is standing by their table, his arms crossed over his chest.

"I just thought it should be hotter," the man in the pink-striped shirt mutters.

"Out," Liam says. Which surprises me. I didn't think he'd take my side on this, and I find myself feeling a little better.

The three men walk past me and make a feeble attempt at sniggering at me, but you can tell their heart isn't in it anymore. One of them raises a hand, says, "Thanks for the wine," then whispers, "suckers!"

And they all laugh on their way out the door.

"I'll pay for the lobster," I say to Liam.

"You'll pay for half the lobster. Ben told me he's paying

with you. And we're doubling the discount so it's twenty dollars each."

I can't help but smile while he scribbles what I owe and hands it to me. When I look up, I catch Ben's eye outside the kitchen. He's shaking his head at me, laughter in his eyes.

Don't look at me like that, Ben. Don't you dare like me, or have expectations of me, and certainly, under no circumstances, fall in love with me. You don't know what I'm capable of. You don't know who I really am inside.

I turn away and return to work.

Later when I get back to Emily's apartment, I find the place is in complete darkness. I fumble around for the light switch but can't find it, so I give up. I use the flashlight on my phone to make my way up the stairs, careful to remain dead in the center.

I turn on the light in my bedroom. There's a letter on my pillow.

Iris,

*I don't want us to start on the wrong foot, but I'm a little disap-pointed that you would choose to go out when you know I don't like being alone at night. Also there are times in the evenings when I might need you. That's because this job is <u>very</u> reactive. I realize you don't know that because you have precisely zero experience, but I expected you at least to be willing to learn. Also on a more personal level, I have deep —*underlined twice—*abandonment issues, and your behavior tonight was a big trigger for me, especially after what happened with Matt.*

I hope I haven't made a mistake in welcoming you with open arms <u>into my home</u>.

Signed, *Emily.* No butterfly blob.

· · ·

I take off my shoes, lean back against my pillow and reread the letter. After the initial shock—which is substantial—I decide to look for the silver lining. Now that I've had time to digest it, I realize it's not so bad. I mean, most people would scheme and plot for days to achieve this kind of misery in another person. I do it standing on my head. I should think of it as my superpower. I can make Emily suffer just by *not* doing what she wants me to do, no matter how trivial. A trigger is a trigger.

I fold the letter and put it in the drawer of my side table as a keepsake. Something to cheer me up when I feel down.

CHAPTER 18

"I'm sorry about leaving you that letter," Emily says the next morning. "I'm just not in a good place at the moment. Coffee?" She lifts a mug decorated with a million little butterflies.

This is unexpected, but I decide to roll with it. "Yes please, and that's okay. Don't worry about it." God, I'm good. I actually sounded like I meant it just then.

"Still friends then?"

I shudder. "Absolutely. Still friends."

"Thank you. Let's get to work."

We check the social media comments, take a million photos of Emily, call random bookstores to order the book. It's becoming phenomenally boring.

Around four she says, "Let's go out and have some fun. Do you have something to wear?"

"Wear?"

"We'll go to Jack's. It's a cocktail bar. I always go there on Fridays. You don't know it? You're going to love it!"

And while she rambles on about this bar, it's all I can do

not to do air punches on the spot. *Oh my God. This is it. Thank you, God. She's going to be out of the house.*

"I'm sorry," I say, my mouth turned down. "That sounds like so much fun, but I'm not feeling well. I think I'm coming down with something. I don't think I'll be able to go."

"Oh, no! Iris! What's the matter?"

"The flu maybe? I feel very hot."

And before I know it, she's put the back of her hand on my forehead. I stand there, frozen in place, the way you might if a python started slithering up your leg.

"Nope! You're fine. Come on. I'll lend you something to wear." And I just know I'm not going to win this battle.

I swallow a sigh. "I have my own clothes. I'll find something to wear."

"No offense sweetie, but you look like something the cat dragged in. Did the cat drag you in, Iris?"

"I don't know, Emily, I don't think so. I suspect that's the way I look naturally."

She laughs. "Come on, sweetie. Let's get ready."

Jack's Bar is noisy and hot. Emily seems to know everyone here. People wave at her and greet her warmly. Tiffany is there too. She looks different in tight animal-skin pants and a sequin top, her curly hair down. I wonder if she'll take it out on me, the fact that I'm staying with Emily, and she was out in the cold for a couple of days. Hey, I don't care. Bring it on.

But she just smiles at me and waves.

"This is my young new friend, Iris," Emily says to no one in particular then orders a bottle of Prosecco for the table.

I sit down then watch her dumb friends fawning over her because they think she's the coolest thing ever, because she's famous and she's rich and she's paying for all the Prosecco.

They talk to her like she's Hemingway or J.D. Salinger, like she's cracked some literary code, like she has a real gift. They want to know how she managed to put herself in the head of a thirteen-year-old girl and make it so *convincing*!

Emily takes selfies with all her friends, of course, and they take selfies with her. At one point, I fear I'm in the background of the shot, and I quickly comb my hair over my face.

"So how did you two meet?" a woman called Cassidy asks.

"Iris came to my book signing," Emily replies, putting her phone away. "Twice. She's quite the fan, aren't you, sweetie? She knows all my content by heart. Don't you, sweetie? And my book. You love my book, don't you, Iris?"

I nod. "Yes, I do. Very much."

She smiles at me. "It's very sweet." And for the next ten minutes, the conversation revolves around how much I love Emily, how much I love her brand, and how much I love the book. I've drunk a little by then and I find myself getting right into character. I show off my impeccable knowledge of her magnum opus like I'm on a quiz show. I know all the answers, I'm a super fan, and give me a buzzer already.

"That's really great!" Cassidy says. "I love Emily's book too. So good!"

"She's a genius," a man called Otto says.

They go on like that for a while, showering Emily with compliments and telling her what a dark horse she is, that they had no idea she'd been working on something like that and that she's *so clever*, and how quickly she went from self-published to an international bestseller, and how long did it take to write such a masterpiece?

"A few weeks," Emily says, touching her hair.

"Is that all!" they exclaim.

She does a coy little shrug. "Once I'm in the zone, the

words just fly out of me. It's like taking dictation from a divine entity. What can I say? I'm very lucky that way. Also I'm a very fast typist. Self-taught too."

This charming modesty is enough to make anyone want to shoot themselves in the head—or it is for me, anyway—but her friends will have none of it.

"You're a genius," Otto says, nodding gravely. "I don't care what you say."

"I couldn't agree more," Cassidy says. "I bet you'll win the Booker Prize for this."

Emily laughs charmingly. "Don't be silly," she says, flapping her hand. "I'm nowhere near good enough to win *that!*"

They all assure her that *of course* she's good enough. Is she kidding? She's the absolute GOAT!

It takes a fair amount of effort to sit there and smile, and once I get there, I can't stop. My face muscles have seized, stretched to breaking point, and still I don't stop smiling. When I take a sip of my Prosecco, I'm still grinning like I'm insane, like my mouth is encased in plaster so that half my drink dribbles down my front.

Emily frowns at my top. "Iris. Again. You need to get this looked at, you know?" She turns to Cassidy. "Iris has a condition. She's always dropping things."

"Oh?" Cassidy says. "I'm sorry. Is it neurological?"

"Maybe," I say, still grinning. I can't stop now. I'm stuck. I start to worry that if a volcano erupted this second they'd find me years from now under the fossilized ash with my mouth wide open, baring teeth, my cheeks pulled next to my ears, and for decades afterward, archaeologists would ponder what I found so funny when everyone else was running for their lives.

Suddenly, and with no warning whatsoever, Emily starts to talk about her parents. She calls them by their names, John and Marjorie, and I stop myself just in time from asking, *who?* Since of course I know Emily's parents' names. I'm a super fan.

Emily explains in great detail how difficult it's been for her to reconcile with them, that they took a long time to accept responsibility for her downfall, and that while she is strong and proudly so, she is still struggling with that.

"Of course you are, babe," Cassidy says.

This is clearly a topic close to Emily's heart, and we stay on it for quite a while. The crux of it seems to be that if John and Marjorie had been more present, better parents, she would never have joined the gang, as she calls it, making it sound like she was let loose on the streets at a young age, scavenging for food while working as a child pickpocket for some shady crime boss.

"They just didn't care," she says, staring down her drink. "Back then, I mean. We're okay now. They're very sorry, of course. Very regretful. They adore me and they're very proud of me and of my many achievements, but it was a long, hard road."

The little group thins out, and you get the impression they've heard it all before. Then it's just me and Emily.

"The problem is," Emily says, a little tipsily, "life is backstory. So when people say to you, that's a lot of backstory, Emily, it's because they don't get it. Backstory is all there is. That's it. That's your life. Backstory. So you know, be nice to your kids because that will be *their* backstory one day."

I nod along even though personally I can't think of anything worse than backstory. We riff on this a while, and Emily pulls out a dripping bottle of Prosecco from the silver bucket and pours it more or less into our flutes. It occurs to me that if I did it as badly as she did, she'd urge me to go talk to a specialist. But when she does it, it's totally fine.

"Okay, Iris. What's your backstory?" She takes a slug of her drink.

I shudder. "You know my backstory. Happily married parents, small-town Wisconsin."

"Oh, come on. There's got to be more to it than that."

"Not really, no."

She narrows her eyes at me. "Iris, sweetie. Everyone comes to my content because they have baggage, and they need the courage to forgive themselves." She takes another gulp of Prosecco. "What do you have to forgive yourself for? What did you do?"

What did you do, Rose?

The room tilts, just a little, as something very cold, very slithery, crawls over my skin.

"Come on, Iris. I've shared. You know what bad things I did. Everybody knows."

I know already how this is going to play out. She can smell blood, and I need to give her something.

"When I was in high school, I took a naked selfie and sent it to my boyfriend. He sent it on to everyone in the school."

A complete lie. No one's ever asked me for a naked selfie.

She rolls her eyes. "Oh, please. Everybody's done *that*!"

"Oh, okay. I didn't know."

I look away, wracking my brain for some juicy tidbit of guilt porn—*I did something really bad*—and it's not that I don't have a dozen choices to pick from. I'm a walking buffet of really bad things I did. I could keep her riveted for days.

Is it because of all the Prosecco I've drunk? I don't know. All I know is I hear the words tumble out of my mouth before I have the time to swallow them back. I'm not sure why I do it—maybe it's the way she's looking at me with genuine concern in her pretty eyebrows—but suddenly I hear myself blurting it out.

"I killed the class pet once."

Most people would jerk back, blink with shock, mutter

something about a forgotten appointment, but to her credit, Emily is made of stronger stuff.

She nods slowly, her face awash with understanding. Like killing the school pet is something she comes across a lot. "What happened, sweetie?"

"I don't know, exactly," I say. I'm smiling but my lips are trembling, which is completely unlike me. I never cry. I haven't cried for eight years. I used to cry a lot when I was a kid. I'd cry like I had two little taps where my eyes should be. I'd cry the way other people sneezed: suddenly, loudly, and for no reason whatsoever. But I'm a psychopath now, and psychopaths never cry. We are cold and callous with shallow emotional lives.

Anyway, all that to say, this is not going at all the way I'd expected. "I have a part of my brain that does stuff," I explain, "but the other part—the reasonable part—doesn't know of it until it's too late. I used to have blackouts where I'd do things..." I stop.

"The class pet," she prods gently. "What was it?"

"A hamster. His name was Pauly—we got to name it. We kept it in a cage in the classroom, and every morning we fed him lettuce and carrots. When it was my turn to feed him, he'd take the food right out of my hand. I was the only one he would do that with. We gave him a little wheel to run on, and he'd do that all day, run on his little wheel to nowhere. On weekends or vacation breaks, someone would take Pauly home. We'd take turns to have him."

"Did you take Pauly home and hurt him, Iris?"

I shake my head. "I never got my turn. One day I walked in and took Pauly out of the cage, and I strangled him and then hid him in my locker. The next morning there was no Pauly in the cage, but there was his little foot sticking out under my locker door." I lift my elbow and let my hand hang, illustrating Pauly's little foot. "When I arrived, everyone was standing in front of it, waiting for me to open it. So I did, and Pauly fell out. He had brown fur with a funny white patch…" I pat my own shoulder. "There. You would have known him anywhere." I look at my hands. "They buried him—I wasn't invited to that—so I don't know where. I kind of wish I did, so I could tell Pauly I was sorry."

CHAPTER 19

I'd never told that story to anyone, and now I'm unstoppable. I think about Lola, poor Lola, who was still desperately wanting to be my friend. The night before, we walked home together, and she'd been at me the whole way to go riding our bikes on the trails, like we used to. "Maybe go fishing too?" she'd said, but I put her off. I said my mother didn't want me to go out after school anymore—as if—because all I wanted was to write a stupid poem for Mr. Bellamy or practice putting on makeup before my mother got home from work. We separated at the crossing to go our separate ways, then the next day I saw her walk ahead of me. I called to her, I ran to catch up with her, but she ran ahead and ignored me. We were never the same after that. I mean, she saw me kill Pauly. I think about the look of horror on Mr. Bellamy's face when I confessed to the crime, my own face scrunched up into an old raisin.

"I'm sure you didn't mean to," Emily says softly.

I'm about to tell her that I did, because I used to do crazy things all the time, like the heart I carved into my desk, but then remember just in time that that's in the book. (*Oh really?*

You did that? Uncanny…) Fortunately, the little Pauly event is not in my diary because my diary was my happy place. Also my incredibly tortured place, but when you're insanely miserable in love you're also incredibly hopeful. And back then I had truckloads of hope.

Anyway, I'm about to explain about the part of my brain that doesn't work properly, but Cassidy arrives back at our table with her phone.

"I'm sorry," she says, tilting the screen to show Emily.

I crane my neck to look. It's a picture of Matt and his beret, standing next to a pretty brunette. They seem to be at some kind of restaurant. Matt has his arm around her shoulders and is raising his glass in a toast.

"I'm sorry, babe," Cassidy says. "He posted it just now."

Emily dabs at her eyes with a handkerchief she seems to have whipped out of nowhere. "So that's it," she says, her voice breaking. "We're really over."

I crane my neck to see. Why she ever thought those tits belonged to Tiffany is a mystery. The woman next to Matt has curves in all the right places, especially on her generous bosom which is advantageously set in her ample décolletage. Tiffany is more the willowy, gazelle type.

"Oh babe…" Cassidy coos, putting her arms around Emily. Tiffany is here too now, her arms also encircling a weeping Emily, oblivious that for a moment, *she* was the suspected evil mistress.

It goes on for a while. I glance around the room, wondering if I should join in the commiseration. Then I remember that I love Emily and I should probably stay in character.

I raise my hand, it hovers over her back. *Go on, Rose. It's just a little pat pat. It's not going to kill you to show a little affection to this nutcase. You can do it. Go on. Deep breath.*

But suddenly Emily stands and declares that she is too

sad and we have to leave. I still have my hovering hand and am still wobbly from telling my story while Emily seems to have sobered up dramatically. She's marching toward the nearest cab, and I'm teetering behind her. We ride back in silence, and it occurs to me that maybe I screwed up. Maybe I've shocked her more than I realized with my class pet murder story. Will she ask me to pack my bags and leave? What's my plan? I'll ask to stay the night, at least. I'm very safe, I'll say. I only strangle small animals, never people. Obviously, that's not true, but I won't tell her about that part.

Back at the apartment, Emily goes straight for the refrigerator.

"Everything okay?" I ask.

"I just got really sad about Matt, that's all. But I'm okay now," she says.

"Oh good," I say. I stretch my arms over my head. "Well, that was fun. I think I'll go to bed now."

"What?" She looks up at me. "But it's only seven o'clock!"

"Oh, is it? Well, anyway, I'm really tired. And I've drank a bit too much so…"

"Oh come on, sweetie. Don't be silly. We have work to do."

"We do?"

"You and me are going to record the first episode of my podcast. I'm very excited." She pulls out a bottle and studies the label. "You want Chardonnay? Or Prosecco?"

I'm going to be sick. "Nothing for me, thanks."

"Don't be silly." She hands me a glass of Chardonnay. I sigh and take it from her. For some reason, drinking is like breathing in this house. If you don't do it, you will die.

"It's my new project. I'm calling it Freedom Project. I'm dying to know what you think."

I nod. "I like it so far."

"Oh, sweetie! I haven't told you what it's about yet."

"Oh, right. Sorry. Keep going."

Emily paces around the room, glass in hand. "You know how my mission is to help people embrace self-forgiveness, right? What if…" She sits down. "What if I invite celebrities —it has to be celebrities, it won't work otherwise—and get them to confess to the worst thing they've ever done. My listeners would think, 'Well, I must be okay. If this famous person or that famous person did these terrible things, and they're still rich and famous and not canceled, and they still have great lives and make a lot money, and they're still admired, then I must be okay, right?'"

"Absolutely. We are okay. I love it."

"I've been telling people about it and getting excellent feedback, which makes me think I need to move fast or someone else will." She shakes her head at me. "You have no idea how many people will steal your ideas. It's dog-eat-dog out there, Iris."

"You don't say," I mumble, taking a slug of wine.

"Anyway, I thought, I could start. Since I'm famous, you know, and I've done bad things… I'll do the first episode because I think people will be more willing to participate if I do it. And I'm doing video because everyone is doing a YouTube channel with their podcasts these days." She grabs her mirror from the table, checks herself, and touches her hair. "I'm just going to fix my makeup. I'll only be a few minutes."

"Okay," I say.

She's gone for ages. After a while I turn on her computer to check if there's anything new from Lola. I open Emily's

Instagram, and that's when I notice the video of her reading a chapter of my book.

"Today in Creative Writing Mr. B. told us about a story called The Bad Seed in which the main character is an evil child but she's super smart. When the class ended I was slow to leave, taking my time putting my things away like I always did, just so I could have even a minute with him alone. That's how I fill my days now: finding ways to be with him, alone. Which sounds stupid because it's not like we do anything, but I don't care. I love him more than anything in the world.

"She reminds me of you," he said. "The girl in the story." He looked at me. "I mean this in a good way, Emily. She's willful, like you. She's defiant, like you. And she's extremely intelligent, like you."

He was putting his books back in his bag. I could tell he was about to leave. I didn't want him to. I wanted to hear more. I said, "What else is she, that is like me?"

He smiled. "She always gets her way."

I kind of felt deflated by that. "I never get my way," I said.

He laughed. "Come on. Stop pouting. You'll get your own way. You just have to be braver, Emily. Brave and bold."

I felt myself blushing, but I held his gaze. I knew he was telling me I was special. That's one of the things I loved most about Mr. B. He really saw me. He encouraged me to be who I really was. Over the past few weeks I'd gone from being invisible—to my dad, anyway—to being someone people called willful and defiant and brave and bold. I was becoming someone special. Someone who always got her way.

"Of course, Rhoda is a very bad girl," he finished. "You're only a little bit bad." He winked.

And someone a little bit bad.

. . .

I'm going to die. If Mr. Bellamy sees this, I am dead. And I thought that was the worst part, until I see the comments below the video.

Is this real, Emily? Because this is super creepy! Who the hell is this guy?

"Emily?"

She's coming back down the stairs, looking exactly the same as she did when she went up. She stops behind me to look at the screen. "What?"

I point at the comment. "They think it's real! Your fans!"

She straightens out, her hand on her chest. "Oh, God. I thought it was something serious."

"You don't think this is serious? Someone is suggesting everything in your book is real! We must delete this comment, Emily, right now, before it spreads."

"Oh, Iris." She fiddles with one of her earrings. "What does it matter if people believe it's real?"

"It matters, Emily! It really, really matters!"

She shrugs. "Why? Would it hurt the sales if people thought this awful story had actually happened to me? And it could have, you know." She touches her hair. "I was a very pretty child. And anyway, it's got over fifteen hundred likes. It's the most liked comment on that video."

Fifteen hundred likes? "Emily, please, I'm trying to help you out here. If people think it's true, they'll search for the guy, they'll search for Mr. B. It's what the mob does. They go after any old teacher who happened to teach at your school."

We don't want your fans to go snooping, Emily. We do not want your fans to go sleuthing and figure out that xVille, Kentucky is really Pike Creek, Kansas and that Mr. B is really Mr. Bellamy and nine years ago there was a rumor about a junior who had a crush on her teacher, and do you know what happened to his wife?

She takes a sip of herbal tea. "There is no Mr. B., Iris.

There's no one to find, so you see? Problem solved because problem nonexistent."

My heart is pounding but I nod anyway, like she's got a fucking point. "I'm just thinking of defamation risks," I say finally, like thinking of defamation risks is something I do standing on my head, and frankly, I'm bored already. "We don't want your old teachers to take you to court for implying they weren't always proper. I'm just thinking of you here."

She clicks her tongue and breaks into a smile. "Wow. You really care. I love that. People don't care enough, don't you agree? One day you'll be part of my backstory, and that'll be a really special part to me."

Over your dead body. "Absolutely. I'm just looking out for you here."

"I know you are, sweetie. But it's an old comment, so who cares?"

I look at the date. The comment is two months old, which—it should go without saying—makes it even worse.

I am dying. I quickly scan the other comments attached to that video. There are hundreds. A stream of people who all say more or less the same thing, that they love the book and they love Emily and where can they buy a butterfly like the one she's got in her hair? And Emily—or rather Tiffany —has replied to each of them with *Thanks!* And *So glad you liked it!* And *Thank you beautiful!* And lots of heart emojis and, of course, butterflies.

I guess that's why I didn't notice the other comment right away, camouflaged in a forest of words.

Is this you, Rose?

CHAPTER 20

The room tilts. I must have stood quickly because there are black dots dancing in front of my eyes.

"Jesus, Iris! Now what?" Emily asks. She's righting my chair, which went toppling back. I take a breath and snap the lid shut.

"It's nothing," I say, my heart pounding. And I'm thinking, if I can't delete this comment, I'm going to delete the video. I'm going to delete her entire account if I have to. I don't care. I'm going to set fire to this apartment. I'm going to burn everything. Her computer, my laptop. Her too. I'm going to lock her in and set the whole thing on fire.

She's staring at me, eyes narrowed.

"Sorry. I just realized something I'd forgotten. But it's fine." I sit back down.

"Leave it alone," she says. "Come over here, and let's do my podcast."

"Sure," I say. My hand is shaking as I proceed to shut down the computer. But before I do, I surreptitiously delete the post. And it's only later, when I've calmed down somewhat, that I realize that in my panic, I didn't check who posted the comment asking about me.

Emily directs me to sit down on an armchair while she puts her video camera on the coffee table, pops out the little screen on the side, fiddles with the tripod.

"Okay," she says, satisfied. "You interview me. Ask me questions."

She has topped up my glass and I take a sip of my drink. Anything to calm myself down. "Sure." I try to think of something. *When did you become such a total fraud? Do you ever wake up at night and feel remorse?*

"What's your star sign, Emily?"

She smiles at the camera. "Gemini."

Of course you are, you two-faced nut job.

"And what are your favorite hobbies?"

"Iris, please. Try to be professional. Ask me what my biggest regrets are."

"Right." And so I do, and immediately realize that the whole point of *Project Freedom* is to create a new opportunity to showcase *Emily Harper: My Story, My Bad, My Redemption.*

"I don't want to blame my parents for my mistakes," she begins, "but I was left alone a lot."

It's a challenge not to fall asleep as she recites the same story, almost word for word, as the one I read in *Darling* magazine and in the series of confessional posts on her Instagram and the conversation we had earlier at the bar. In fact, I'm so bored, I don't even notice when she finished.

"Iris? Are you going to ask me anything else? Ask me about the time I had to do community service."

"What about the time you had to do community

service?" I slur. I look at my glass. It's empty. Emily leans forward and refills it.

"Ah, yes. Community service." She sits up straight smiles into the camera. "I wish my parents had made me do community service when I was a child. Every child should do community service. It changed my life."

I'm really very tired, and unsurprisingly, very drunk too. Emily seems fine and I wonder how she does it. Maybe she has built up some kind of immunity to the effects of alcohol.

Meanwhile, Emily rambles on. I finish another glass. I feel myself slipping, my eyelids drooping, snatches of dreams appearing against my eyelids.

And then it's over.

"What did you think?" Emily asks, hands together.

"That was great, really great. Well done. I'm going to bed."

"Don't be silly. It's your turn now."

"I don't think so. I'm not famous."

"I know, but I need to practice. I've never interviewed anyone before. Let me try it."

I don't know. I guess I just think it's easier and faster to give in, so I do it. We swap places and I sit with my chin in my hands. She asks me questions as if I were a famous movie star, and I make up stories about all the crazy bad things famous people do, like going to the Met Gala on acid or whatever.

I don't know what happened after that, but when I wake up, I'm still on the couch, folded over like an old sack of potatoes. I am disoriented, my head woozy, my tongue furry. I pull my sticky eyes open and make out the bottle of wine on its side on the coffee table. It's empty. Emily is gone, but the camera is still there, blinking red. There are tissues on my lap. Dirty scrunched-up Kleenexes, like I've been crying.

And then I remember. I was crying.

Well, I don't *remember,* remember. Only the tears, the blowing of my nose, the wailing. Was I wailing? I think I was. I haven't cried in years—what self-respecting psychopath would?—and it's scaring me. Why did I cry? What did I say? All I can remember is Emily sitting in front of me, interview style. "What happened, Iris? Why did you hurt little Pauly?"

And then I explained everything.

CHAPTER 21

"I used to have blackouts. Did you ever have blackouts?"

I'm watching myself on the little screen that pops out to the side of the camera. I just can't believe what I'm seeing. I want to throw the camera against the wall, but I know I have to watch it. I have to know what I said.

"Blackouts? No…" Emily replies.

"Maybe you had blackouts about having blackouts?" I slur, grinning. Jesus. How much did I have to drink? I watch myself tilting my head to the side but doing it a bit too much, so that I lose my balance and fall sideways on my elbow. "Oops," I mumble, righting myself. "I think I should go to bed."

"So you had a blackout?" Emily asks off camera.

I watch myself drag my hands down my cheeks. I look like my face is made of rubber, like a mask, a ghost face from horror movies. "I'm a bad person. I do bad things."

"Did something happen to make you hurt Pauly? Was it only Pauly?" Emily asks.

I'm scratching my scalp so that now my hair is standing up on one side. "Why are you asking me about Pauly?"

"We're just practicing, that's all. Is this thing on?" The camera tilts. "Oh, yes." The camera rights itself. "You can talk about whatever you like, Iris. What would you like to talk about?"

"You want the moon? I'll give you the moon!"

"Okay." Emily sighs off-screen. "I think we should go to bed."

And then, for some horrible, twisted, weird, deeply disturbed reason, I say, "I loved him, you know. I really, really, really, really, really loved him." I make a sound. Like a strangled sob.

"Pauly?" Emily asks.

I snort a laugh. "No! I mean yes. I loved Pauly. I really loved Pauly. But no."

I drop my head—in real life, right now—and put my hand over my eyes. I hear myself mumble on camera. "Everybody knew. Because of the heart."

"What heart, sweetie?"

Oh, my God.

I'd gone to feed little Pauly because it was my turn. He did what he always did. Nibble on a leaf of lettuce I was holding. He'd come right down to my fingertips until they tickled. I could hear the giggles behind me, and at first I thought it was about Pauly, but then I could tell it was something else. I stood up and everyone giggled again, a bit louder, and Mr. Bellamy told them to cut it out, and you could tell he wasn't kidding. I went to sit at my desk, and that's when I saw the heart. I'd carved it into the desk. It was deep and smooth. And huge. Inside I'd carved the words, *Rose + Mr. B. 4ever*, in big letters, right in front of where I sat every day. My classmates kept stealing glances at me, giggling behind their hands. I pulled out my schoolbook and my notebook and my pen like everything was normal, like there was nothing wrong at all, like declaring my love for Mr. Bellamy for all to see was no big deal. Then I made a list of all the dumb things my classmates had done. Like when Carol wet herself last year in geography, or the time Marcus fell over and hurt his knee and cried even though there was no blood. I concentrated on my list for the whole hour, and by the time the bell rang I'd counted thirty-eight transgressions of varying severity. I tore the page and stuck it in the pocket of my skirt. I figured next time someone laughed at me I'd have something to throw back in their face.

When class ended, Mr. Bellamy asked me to stay back. He was annoyed with me, but then he'd been annoyed all class. He'd called Joshua an idiot for asking a question, and he'd snapped at us to be quiet four times, at least.

I can see myself sitting at my little desk in class like it was yesterday. My classmates filed out, barely holding back giggles. Mr. Bellamy snapped at them to cut it out, then he came to stand next to me.

"What on earth do you think you're doing, Rose?" he bellowed.

I shrank back. He'd never shouted at me before. I started to cry. Soon tears were blasting out of my eyes.

He sighed. "Hey, Rose, come on. Don't cry."

But I couldn't stop. I knew what I'd done, and I knew it was stupid. I was crying like a toddler with my eyes scrunched up, my nostrils burning, my mouth twisted.

"You're not a child, Rose. It's simply not appropriate for you to do things like that. It's embarrassing. And not just for you."

I nodded. "I'm sorry."

"It's inexcusable. For Christ's sake. I thought you were more mature than that."

"But I am!" I cried.

"Then stop crying."

I was crushed. He was the only person in the world who was nice to me. He'd helped me with my grades. He gave me his laptop. He helped me with my short stories. He said I had talent and found competitions I could send my stories to. He made me want to be a better person.

And now it was over. I'd done something stupid. I'd ruined everything.

"Are you listening to what I'm saying, Rose? Because sorry is not enough. You have to promise never to do such things again. Otherwise, I can't have you in my class, you understand? There are rules, Rose."

I wiped snot from my top lip with the back of my hand. "I don't know how."

"What do you mean?"

I looked up at him and whispered, "I don't remember doing it."

"Rose. Please don't lie. Everyone saw you do it. *I* saw you do it."

"I know I did it," I said. I recognized my own handwriting. I could see myself doing it. It was the kind of thing I did all the time, draw hearts and link our names together, but I didn't realize I'd drawn it on my desk, with my ballpoint pen, over and over until I'd scratched indelible grooves into the wood.

In the end I promised not to do things like that again, even though I knew I couldn't keep the promise. I was out of control.

For the rest of the day my classmates made kissing sounds as I walked past. "Rose is in love with Mr. Bellamy!" they'd sing out, drawing out the word *love*. Hands would furtively pinch my ass as I turned away, and giggles would precede and follow me everywhere I went. An older boy with a pimply, round face wouldn't move out of my way as I walked along the corridor.

"So Rose, we were wondering, do you just want to fuck Mr. Bellamy? Or will any of us do?" Raucous laughter behind him.

"Let me through."

He leaned forward, and in a very soft voice, he said, "What about all of us together? Would you like that?"

I punched him in the face, which sent him and his bleeding nose to the hospital. After that, they all looked away when I passed, but I could hear them anyway. *Watch out, it's crazy Rose.* Even Lola started to keep her distance.

"And then, I saw them," I mumble.

"Who?" Emily asks.

"Miss Amy."

"Was she another class pet?" Emily asks softly.

Was Miss Amy another class pet? I'm clearly pondering the question. Did Mr. Bellamy think she was another class pet? "It was the first time I saw them together," I slur.

"Who?" Emily asks again. I don't reply. I'm gazing in the middle distance. I'm back there, I can tell. I'm thirteen years old again, and I've been summoned to the principal's office for punching the boy. I'm walking past the teachers' lounge when I catch Mr. Bellamy's profile through the open door. He's sitting with Miss Amy at one of the gray Formica tables. She's only been at the school for a few weeks, and I don't like the way they're sitting together, their heads so close they're almost touching. They're alone, reading a newspaper spread out on the table. At one point he gazes up at her and smiles, and I step back and flatten myself against the wall. But I can still see them, and I am watching like a hawk as he tucks a loose strand of hair behind her ear.

In the background, Emily sighs. "I think we should go to bed."

I close my eyes. I am so relieved I could cry. I mean, it's not ideal. I said some things, too many things, but I don't think she understood the significance. She must have put the camera down, because I stare at my puffy face sideways, my eyes drooping shut, my skin pale with red blotches. I look like a Spanish omelette. Or a pizza. Then there's a long shot of the ceiling before the screen goes dark.

CHAPTER 22

And now it's daylight. I must have crawled into bed at some point, because I wake from a dark torpor, running from nightmares I can no longer remember. I make vague plans to drag myself out of bed, but it's all too depressing.

My arm is dangling on the side like an old rope. I feel around the carpet with the tips of my fingers until I find my phone. It's two o'clock in the afternoon.

"I thought you might be dead," Emily chirps happily. If only, I think. She's all dressed up, looking fresh and rested, checking her purse. I've just come out of the shower and my hair is damp. My head hurts. I glance at the coffee table. Two empty bottles and two empty glasses are still there. Did I drink *that* much? Am I insane?

"Now about the party…"

My stomach lurches. "What party?"

She frowns at me. "What do you mean, what party? I'm having a few friends over, remember? We're making martinis. Dirty ones."

Something reaches my brain through the fog. Emily telling me about that last night. I rub my eyes. They feel like they're wrapped in sandpaper.

"I can't tonight. It's Saturday and I'm working at the restaurant."

"You must be joking! I need you, Iris! Please! You can't leave me in the lurch like this." She touches her hair. "Not to put a finer point on things, but you are living here rent free for a reason. You are helping me with my work and any—"

"Okay, you know what? I'll see what I can do." Which is a lie. I'll just go without telling her.

She frowns at me. "You okay? You don't look too good."

She must be joking. "I'm okay," I mumble. I'm going to be sick. "I'll clean this up."

"That would be great, thank you. I have to go out. I can get in now for a quick massage."

Errr... What? I whip my head around, which was a mistake. It hurts my brain. "You're going out?"

"Yes."

"Now?"

"Yes. But I won't be long. An hour at the most."

She's barely out the door, and I'm already running up the floating steps. I open the door of her bedroom. I've never seen it so tidy. Her bed is made, her silk robe is folded on the side of an armchair. The door to her bathroom is open, but the door to her walk-in closet is shut.

I pull up my sleeves. I've got this. I know what to do. In and out.

I start with the closet.

CHAPTER 23

"What are you doing in my room?"

I laugh. A couple of short cackles like a mad rooster. I put my hand on my chest. It feels like there were bits of shrapnel flying around in there. "You're back!"

I don't know how long I was in Emily's room, but it must have been a long time. I just didn't notice. When she said my name just now, I was crouched by her little desk with my back to her, frantically trying to unlock the little drawer. And that drawer is the size of a paperback so it was unlikely to contain my laptop, but that's how desperate I was. Because *I had searched everywhere* and I was going out of my mind. I still am.

When I came into her bedroom earlier, my heart full of flight and fancy, I immediately went to her closet and went through her million handbags, even those that were too small. I patted down cashmere sweaters and silk tops, jeans, and scarves, and rummaged through travel bags and Chanel suitcases and hat boxes and even shoe boxes. I ran my hands down coats and jackets and dresses on hangers and felt under the shelves with my fingers in case she'd taped it under there.

I went through her bathroom and through her vanity where she keeps all her makeup, and I resisted the urge to swipe the sleeping pills, and I checked behind her toilet because I know all the tricks, and I felt under the mattress, and every time I came back empty, a little chunk of my heart splintered off. And still I looked in the most desperate of places, like the little drawers of her bedside table where I found a little pink-and-white gun in a little pink-and-white purse holster and I don't know why I was surprised because she's mad, totally mad, and I checked behind the mirror on the wall and I was tasting blood by then, from twisting and biting the inside of my cheek, and the only place I hadn't been able to look in was the little drawer on her stupid little antique French desk because it was locked and I tried to break it open with my fingernails which broke off and the skin under them started bleeding, and I ran to the bathroom for something I could use to pick the lock and came back with one of those little brush toothpicks and now, she's here.

I've stood up so fast I've given myself a headache. Like my brain got flung against my skull. "I didn't hear you come in!"

"Clearly." She's frowning, her mouth turned down. "What are you doing, Iris?"

"I was looking for something to wear for the party. You said I could borrow something."

"Did I? I don't remember that." She glances at my fingers speckled with blood, at the toothpick I'm holding, then at the cute little French desk behind me.

"But I haven't found anything," I say. "To wear, I mean. Actually, sorry, I need some air."

I hurry past her and down the stairs and straight out the front door. I don't even take my keys. I have to get out of here. I have to think. I have to scream, and I don't trust myself to hold it in. In the elevator, I hit my forehead against the mirrored wall the whole way down.

I don't think I ever seriously considered I would *not* find the laptop. But it's happened. The laptop isn't in her apartment, so I'm not going to find it, and now I don't know what to do. I don't know what's going to happen to me, and I am thinking of my mother. I'm thinking that I should tell her before she hears it from someone else. Like the police. It's only a matter of time.

The lift doors open. Tiffany, Otto, and Cassidy stand there.

"Iris! Hi!" They're holding brown paper bags with bottles and bags of chips sticking out. Cassidy pushes her sunglasses to the top of her head. "You look upset, Iris. Everything okay?"

"Everything is fine. I'm just getting some air, that's all. I'll be right back."

"Okay, see you later."

I get out of the elevator, and they get in. Behind me, Tiffany calls out. "Iris! Wait!"

I turn around.

"In that case…" She jams the door open with her foot while fumbling with her purse. "On your way back up… would you mind going down to the storage cage in the basement? There's a cardboard box marked *Special Glasses*. It's not heavy or anything, just cumbersome." She hands me a butterfly keychain with two keys. "31B. Is that okay? It's just we're carrying a lot, saves me going back down."

I stare at the key in her hand and reach for it slowly,

"It lives in the kitchen drawer, by the way. I just forgot to return it last time."

I look at it in my hand, my spirit too battered to be hopeful.

"Sure," I say. "I can do that."

CHAPTER 24

The basement smells of gasoline. I press the light switch, and fluorescent lights buzz to life. The storage cage is exactly that, a wire cage, approximately six by six feet all the way to the ceiling and wedged between similar wire cages. Most other people have skis and bicycles and even surfboards in theirs. Emily has two layers of hanging racks covered by large sheets of white canvas. They smell of mothballs. I peek under the canvas. Winter clothes, by the looks of it. Lots of winter clothes.

Against another wall of the cage are half a dozen cardboard boxes. I stare at them. Some of them are labeled (Special Glasses), and some of them are not. I take a breath, open the first unlabeled box, and for a moment I think I'm dreaming.

It's my old Christmas sweater.

I put my hands on it. There's something under it, something hard and flat. I lift it out and unwrap it carefully, and there it is. My laptop. I wait for the feeling of elation to envelop me, but it doesn't come. I just feel sick. And then I remember. I hate that thing. I hate it passionately. It represents everything that is wrong with me. Other people might see a piece of hardware, but what I see is a deformed, oozing, vile testament of my malevolence.

I close my eyes. *Cut it out, Rose,* I admonish myself. Why are you even thinking like that? I am what I am, and who cares? Not me, that's who. But let it be said that I can't wait to get rid of that thing and that in my new life, I will do my very best not to hurt anyone ever again. Also, I haven't hurt anyone in almost ten years, so clearly I'm better. On the psychopathic scale I'm probably a five out of ten. If I keep at it, then maybe one day I'll be a one.

But before I do anything else, I'm going to trash that document, because let's face it, it would be just my luck to lose the laptop, again, on my way to the nearest landfill.

I press the power button. I don't know for sure that it's charged, but I imagine Emily charged it at some point since she stole its contents, and I figure it was still charged when she turned it off and stored it down here. And just as I thought, it whirs and clanks to life. I stand there, gnawing on a fingernail, waiting for it to come fully alive. Meanwhile, I plan my next move. I still have my things upstairs, so I have to go back and get them. I'm thinking again of Ashley's passport. I know where she keeps it—in the dresser in her bedroom. I saw it when she was out and I was riffling through her things, looking for the necklace Ben had given me in case she'd stolen it. I didn't find my necklace, but I found her passport. I could go back there, say I need somewhere to stay for the night. I'll pay a hundred dollars, I'll say. Do I have a hundred dollars? Because Ashley will want to see the money up front. Yes. I do. Also, I could totally kill Ashley if I have to. That's how much she annoys me. I could start my new, harmless life the day after.

The laptop finally turns on. A bunch of error messages pop up. No Wi-Fi, the operating system requires updating...

The battery is very low, but I don't need much. All I want to do is delete my diary and empty the trash.

I'm about to do just that, my finger hovering over the mouse pad, when another error message pops up.

Unable to sync document to SkyDrive.

I stare at the message. Sync document? Sync where? Did Emily set this up? Is she syncing my diary to the cloud? If that's the case, she's got multiple copies. The thought makes my stomach curl.

I'm about to close the pop-up when the laptop goes black. I press the power button repeatedly, but it's no use. The battery is dead.

I consider what to do now. I'm wearing jeans and a T-shirt, so I can't hide it on me. I'll just have to come back for it. But that's okay. I know where it is now, and that's the main thing. Heck, that's *everything*. I won't go to the restaurant tonight. I'll go back upstairs with her box of glasses, put the key back in the kitchen drawer, and text Ben that I'm sick. Then later when she's asleep, I will leave her a note saying my mother needs me or something, and I will sneak out in the dead of night and take the laptop on the way out. The key to the basement will be missing, but who cares? She might think I kept it by accident, or just that it got misplaced.

Okay. Good plan. Easy. I grab the box of glasses and go back upstairs.

They're all in the kitchen unpacking the groceries. I put the box of glasses on the corner of the counter and make a show of dropping the key in the top drawer.

"Thank you, Iris," Emily says, opening the box.

"No problem," I say cheerily. I'm so happy I feel dizzy. "I'm just going upstairs for a sec, then I'll come down and help."

"We've got plenty of time," Emily says. "I still have to get ready."

I go to my room and pack my things into my duffel bag. I want to be able to leave quickly when the time comes, and I don't want to leave anything behind. And I'll ditch my cell phone and get a new prepaid one, and then I'll... Ben's face pops into my mind. I mentally shoo him away. I'll have to think about that later. I just want to get through the next few hours and get out of here. Meanwhile, my motto is *act normal.*

I put my bag in the closet and go back downstairs to the living room where I proceed to tidy up. I have to keep myself busy, away from the others so I don't have to talk to anyone because I think if I opened my mouth right now, I'd just laugh like some crazy demented clown. Even now I'm grinning so hard I have to bite my bottom lip to make myself stop. Emily has taken all her bits and pieces upstairs, and all that's left on the table are some magazines, which I gather into a neat pile.

Emily returns, looking fabulous in a gold lamé dress, with her hair styled in an elaborate updo held in place by a gold butterfly, tendrils of blond curls framing her face.

"You look amazing," I say. I'm in such a good mood, I want to make everybody as happy as I am.

"Thank you, sweetie," she says.

"Where's Tiffany?" I ask.

"I've sent her away for more supplies. Would you mind putting chips in bowls?"

"Sure," I say, plumping cushions on the couch.

"That looks great. Thank you, Iris. You're very sweet."

"No problem!" I say, smiling broadly. I move to the kitchen and get bowls out of the cupboard. Cassidy is chopping carrots into sticks. I smile at her as I make a space on the counter next to her.

"We're making martinis," Otto says. "Dirty ones." He

hands me one. "Here." I notice they all have one. I don't want a martini. I don't want to drink anything tonight. I need to stay focused. But I also don't want to make Emily suspicious. *Remember the motto. Act normal.*

"Thanks, that looks great." I put it aside and empty bags of chips into bowls. When I'm done, I put them on the table, then I take a sip of my drink.

Emily puts on a record on the player. When she drops the needle, it makes a scratching sound. "Iris is from Wisconsin," she says to no one in particular. "And so is Otto. Isn't that a coincidence?"

"Really? Where about?" Otto asks.

"Small town," I mutter, taking a sip of my drink.

"Which town?" Otto says.

I put my martini glass down, shove a handful of chips into my mouth, then rearrange the pile of magazines I've already rearranged twice. "Green Falls," I say, my mouth full of chips, so that it comes out as *Eenfflls.*

"Huh. Never heard of it, I don't think. Is it in Green County?"

"Mmm…" I say, which could mean anything, really.

"These small towns, they can have very dark undercurrents," Emily says. "Some of the worst murders happen in small towns. Have you read *In Cold Blood* by Truman Capote? That was in Wisconsin, wasn't it?"

"Kansas," Otto says gravely. I pick up my martini glass again. I am wracking my brain for something to say, something that will propel the conversation away from Wisconsin and Kansas and small-town murders, but nothing comes.

"Oh yes, Kansas, that's right," Emily says. "Actually, it's funny we should be talking about Kansas. I was reading about the most horrific murder that happened there nine, ten years ago. Some poor woman was strangled in her bed while her husband was at a baseball game. Who would do such a thing? They never found who did it. Have you heard of that murder, Iris? What was the town again..."

She clicks her fingers. "Oh, I know. Pike Creek!" And my drink slips through my fingers and shatters on the timber floor, spraying shards of glass everywhere.

CHAPTER 25

We're back in my room. I'm folded over on the bed with my arms around myself. I'm going to be sick, right on her velvet-pile carpet.

Emily is leaning against the door, her eyebrows knotted together. "There's no need to get so upset, Rose."

"My name is Iris. You have me confused with someone else."

"Really? I wonder what this is?" She whips up a piece of paper from her pocket like a magician pulling a rabbit out of a hat. I look up at it.

TO ROSE: 1/2 lobster mornay with staff discount: $20.

"You went through my stuff?" I'm on my feet, reaching for it, but she puts it back in her pocket.

"Rose. Please. You've been going through *my* stuff ever since you got here."

I sit back down, deflated. "How long have you known?"

She looks up, taps her finger on her chin. "Erm...let me think. Oh yes. From the day you sent Tiff to buy flowers. Tiff left me a voicemail to say some strange young woman outside gave her the message. And just like that, I knew. Iris.

Just like the flower! Clumsy Iris, who came *twice* to get my book signed. Was Iris the owner of the laptop I found, and the author of the diary? I was curious. I texted Tiff back and told her yes, please go and get the flowers. And then I went outside to meet you. My biggest fan. So sweet." She pouts prettily. "You made such a big show of wanting to come back with me, and you flattered me in all the right ways. I was very impressed. When we got back to the apartment and you went to the bathroom, I texted Tiff to tell her I was going to play a little joke on my friend Iris. I told her, when you bring the flowers, I will pretend to be angry with you and ask you to leave, but it's not real and I'll explain later. Just be a honey and play along."

"So the whole Matt thing, you made it up?"

She touches her hair. "Oh, no. Matt's real. And he's an asshole. He did have an affair with that stupid cunt Maria. But it had nothing to do with Tiff."

Oh my God. I just can't believe what I'm hearing. I feel like such an idiot.

"Look, if it makes you feel better, I knew you'd show up at some point. The book became much more successful than I'd expected, so I assumed that sooner or later, the owner of the laptop would come asking for an explanation. And it was not a nice feeling, waiting for you to show up. You could ruin my life with a single phone call to my publisher. You could turn me into a laughingstock. God, what would my parents say?" She shudders.

"But you could have written your own book! You had so much going for you! A hundred thousand followers like you! They would have bought whatever you published! You didn't have to steal my book!"

She studies her fingernails. "Actually…"

"What?"

"I bought most of those."

"Excuse me?"

"I had maybe five hundred people follow me and comment on what I wrote. And it was wonderful, but I wanted more. I wanted to show my parents that I was someone people looked up to. I wasn't the loser they made me feel like. So I bought followers." She shrugs. "Everybody does it."

"Really? I don't."

"No, well, you wouldn't. You barely know how to upload a photo, so…"

"And you got a book deal and a big advance on the basis of a hundred thousand fake followers, and you couldn't deliver, so you stole my diary. Nice work, Emily."

"Well, they're not all fake now! I meant I bought the first fifty thousand, then the rest followed. As followers do." She smiles. "Oh, and the book deal? I made that up. I was trying to manifest one, and the way to manifest your desires, as everyone knows, is to pretend they've already happened. I put out there that I had a book deal and waited for the universe to respond."

"That's just insane."

"Well, I found your diary, didn't I? Who's laughing now."

And I'm thinking, okay, maybe she's got a point. Maybe I should try manifesting things. Pretend they've already happened. Like she's already dead.

"I'd been telling my parents about the book deal as part of my manifestation exercise. But then a year went by, and my mother would ask me, 'Emily, what happened to that book deal of yours?' And the way she said it, I knew *she* knew that I'd made it up. You see, for maybe ten minutes she was impressed. Her wayward daughter was going to be a published author. But then she understood there was no advance and no book deal, and at some level, I think she was glad. Like the world had realigned itself to the way things should be. I was back to being a disappointment and a failure, and now I'd managed to fall even further down her esteem, which, you know, took some doing. So I tried to write something I could self-publish, but I couldn't come up with anything. And one day I was at LaGuardia waiting for a flight and I was early, so I bought a latte and paid for it. And as I was leaving, the woman behind the counter called out to me and said, 'You forgot this!' It was this horrible Christmas sweater, and I was, like, I don't think so, but when she picked it up, I could tell there was something in it. So I had to take a look. It was too interesting a situation to pass up. And I'm glad I did. Oh, don't look at me like that. You would have done the same. I know you would have. And anyway, all there was on it was that one document, and it was good, Rose. Really. I couldn't stop reading."

"So you stole it."

She pats her hair. "I believe the more accurate description of the situation is that you lost it, and I found it. You should take better care of your things. Oh, by the way, don't bother looking for it in the basement. It's gone. As soon as Tiff told me she sent you down there to get the glasses, I knew you'd find it. When you came back, I could tell that you did. It was written all over your face. Also, you were smiling, and I'm not sure I saw you smile like that before. You're quite pretty when you smile. You should do it more. Anyway, when you were up here, I sent Tiff down there. I asked her to take the laptop away, to a secret place. Secret to you, I mean. Not to her, obviously. She has no idea why it's special or what's on it, just so you know."

I look at her. I wonder how someone so pretty can be filled with so much ugliness. "What's to stop me from calling your publisher and telling them what you did?" I say with way more bravado than I feel.

"That's an excellent question, Rose. What's to stop you?

Well, let me spell it out. You see, I didn't know whatever you did that was so"—she makes air quotes—"terrible, but I knew that you'd gone to see your teacher's wife, just like you wrote about, and told her about your imaginary love affair. No, wait. It was imaginary, wasn't it? Yes. Of course it was. Anyway. You know what I thought? I thought you'd gotten him fired. I thought that was the"—again, air quotes—"terrible thing. But then, your little friend Lola started messaging me, asking about Rose Dunmore." She puts an index finger on her chin. "And I started to wonder. I went searching. I didn't actually find anything about you, which was interesting in itself. But I had to be prepared for the very likely eventuality you'd show up on my doorstep. I searched deeper for any scandal related to a high school teacher fired after having an imaginary affair with a student, which led me nowhere, at first, but eventually, I found an interesting item about Pike Creek."

She traces a headline in the air, like she's reading a billboard. "Teacher's wife murdered while husband is at a high school baseball game. I thought, surely not. I called your old high school saying I was from NYU and I was checking graduation records for one of our prospective students. And guess what? You never graduated!" She laughs, then stops abruptly. "Oh, sweetie, you're crying!"

She comes to sit on the bed next to me and puts her hand around my shoulders. I try to jerk away, but she just holds me tighter.

"What do you want from me?"

"We'll come to that. Have I told you about the four Rs of self-forgiveness?" She wipes tears off my cheek with the back of her fingers. "Responsibility, remorse, reparation, renewal. You're at like, step zero. It's time to take responsibility, sweetie. I know it's not pleasant to think about, but that's what being an adult means."

I feel my face distort. I am terrified. She's completely insane. I know that now.

There's a knock at the door.

"Yes?" Emily says.

It's Cassidy. "Your guests are arriving. Oh! Everything okay, you guys?"

"Oh, thanks, sweetie. We're fine. Iris was confiding in me about some terrible things in her past, but she's okay now. Aren't you, Iris? Poor thing. Do you want to borrow something of mine for the party? Would you like that?"

I brush my cheeks. "I don't want to stay," I whimper.

"Now, now." She clicks her tongue, turns back to Cassidy. "Iris is embarrassed. You don't need to be embarrassed, sweetie. You're among friends here."

"Of course you are!" Cassidy says. "Come to the party, Iris. It will cheer you up. Oh, honey... You look really upset. You're in good hands here." She smiles at Emily. "I will leave you two to it. Let me know if you need me. I'll take care of things downstairs."

"Thank you, Cass. We'll be right down."

She closes the door.

"For Christ's sake. Stop crying, Rose. You look a mess. What will my friends say? Come on. Dry your tears. I have a proposition for you."

CHAPTER 26

"A proposition?" I try to keep the eagerness out of my tone, but I can't. I want her to tell me. I don't care what she wants, I'm doing it. I'm absolutely taking the deal. Bring it on.

She gets up, stands in front of me, and crosses her arms. "You tell me exactly what you did to Mrs. Bellamy—" she makes a sad face "—on camera."

Okay, maybe not *that* deal. I snort a laugh. "You're insane."

"Now, now. Let's keep it nice, okay? And look, it's a shame it didn't work out last night when I taped you for my fake podcast. I fed you a couple of my sleeping pills to loosen you up—that's what happens when you mix it with alcohol— but maybe I gave you too much. You stopped making any sense, and then you fell asleep. Anyway, never mind. I think this is better, don't you? I don't like tricking people into doing things. So. You tell me what you did, and then you can be on your way."

"But I didn't do anything!" I lie.

"Sweetie, please. We're way past that. My problem is, the way things stand, any day now, people will learn that I didn't write *Diary of an Octopus*. Your little friend Lola. She's been at me for ages. Is it Rose? Do you know Rose Dunmore? I haven't spoken to her, but little Lola is going to tell someone. Pretty soon it will be out there that *Diary of an Octopus* is actually Diary of Rose Dunmore." She sighs. "Anyway. It's too late now. No use crying over spilled milk. By the way. Something I'm curious about. Lola read the book, so she knows you went to visit Mrs. Bellamy while the game was going on. You and her had a fight just before and you wrote about that. And of course she knows Mrs. Bellamy died that night, so why hasn't she put two and two together yet? Is she...you know...not very bright? Because it's hard to understand why she's taking so long to bring the police into it. She was a good friend of yours, wasn't she?"

I wipe my nose with my sleeve, nod.

"I suppose that's why. She wants to talk to you before she goes to the police. Sweet, really. I like that. Anyway. The way I see it, the only way out that I can think of—and I've thought a lot about this—is to say that I found your laptop, I read the diary, and did some online sleuthing. I understood then that what I had in my hands was possibly the clue to who killed poor Mrs. Bellamy." Another sad face. "I felt very strongly that I had to do something to bring justice to this poor woman. I could just turn the laptop over to the police with everything else I found out online, but is it enough to arrest you? Maybe everybody knew you had a crush on your teacher, and everybody knew you likely killed his wife"— sad face—"but if there's no proof, the police will say there's nothing they can do. So I thought—" She puts a hand on her chest. "What if I published this diary? Then the culprit would come after me! They'd want to retrieve their laptop, and then they'd try to kill me. Case closed. The police would have to arrest you for the attempted murder of me, which would also prove you killed poor Mrs. Bellamy. I would be a heroine. Dangerous? Absolutely. I would be putting myself out as bait to bring justice to a woman I'd never met. And I would put my trust in God to keep me safe. What do you think?"

She crosses her arms over her chest. I am speechless.

"I know, it's a stretch, sure. But I think it will work, don't you?" She puts a finger on her chin. "I wonder if they'll commission a Netflix series about me. My terrible ordeal with my stalker Iris. How I put myself in the face of danger to avenge a woman I'd never met. Anyway, here we are. Now I realize you need a little incentive here, so what about this: If you confess, on camera, and also explain that you infil-trated yourself into my life pretending to be a fan and calling yourself Iris because you wanted your laptop back, I will give you ten thousand dollars, in cash, and I would let you go before I took your confession to the police. I'll give you two whole days. You can get quite far in two days, you know? You can get all the way to Australia in a day. So win-win, see? I'm the heroine of the story." She pats her hair. "Even if I acci-dentally let the murderer get away. But I don't think people will hold that against me, do you? And you can start over in Australia or whatever. What do you say?"

"You're insane."

She sighs. "Sweetie. I understand you're in shock, but there's no need for this kind of language. And I'm not without compassion. I realize you might want some time to think about this. What about one week? Would that work? If after one week I don't have a recorded true confession of how you killed poor Mrs. Bellamy"—sad face—"then I'll have no choice but to take the laptop to the police. I will explain what I was trying to achieve, and that I now realize that the woman calling herself Iris and pretending to be a fan of mine, i.e., my stalker, was, in fact, the murderer I've been baiting all this time." She looks at me, head tilted. I'm going to be sick.

"I'll be honest with you," she continues. "It works better for me if I have your confession. Unfortunately, your diary does not go into the specifics of what you did. It would be extremely disappointing if you got off on a technicality. Also, a confession would make for great content for my feed." She checks her watch. "You think about it, sweetie, okay? One week. Now I don't want to rush you, but we are having a party and you look terrible…"

"I want to go home," I whisper.

"But this is your home, sweetie!"

I bury my face in my hands. "All I ever wanted was my laptop, okay?" I cry. "I would never have told anyone about what you did. I don't care! I just wanted my laptop back and to be left alone!"

"Yes, well, unfortunately, it doesn't work that way. Finders keepers, sweetie. Just tell me how you killed Charlene Bellamy, and you can be on your way. Come on. Stop crying. I'll fix you up and lend you something nice. It'll be fun!"

PART II

CHAPTER 27

Rose. My sweet little Rose. My sweet, sweet Amelie... Chet Bellamy smiled to himself at the sight of Rose walking into class. *My little Rose by any other name... If you didn't exist, someone would have to invent you.*

And not because Chet was attracted to Rose. Chet had never been attracted to children, although his wife would dispute that. No. Rose wasn't his type. She was too pale, too weird, and yes, too young. But Charlene had been suspicious —to put it mildly—of Chet's denials on that score. Sometimes when they argued, Charlene would call him a monster, a creep, a pervert, and Chet knew part of her shrieking insistence was so that she could justify to herself why Chet never touched her anymore.

They had been too young when they got married. That was the problem. They met in college, in California, where Chet was majoring in English and psychology, and Charlene in social work. She was a waitress at the college bar where Chet and his friends would drink most nights. She was cute, with her curly hair and her pink headbands, her small hands

—Chet loved small hands—and it was only a matter of time before he asked her out. And for a while, he was in love.

But that was fifteen years ago, and now, most days, it took all of Chet's willpower not to tell Charlene the truth, which was that she was an old harpy who hated everything about him, that once she'd been sweet and pretty and loving, but now she'd become old and bitter and ugly, and that he'd rather eat glass than make love to her.

It was because of Charlene that they moved to Pike Creek. At his last job, Chet had enjoyed a brief fling with a seventeen-year-old, which no one would argue was akin to cradle-snatching, except Charlene. Chet had always been lucky with women. His whole adult life he'd been called charming and charismatic, remarked on for his green eyes, told he was handsome, and complimented on his boyish good looks. Women liked his self-deprecating sense of humor. Women liked everything about him, especially the way he would make them feel special. They went out of their way to get his attention, and seventeen-year-old girls were no different. Seventeen-year-olds knew exactly what they wanted and how to get it, and this one had wanted Chet, and she got him. Sure, he didn't mind. She was gorgeous and young and supple, just the way Charlene was when they first met, back in the dark ages. Anyway, it was just his luck that he happened to leave his phone lying around and walked out of the room before the screen had a chance to lock itself. Charlene grabbed it and found all the texts and photographs he and the girl had been exchanging. Charlene threw a fit of rage and called the school principal. Chet was summoned to a meeting and told to pack his bags and find work elsewhere —in another state, preferably. The man didn't want a scandal any more than Chet did. Although in Chet's case, it would have been a tad more than a scandal. A felony, probably. Especially considering the pictures he and the seventeen-year-old girl had been exchanging.

Pike Creek was the only high school that would hire an English teacher without references, and as Chet discovered, the last miserable hellhole at the bottom of the earth. It would be an understatement to say that he hated it here. He hated everything about the place. He hated the town and its inhabitants. He hated the miserable school and the other teachers with their sloppy tracksuits and the way their stomachs protruded over their belts. He hated the students who had no hope of achieving anything and still had to be taught the curriculum. He hated his miserable house with its cheap drapes and stained wallpaper. He hated the yard where the grass had stopped growing.

But Charlene had his old phone now. Not with her—she wasn't that stupid—but in a secret hiding place. She insisted she could whip it out any time she liked and have him thrown in jail by clicking her fingers. So Chet had to convince Charlene that he was a changed man and that he loved her very much, and this was their chance to start again, which took a superhuman effort. Charlene was a bad drunk, that was the problem. A bad, bad, drunk. She'd start to cry, then call him names, scream at him that he couldn't even *get it up* anymore—*oh, I can get it up, Charlene, just not for you*—and sometimes even slap him. And Chet, mindful of the evidence in her possession that could send him to prison at the click of her fingers, would talk her down. He'd whisper tender words in her ear, apologize for not being affectionate enough, assure her that she was the love of his life, that he was having difficulties adjusting to this new town, that was all, but that everything would be okay in the end. And Charlene would sulk a while then let herself be coaxed out of her mood, and they would hug and cuddle and maybe even kiss, which was by far the most repulsive act Chet could possibly engage in, but, hey, had to be done.

Then life would drag on miserably until the next meltdown.

So sure, a young girl like Rose falling in love with Chet before his eyes was vaguely entertaining. Ever since her father left, that kid had walked around with a great big hole where her heart should be, a hollow well longing to be filled. Chet was bored, so he filled it. He could play the kindly, caring teacher when he wanted. It was entertaining to tell her she was bright (she wasn't), that she was a good writer (she wasn't), that she should take the elective unit because she had talent (she didn't). And when she told Chet that she was behind on her homework because her laptop was broken, it amused him to lend her his old one and have her look at him like he was Prince Charming and he'd just handed her a glass slipper. It made a nice change from the forty-year-olds with their dark roots showing and their fingers stained with tobacco who'd flirt with him because he happened to smile at them. Sometimes Chet would pretend he had a teacher's meeting over an evening just to get away from harping Charlene, and he'd go to the Longstaff Bar & Grill, the only passable watering hole for miles, where single women would sidle up to him with their loose tops falling over one shoulder and their high heels and brand-new nail polish on their stubby nails. They were the sad, lonely ones, desperately hanging on to the fantasy that they still *had a chance at love.*

Not with me, you don't. Get the app and swipe left, you old hag. But they believed Chet was lonely just like they were because his wife never went out with him. They thought because he got to fuck them in their sad old trailer, that he would be grateful. They thought he would fall in love with them and leave his wife for good.

They were dreaming. Charlene would never let him go.

And then, Chet discovered Rose's diary. He was looking for a file on his computer when he saw it among his documents saved to the cloud. *Mydiary*, it was called. Later, for reasons that only Rose's pea soup brain could possibly explain, it would become *Diary of an Octopus*.

He opened it and started to read at random.

Dear Diary,

Mr. B. took me and Toby home in his Corvette after school today, because it was raining and it was late. I sat in the front and Toby in the back and we dropped Toby off first because he lived closer.

Afterwards we stopped at the railroad tracks to wait for the train to pass. I pointed to my house. I told Mr. B. about the fish tank in our living room, about how when the train rolls past the water will quiver for a full minute. "To a goldfish, it must be like a tsunami," I said, and he smiled at me, like I'd just said something sweet but also clever, and I felt a gliding sensation in my chest.

He turned back to wait for the crossing, and I studied the side of his face, his jaw, strong and masculine, his lips the color of ripe plums, the little coarse hair growing over his Adam's apple. I imagined him looking at me that way again, the gap between us closing, his lips suddenly close to mine. I imagined him caressing the corner of my mouth with his thumb. I imagined him whispering, "I love the way you think."

I love him so much!!!

Love, Amelie.

It's fair to say that Chet hadn't laughed like that in years. In fact, he laughed so much he could have given himself a hernia.

Every day after that he would wait for the next installment with an eagerness he hadn't felt in months. The imagination of a thirteen-year-old is something to behold, but Rose was next-level weird. To be the subject of her fantasies was fascinating and repulsive, in equal parts. Of course, he knew he'd have to put a stop to it eventually. The very last thing Chet needed was for Charlene to think he was fucking another student. A thirteen-year-old to boot. Christ. The thought made him sick. Charlene would for sure whip up her receipts, as she called them. (*I have receipts, Chet, remember that. How could I not, Charlene?* was how that conversation went.) So yes, Chet would absolutely have to put a stop to Rose's romantic descriptions of her inner fantasy life with Chet, but there was so much fun still to be had, so he decided to enjoy himself a little longer.

CHAPTER 28

Emily gets me to unpack my duffel bag and put my things back where they were, which feels not unlike having to dig your own grave while your would-be killer watches on. Then, she takes me into her room and sits me down in front of her dressing table then stands behind me and lifts both my arms at my side.

"Look at you," she says, meeting my eye in the mirror. "You look like a scarecrow."

This is it. I'm going to die. This woman is insane, and she's going to kill me, I just know it. It's only a matter of time.

Emily drops my arms and sighs, then starts brushing my hair. "You really need to use product on your hair, Rose."

I don't reply. She keeps brushing, and after a few minutes she admires her handiwork. "Much better," she murmurs to herself.

I take that as my cue. "Thank you," I say, standing on wobbly legs, but she gently pushes me back down.

"I can't let you go out looking like that, sweetie. My friends will think my fans live in trash cans."

She picks out a small jar of foundation from the dresser and starts to rub it on my face. When she's satisfied my face is caked enough, she puts down the foundation and picks up a tube of mascara. I vaguely wonder if she's going to stab my eye with it, but she doesn't. She rubs a little blush on my cheek, some lipstick on my mouth, except she's not doing it right, so I look like a drunken lush, and the whole time I'm thinking, *Take the money, Rose. Do what she wants and take the money. I can go to Texas, or Colorado, big, wide-open spaces where I can lose myself. I'll call myself Tana. I always liked the name Tana. I'll get a waitressing job, cash, and move into a rooming house. Ten thousand dollars is more than enough to start a new life. Just take the fucking money and get the hell out of here.*

"There. What do you think?"

I stare at my sunken eyes, at the skin below them stained purple, at my hair stiff like black straw. I still look like a scarecrow but one with a painted face and butterfly barrettes in its hair. Emily goes to her closet and pulls out a blue wrap dress. "It will match your eyes nicely," she says, holding it up against me. I don't even look at it.

"You're welcome," she says with a sigh. "I'll see you downstairs shortly, okay?"

She's almost out of the room, her hand on the doorknob. "You're not going to murder me in the night, are you?" She raises an eyebrow.

And I'm thinking, I could kill her now. Get it over with. Quick twist of the neck. No one will know until later, and I'll be long gone by then. I just need a good blackout, that's all.

Except this is the thing about blackouts—or fugue states as Mr. Bellamy used to call them—they're like taxis. You can never get one when you really need it.

"Because there's an outgoing email in my outbox addressed to Tiff," she continues. "Every day I change the scheduled send date to the following day. If I miss a day, Tiff will get the email. She'll know who you are and what you did and that it's highly likely you murdered me too. We don't want that, do we?"

Oh well, that's that then.

It's a full-on rave down there. There must be a hundred beautiful people who wear hats and sunglasses indoors, wear jumpsuits and platform boots and dresses that are barely there.

I stand in the corner, my arms crossed, desperately trying to think my way out of this nightmare. Then I become aware of Emily prattling on in the background.

"Yes, thank you. I'm very proud of it. That book is my salvation, you know. My way of giving back to the world."

My stomach fills with lead. I'm waiting for her to say it, because she is that kind of horrible person. *And you know the funniest thing? It's actually a true story! And not only that, but Iris, here, my stalker—have you met my stalker? Anyway, she is the Emily character in the book! Yes! And her name is Rose! And she killed her teacher's wife! Isn't that a hoot?*

"That's why I published *Diary of an Octopus,*" Emily continues. "To make the world a better place. Oh, thank you. You're too kind. Oh Iris, sweetie, can you bring me a fresh martini, please? This one's a hair above room temperature."

I push myself off the wall and do as I'm told. I don't actually know how to make a martini, so I just slosh whatever alcohol is on the kitchen bench into her glass and add in a spoonful of salt, a couple olives that I drop on the floor first and squash a little with my foot, and a lime quarter. There. That should be dirty enough, I think.

"She's my little protégé, you could say. That's French, you know. I love everything French, don't you? So sophisticated. No, Iris isn't French, but she's very sweet. Absolutely adores me. Worships the ground I walk on."

"Where did you find her?" her friend asks.

"She's one of my fans. She bought my book twice. Isn't that the sweetest thing? Begged me to sign it for her each time. She'd do anything for me. It's very touching, really."

I hand her her drink with my jaw set like it's rusted shut. Every time I glance at her after that with her fake sweeties and her fake face, it's like the mask has melted off and all that's left is a bunch of electrical wires and a handful of cogs.

Take the money and get the hell out of here, Rose.

The dining table is covered with martini glasses everywhere you look. I can't be bothered getting myself a drink, so I pick up one at random and take a sip. Then I take another sip of a different glass and I keep doing that until they're all gone. Someone passes me a joint and points at a woman with a crown of roses in her hair. *Can you give this to Poppy, please?* No. I can't. I keep it for myself. Screw the lot of you.

At one point I go upstairs to the bathroom because people are snorting cocaine in the downstairs one and I can't hold it in anymore. My bedroom is swathed in a fog of cigarette smoke and packed with guests, some of them idly going through my things like they're at a garage sale and all the best stuff has already been snapped up. They're so stoned, they think they're underwater, swaying to the music with their eyes half closed and their arms over their heads, like a giant kelp farm. I have a sudden urge to throw a great big net over them then watch them struggle to get out.

I slip into the bathroom and do my business, and then I sit on the toilet lid and check my phone. I have four texts from Ben.

Oh God. I forgot. I was supposed to work tonight.

Everything okay? ... You're still coming? ... Where are you? ... Getting worried, call me.

I press the heel of my hand against one closed eye. I type, *Sorry. I'm sick. I'll call tomorrow x* but then I delete it and start to cry. I'm thinking that I will never see him again because I'm taking the money. I tell myself that Ben deserves better than me and that all I'm doing is giving him his freedom back. *If you love someone, set them free!*

But it doesn't really work. Instead I find myself—and not for the first time—resenting all the normal girls out there. The good girls with their smooth skin and shiny hair and sunny smiles, girls who go through life never doing anything wrong and who get to pick out babies' names and nursery wallpaper and honeymoon destinations and who would *never* take the money. But I will because I'm bad, and bad people can't have nice things.

Someone knocks on the door and I look up, catching my reflection in the mirror. I've got mascara tracks running down my cheeks and butterfly barrettes hanging limply halfway down my hair. The person knocks again. I ignore them. I'm busy going mad in here. Go use Emily's bathroom or wait your turn for the downstairs one because I'm never coming out. I'm going to die in here. Screw you, world. I'm done. Game over.

I tell myself it doesn't matter about the laptop anyway since she saved the document to the cloud or whatever that SkyDrive pop-up message was.

I freeze. SkyDrive. Syncing. The words light up through the fog in my brain. My pulse is racing. As far as I know, if you delete a copy on one device, then it gets deleted on all devices and on the cloud. What if I log on to her computer here, find the SkyDrive cloud, and delete my diary? Then once she re-connects my laptop to the internet, that copy will be gone too, right? That's how cloud storage works, doesn't it? Delete once, delete everywhere?

Oh my God. I feel like I've been trapped under ten feet

of earth, and after hours of scratching with my bare hands, I can just discern a sliver of light. A tiny bit of hope—barely there, sure, but that's a lot more than I've had recently.

I have a plan: Delete my diary from her computer and from the SkyDrive cloud. Then I'll give her a confession, but I will include details that never happened. Something easily disprovable, except she won't know that. Then I'll take the cash and run. Two days later when she gives my confession to the police, they'll know it couldn't have happened that way. And when they check the laptop, my diary won't be there.

She'll have nothing.

I clean my face, straighten my dress, and return downstairs. I must have been up there longer than I realized because everyone has gone except for a few stragglers on the terrace. Emily is lying in her hammock, chatting to her friends, laughing her fake laugh.

She points to me. "Have you met Iris? Of course you have. Iris is my biggest fan. She's such a sweetheart. You know my book by heart, don't you, Iris?"

"Mmmm," I say.

She brings her hands together on her lap. "What's your favorite part?"

"What do you mean?"

"I thought that was a simple question, Ro—Iris!" She gives a small mocking laugh. "Come on. Don't be shy! Indulge me."

I know what she's doing. She did the same thing when we were at Jack's Bar. She's getting me to perform for the crowd, describing in great detail chapters of the book, marveling about how I *know so much about it*. Later, when I've been revealed as the murderer that I am, she will tell her friends, "I thought it was odd she could recite the book by heart.

Only the killer would know the book by heart, when you think about it."

But hey, I can do this. I remind myself that I'm a psychopath, and frankly, it's time I started behaving like one. We are callous and emotionally deficient. I know this because I looked it up. And we sure don't go around kneading our hands and hyperventilating every five minutes.

I pretend to think about it. I do it the way she does it, my eyes looking up and my finger tapping my chin.

"I think it's the part where you go to his house to tell his wife you're in love with him, and you thought he wouldn't be there, but he is. In fact, he's standing next to her with his arm around her shoulders. He tells you that he's confessed everything about the two of you, and she's forgiven him. Oh, and that he's realized he loves her more than he could ever love you. Yes. That's definitely my favorite part."

It's also the part I didn't write, so stick that in your Champagne flute. Rose—1, Emily—big, fat zero.

Emily narrows her eyes slightly. "You know, you are so right. I think that's also my favorite part. It's the chapter where her heart is truly broken."

Whatever, I think. Nice try and all that. I just want access to her computer. "I'll tidy up down here," I say, jerking a thumb behind me.

"That would be great. Thank you, sweetie," she says through tightly stretched lips, and it's all I can do not to skip like a child all the way back to the kitchen.

The last guests leave shortly after. Emily watches me mop the floor and pick up cigarette butts from potted plants. After a few minutes, she says, "I'm going to bed. Good night, Rose. Oh, and remember. I have an email scheduled to be sent out tomorrow that you don't want me to send. So don't kill me in the night."

"Haha, that's funny," I say, and I have to try really hard

not to grin. Why would I kill her? I'm taking the money and I'm running. And only later will she realize that she has nothing but a fake confession.

Rose—2, Emily—still big, fat zero.

When she's disappeared inside her bedroom, I fire up her computer, and first, I log onto her email and search for the scheduled one, but I can't find it. Which tells me she's either lying—probably—or she's got a different email account I don't know about.

Anyway, I don't care. I log out and search for *SkyDrive*, drumming my fingers on the table, smirking to myself.

Nothing. Hey, I'm just getting started. I've got all the time in the world. I just need to dig a little deeper, that's all. I search for *SkyDrive Cloud*, then for the title of my diary, then for *cloud*, and by the time I've combed her computer with every variation of SkyDrive Cloud Storage I could possibly dream up, I'm gritting my teeth so hard they're threatening to come up through my eyeballs.

I drop my head in my hands and cry. It really is over. I will never wake up from this nightmare. I killed someone, I am a bad person, and I will never, ever be free.

CHAPTER 29

It was lunchtime, and Chet was in the teachers' lounge with all the other teachers. Penny—history and geography—was heating up chicken fried rice in the microwave that, to Chet, smelled like old socks. She offered him some, and he declined. He'd had his ham sandwich, but *thank you Penny, you're very kind,* and then winked at her, and she giggled and blushed.

He was reading a newspaper that had already been smeared with greasy fingers, probably by Rob, the math teacher whose round, bloated body reminded Chet of a dead rotting porpoise he'd seen on the beach once as a kid. He was turning a page by its edge with only the utmost tip of his fingers when the school principal, Janice Morales, entered.

"Hello, everyone!" And Chet braced himself. Janice Morales could talk your ear off. If she happened to catch you in a corridor, you'd be lucky to get away in under fifteen minutes. That woman didn't know how to take a hint.

But Mrs. Morales wasn't here for a chat. She stood aside. "This is Amy. She's our new Mary. I'm sure you'll all make her feel very welcome."

Chet sat up straighter then leaned back into his chair, admiring the vision that stood shyly in the doorway.

"What happened to Mary?" Penny asked, putting down her chopsticks.

"You haven't heard?" Janice Morales asked. "Poor Mary. Her father is very ill. She's gone home to Denver to help look after him. It was very sudden."

Chet wasn't going to miss Mary, a middle-aged bore who flirted with him by bringing him pears and peaches from her orchard. But this was something else. A breath of fresh air. A ray of sunshine through the dull, gray clouds.

And where did you come from? Chet wondered to himself.

Amy was very young, twenty-three, he learned later. Almost a child. She had big blue eyes, peach-colored cheeks like a porcelain doll, and long blond hair held in a high ponytail with a pink ribbon. Chet invited her for a drink after class that very evening. "The Longstaff Bar & Grill. It's not much of a bar, but we simple folk like it," he said, making it sound like the other teachers would be there too. Then he went home, fed Charlene a couple of Valium in her boxed wine, waited until she fell asleep in front of the Bill Cunningham Show, then went out to meet Amy.

It took half an hour and two glasses of Chardonnay for her to ask when the others were coming.

Chet feigned surprise. He was terribly sorry if there was a misunderstanding, he hadn't meant to mislead…but Amy assured him, with a little color on her cheeks, that it was fine, that she was having a nice time and appreciated that he made her feel so welcome in this new town.

"It's a great little town," Chet said gravely. "The locals

are very friendly. Very welcoming. We're very fortunate to be here."

At some point in the night, Amy asked about Chet's wife.

"Charlene isn't very well," he explained. Then he invented a diagnosis—multiple sclerosis—which was very painful for Charlene, and that was why she didn't go out much. Amy clicked her tongue sadly and put her hand on his.

On their second outing, Chet asked if Amy was seeing anyone. Was there a long-distance relationship maybe? She ran her fingers through her hair (she wore her hair down on that second so-called date, the little slut), and said that no, there was no one on the horizon. And something about the way she said it, the way she'd laughed when he asked, was so flirtatious that Chet didn't hesitate. He leaned in, his lips so close to hers he could smell the fruitiness on her breath from the wine spritzer.

She pulled away abruptly. "Chet!" she cried, her hand at her throat.

"I'm so sorry," Chet said, surprised he'd misjudged the situation. He was yet to meet a female who'd turned down a kiss from him, so this was interesting. "I don't know what came over me." He turned away and knocked back the rest of his bourbon.

"No, it's all right," Amy said, her hand on his arm.

"It's not. I don't know what I was thinking." Then he shook his head sadly. "You're so incredibly beautiful, Amy…"

She looked away, smiling coyly.

"And for someone in my position…"

"What do you mean?"

He took a sharp breath. "I shouldn't tell you this, but I don't have many friends in this town to confide in…" He raked his fingers through his hair.

"What is it?"

"I hope you won't mind my being blunt…"

"Please."

He pinched the top of his nose. "Charlene finds love-making too painful."

He explained that Charlene was far sicker than he'd let on. She was very, very sick. Sweet Amy's eyes filled with tears. Chet felt bound to take care of his wife, of course. In sickness and in health. But it was hard. He was only a man, with everything that implied.

Amy blushed, clicked her tongue, and said she was very sorry too. Chet thanked her, ran his fingers through his hair again—women loved his hair. It was so thick and luxurious. He brought up men's needs again, and that men were different from women in that respect. It had been such a long time… Amy listened with knotted eyebrows, and by the end of the night she was kissing him hungrily in the parking lot. As a favor. Because it had been so long.

Just like Chet thought. The little slut.

The next day at home, he read more of Rose's diary.

Dear Diary,

I can't stop thinking about Mr. B. and me getting married. I think about it all the time. Last night I had this whole fantasy about it. I imagined I was in his office waiting for him to finish marking papers, and I told him.

"I want you to meet my dad."

His eyes are wide with shock, like I've asked him to cut his wedding finger off. "You cannot be serious."

Chet was laughing so hard he spilled some of his bourbon onto his lap.

"What's so funny, Chet?" Charlene called out from the living room.

The sound of her voice grated on his nerves like finger-nails on a blackboard. He took a short breath. "Nothing, babe," he shouted back, brushing the spilt drink off his jeans. "Just remembering our wedding when I almost fell over on the cake!"

"Oh yeah, that was funny. You want some dinner? I'm making burgers!"

Charlene was the worst cook in the world, but at least burgers were harder to fuck up. "Burgers would be great! Thanks, hon!"

He went back to reading Rose's diary.

"I don't think your dad would like me."

"You could ask for my hand in marriage. He'd like you then." I've imagined that scene so many times, all I have to do is rewind and press play.

Me waiting outside, sitting on the low wall that borders my dad's new front yard. When Mr. B. and I move in together, we would have a front yard too. I would grow daffodils. I would wear a red apron with needlework in the shape of a cute house...

He had considered putting a stop to those stupid fantasies. It was getting out of control. But that very morning, Amy told Chet, with admiration in her eyes, what a wonderful, dedicated teacher he was. His, Amy said, was the only class where Rose was so attentive. In every other class, Rose would gaze out the window or fall asleep on her desk with her head on her arms. So Chet decided *not* to tell Rose to cut it out, and instead occasionally amused himself by leaving his hand on her neck a second too long, just like she wrote about ad nauseum, and watching her face turn scarlet.

Two days later, Amy timidly suggested that if Chet wanted...since it had been so physically difficult for him... could she perhaps provide some relief? Chet could come over to her place the following Friday evening? Her room-mate—a nurse—would be on a shift.

Chet nodded slowly, caressed her sweet face, and said that would be wonderful.

And that's when Chet made his first mistake.

CHAPTER 30

I'm rowing a small boat on a lake. My mother is on the shore taking photos with an old Nikon camera. She's waving at me with her free arm fully extended.

Rose.

She's calling out to me, but my boat is filling up with water. I'm starting to panic. I'm too far from the shore, and I forgot how to swim.

Rose.

She doesn't seem to grasp that I'm drowning. She's sounding annoyed with me. She wants me to wave for the camera, even though I'm up to my shoulders in water.

Rose!

My eyes fling open. "Jesus, Emily!" I scurry away from her, slamming my back against the headboard and pulling the sheet over my chest.

"Good morning, sweetie! You're ready for your close-up?"

"What?"

"I want to record your confession this morning since we have a busy afternoon." She flicks her wrists to show me her watch. "It's eight o'clock. You get ready, and I'll make some coffee."

"I don't want to."

She sighs. "Rose! Why? What's the point in waiting?"

"I just need to prepare myself."

"What does that mean?"

"You said I had a week."

"Well, technically it's six days now. But I've changed my mind. Let's say Monday."

"Monday? But that's tomorrow!"

"Seven days was unrealistic. Anything could happen in seven days. Now, it's tomorrow. Tomorrow morning. Okay, sweetie?"

She stands up. "I'm going to make coffee. I'll see you downstairs. And remember we have the book event at two."

I get up, bleary-eyed, head pounding, and step into the shower. Then I stay upstairs in my room until we have to leave for the book talk. I ruminate on my predicament, googling countries that don't have an extradition treaty with the U.S., countries like Russia, Iran, Afghanistan, none of which are exactly enticing. Texas is better. I'll get a bus to Houston. It takes two days, which is good. I could use two days to think.

Eventually it's time to leave. Emily's fraud-fake-author event is called *Emily Harper In Person: Diary of an Octopus*, and if I wasn't so frazzled right now, I would find it hilarious. I find nothing hilarious at the moment. I'm just in pain. Like in my chest. It hurts, and I wonder if it's from a looming heart attack. I hope it is.

. . .

"I am so excited about today," Emily says, putting blush on my cheeks with a brush. She says I have to look my best because I am a reflection of her. By the time she's done, I still look like I just crawled out from under a rock. I walk like a zombie and pick up a box full of books from the table, books that she will dole out at her event like a priest at communion. I follow her out of the building, my arms already aching from the weight of the box. Then I hear my name.

"Rose."

I turn around. Ben is standing there, his fists shoved deep in his pockets, his shoulders hunched, his eyes narrowed.

"What are you doing here?"

"We need to talk."

"How did you know where to find me?"

"The restaurant books and pays for your Uber home, remember? And why didn't you—"

"Oh! Hello, there…" Emily says, giving him an apprecia- tive up-down look. "Have we met?" She pats her hair, blinks a hundred times. Ben looks like he hasn't slept for a week, but he still looks great, with his day-old beard, his white T- shirt showing off his biceps, his crinkly eyes.

"I'm Ben." He hesitates. "I'm a friend of Rose."

"Oh, wow! That's so sweet! I had no idea Rose had friends! I'm Emily." She professes her hand as if expecting Ben to kiss it. "Enchantée," she coos. If I wasn't carrying this heavy box, I would have elbowed her in the stomach. Ben shakes her hand, but his eyes don't leave mine. He goes to take the box from me—ever the gentleman—but I shake my head. "No."

He raises his hands, like, *whatever*. "So, this is your friend Emily."

"Oh, Rose, that's so sweet. You've been telling everyone about me."

"Can I have a minute, please?" I say to Emily.

She clicks her tongue. "I'm sorry sweetie, but, no, you can't." She checks her watch. "We have to be at the bookstore in half an hour."

I grit my teeth. I'm about to insist when Ben says, "Rose just asked you for a minute in private. Would you mind?" Which is the worst thing he could have said. She smiles at him, her radiant, beautiful smile. "I know that, Ben. I'm not deaf!" She laughs. "But we're due somewhere. Aren't we, sweetie. So no. She can't have a minute."

Ben blinks, shakes his head. "Excuse me?"

She tilts her head. "How well do you know Rose, Ben?"

"Cut it out," I hiss.

Ben opens his mouth. "I—"

"Had she told you about the class pet? No? It's a charming story. It goes like this—"

I've dropped the box on the pavement. I shove my finger in her face. "One minute, okay? Just give me one fucking minute!"

"Well! Excuse me! Look who got up on the wrong side of the bed this morning." She touches her hair. "Fine. I was about to call a taxi anyway. I'll be over there." She points to the curb. "Don't be long, okay?"

"What the hell was that?" Ben asks.

"It doesn't matter. You need to go. I'm sorry about everything. But you need to go and forget about me." *Until you hear on the news what I've done, at which point you won't forget about me ever again.*

He narrows his eyes. "If you wanted to dump me, then you should have just said so." He starts counting on his fingers. "You don't show up at work, you don't take my calls, you don't reply to my messages, I have no idea where you are or where you live. I've been worried sick about you."

"You have?"

"What do you think?"

I lay my hands on his chest. "Just go, Ben. Please."

"What the hell did I do?"

"Nothing. You've been great. The problem is me."

He snorts a laugh. "Oh, right. Original."

A wave of anger flashes through me. "Listen. You don't know me, okay? You don't want to be around me. I'm a very bad person, and I'm sorry I wasted your time. Now leave."

I bend down to pick up my box. He grabs my arm. "For Christ's sake, Rose! What are you talking about?"

I take a breath. "It's going to come out that I did things, okay?"

"What things?"

I raise both arms and let them drop. "You want to know? You're sure? Okay. Here it is. I'm a psychopath. I've done bad things. Horrible things. I've harmed people… hamsters… I mean, one hamster."

The corner of his mouth twitches, but not in a good way. "Are you playing games here?"

"Nope. It's all true. You probably got a lucky escape. Who knows?"

"You're not a psychopath, Rose."

"Sweetie?" Emily taps her watch.

"I have to go. Just forget about us. Forget we ever happened."

I bend down again to pick up my box. This time he pushes me back, both hands on my shoulders. "Is this a joke? Is this the best you can come up with to break up with me? You think I couldn't handle it?"

"You don't get it!" I hiss into his face. "It's going to come out. I've done bad things, evil things. I'm sorry I ever dragged you into my life, okay? Now fuck off!"

"Hey! I don't know what you're trying to do here, but I know you're not a psychopath so cut the joke."

"You don't know me."

"You're the savior of rats."

I blink for a second. "Okay, well…these things are not mutually exclusive." I think of it now. I'd only just started to work at the restaurant, and he suggested a drink after work. The place was wild. Low lit, punk rock vibe, graffiti everywhere. We drank bottles of Stella Artois. It was raining when we came out around four in the morning. I wanted to go home to his place and have sex, but he hadn't suggested it. He was walking me to the cab rank, his jacket pulled up over both of our heads. I liked Ben. I figured we were going to be just friends, and that was okay too. And that's when I saw the rat.

It was tiny, just a baby, and it was coming out of a grate on the sidewalk, using its front paws to pull himself out. I stopped and watched for a second because I could tell something wasn't right. It was struggling. Then I realized it was stuck, and frankly, I had no idea how it got in in the first place. Those slots are so narrow. I moved away from under Ben's jacket, found a stick, and tried to get the rat to hold on to that, but it wasn't helping at all. If anything, it was getting more freaked out. So I used my hands to ease it out, wriggling it sideways so its hips would be more narrow. I could hear people behind me making disgusted noises, saying it was gross, and I thought, what's wrong with people? It's just a small animal. It's no different than a kitten. People would fall over themselves to help a kitten.

Anyway, I got it out, and it scampered away. I wiped my hands on my jeans and walked over to the taxi. Ben stopped me. We went home together.

"And you bought Bernie lobster Mornay…" he says.

"You paid for half."

"You buy him dinner all the time…"

"I get a staff discount."

"Bernie told me you're his best friend."

"He did?"

"Rose!" Emily calls out.

"You saved a cockroach once, in my kitchen. You put it in a glass jar and made me take it out to the park."

"That was different. I was drunk. He reminded me of my grandmother. I told you that."

He brings his face close to mine. "If you're a psychopath, then I'm James Bond."

"Rose!" Emily snaps.

I look into Ben's eyes. I have a sudden urge to cry. I tilt my head and attempt a watery smile. "Shaken? Or stirred?"

He takes a step back and raises a hand dismissively. "Fuck you." And then walks away.

"Sweetie?" Emily calls. "Come on! Let's go!"

CHAPTER 31

There were plenty of women who would gladly have sex with Chet—and many who did—but they generally had yellowing teeth and short stubby fingers.

Amy was different. Amy was unspoiled. Amy had small hands and small white teeth and an adorable, heart-shaped mouth.

Friday couldn't come soon enough.

Chet went home after school finished and told Charlene about baseball practice later that evening.

"Coach would really appreciate it if I could be there," he said gravely.

Charlene grumbled as usual (*I never see you anymore!*). He poured her a glass of wine mixed with four or five Valium and went on his way to Amy's apartment.

But as Charlene settled in with her wine, she remembered she'd left a load of washing in the dryer. As she entered the garage, she saw on the shelf Chet's baseball glove, baseball bat, and baseball cap. Silly Chet, Charlene thought. Going to baseball practice without his baseball gear. She would bring them to him. He'd like that. She asked her neighbor, Doris Garcia, if she could borrow her car. Did Charlene genuinely believe Chet had left them behind accidentally? Or was she growing suspicious about his nightly activities and saw an opportunity to check on him? Nobody knows. Not even Chet. But when Charlene arrived at the school, she found it was closed, locked, and dark. She then drove to the baseball field, which was also empty and dark.

So Charlene went home and waited for Chet. When he returned around midnight, closing the door quietly so as not to wake her, Charlene was ready. She swung the bat right into his face. Fortunately, she was a terrible hitter, and by then she was very drunk, but it still hurt like hell.

He'd almost killed her. He'd grabbed the bat from her hands and lifted it in the air, and for a moment he could almost hear the sweet, delicious sound of her skull cracking. It was Charlene's scream that brought him back to reality. He dropped the bat, put his hand over her mouth, and whispered sweet words in her ear while she tried to bite his fingers. *It's me, Charlene, honey. It's me. It's all right.* He glanced nervously through the window at Mrs. Garcia's house next door, wondering if she'd heard Charlene's screams. Those two had become friendly lately—only because Charlene was home all day and had zero friends—and the last thing he needed was Charlene telling her friend Doris that Chet was a pervert who fucked seventeen-year-olds and she had the evidence to prove it.

Already Doris was asking Chet on a regular basis if Charlene was all right. "She often seems very vague, somewhat unwell," she'd say. And Chet would grit his teeth and tell her that Charlene was fine, and she did like to have a glass of wine or two during the day—she didn't, unless Chet encouraged her to—and it wasn't against the law, was it?

But Doris Garcia's house remained dark, and Chet gently released his wife.

It took two hours to calm Charlene down. The story he spun was that he'd gone to Longstaff on his own, like he did on many nights because he was so miserable. He thought he was losing her, he said. He was afraid she didn't love him anymore and he didn't know what to do. He'd spun that one before and it had worked then, but that excuse was getting harder to swallow with every telling. *Don't lie to me! Stop lying to me! You never ask me out anymore! Is there someone else? Who is she?* On and on she went.

"I love you. You're everything to me. But I also know you're unhappy and I know it's my fault, and you deserve so much better!" She softened and put her arms around his neck, her face upturned, and he had to kiss that ugly, stinking mouth as passionately as if his life depended on it. Which it did.

The next day he went to Longstaff and paid Tom the bartender a hundred dollars to say to anyone who asked that he was there all night, sitting by himself on a stool at the far end, looking wretched, which wasn't that far from the truth anyway. Later he would learn that Charlene did call, and that Tom did as he'd asked.

But Chet was at a breaking point. He had spent every second of the weekend playing the romantic, loving husband, assuring Charlene that he loved her, that all he ever wanted was for their marriage to work. That was bad enough, but Chet had found himself thinking nonstop about Amy since their encounter that past Friday night. Something had awoken in him, like a lightbulb had been turned on. Love.

He was in love. He was obsessed. He couldn't wait to see her again, to fuck her again, to kiss that beautiful heart-shaped mouth again, and as he found out when he went back to work, neither could Amy.

But it wasn't going to happen in a hurry. Not now that Charlene's suspicions were at an all-time high.

"It's her illness," he told Amy. He stared right into her eyes. "It's horrible. The pain... I can't leave her in the evenings."

And sweet, kind, lovely Amy timidly said that Chet couldn't remain shackled to sick Charlene forever, that it wasn't fair on him, and had he considered finding a facility to care for her? Wouldn't that be better for poor Charlene?

God, he loved her. He nodded gravely and said he would think about it. Of course what he *really* thought was that it would be better for poor Charlene and poor Chet if poor Charlene fucking died.

It was later that day, while he read the latest installment of Rose's diary to distract himself from his miserable life, that the idea came to him. His pulse quickened. The hair on the back of his neck stood up. Could Rose, with her boundless imagination, her total and absolute idolization of Chet, and the fact that she was weird—understatement—be what he needed to escape the nightmare that was his marriage?

He laughed out loud. There was a way out of this hell-hole after all, and all he had to do was funnel little *Amelie* to the exit.

CHAPTER 32

Emily walks to the small stage, her arms wide, basking in the applause of her adoring fans like she's an inspiration to millions, as opposed to a megalomaniac who found a laptop.

She takes her seat on a high stool, while on the other high stool, holding the microphone, is the manager of the store, a woman named Veronica.

"Emily Harper! Thank you so much for being here!" Veronica exclaims. Emily puts one hand on her chest. The pleasure is all hers, and she's honored and humbled.

I stand at the back of room, sullen like a child. I'm still shaken up by what happened with Ben just now. I've ended relationships before when things started to get serious. I don't remember feeling this empty or this heavy. Or this sad.

Emily gives her spiel about bailing out of writing her biography, like somehow that's a brave thing and a courageous act.

I close my eyes. I need to tune her out so I can focus on what I need to do. Last night I had a tiny bit of hope. Find that SkyDrive, delete the document. The moment that laptop goes back online, the document disappears. It's not much, but it's something. Also, it's all I've got.

I unlock my phone and search online for SkyDrive.

When I look up again a few minutes later, it's like the air has been sucked out of the room.

It's the third entry in the search results that jumped out to me. A link to Wikipedia. The summary was enough to send my heart clattering, even before I clicked on it.

OneDrive, a Microsoft file hosting service, which was renamed from SkyDrive in February 2014…

That couldn't be right. I clicked on the link and read on. And now I can't stop reading and rereading.

SkyDrive was changed to OneDrive in 2014. You can't sign up to SkyDrive anymore. It doesn't exist. It hasn't existed for nine years.

Nine years.

Why did I never see this message about syncing pop up before? Because when I was still in Pike Creek, I'd connected the laptop to the internet, and SkyDrive was still a thing. And when I was at Sacred Heart, I never turned it on. It lived in a trunk under my bed, wrapped in that Christmas sweater my mother knitted for me. I never even turned it on after I left Pike Creek.

Emily and Veronica are speaking on stage, but I can't hear anything except the beating of my own heart.

It wasn't Emily who was syncing my document. It was the man who gave me that laptop. My teacher, Mr. Bellamy.

He was syncing my diary.

An avalanche of thoughts, images, noise, fragments of conversations, memories, tears, threaten to overwhelm me. The noise is making me dizzy. I can barely breathe. I replay that whole year in my mind like a video at top speed. Every exchange I've had with Mr. Bellamy has been turned on its head. I used to feel we were on our special wavelength, that we were connected by a piece of invisible, unbreakable gossamer. He always knew where I was going to be, what I was going to say, what I was thinking. I'd write a fantasy where he'd brush my cheek, and the next day he would brush my cheek. If I fantasized about showing him one of my poems and him saying something like, *You have a uniquely wonderful way with language, Rose,* then that's exactly what he would say the next time I showed him a poem. Sometimes I'd write that he was the only person who could truly *see* me. Two days later he would tell me that he was the only person who could truly *see* me.

I used to think he was reading my mind.

Because he was.

I feel a burning fury rise inside me, and for once it has nothing to do with Emily Harper. I was thirteen years old, for Christ's sake. Did Mr. Bellamy think it was *funny*? Did he laugh when he read my diary? Well, obviously—I mean, that one goes without saying. But my anger isn't about discovering I was the butt of a joke. It's about the deceit and the cruelty with which he carried it out. And what about the heart I'd supposedly etched so carefully into my desk? When Mr. Bellamy saw it, he acted completely dumbstruck, like he'd had no idea. He thundered things like, "Do you think I would have spent time with you, tutoring you, counseling you, encouraging you if I'd known you had a stupid school-girl crush on me?"

Except he did know. He'd known for months. So that little performance that day, it was just that. A performance. An act.

"Iris! Iris, sweetie! Earth to Iris!"

I look up. Everyone has twisted their neck to look at me,

and the room feels more like a meeting of the Meerkat Society than a book reading. Emily has the microphone, and she's pointing at me, gracing me with her sunny, happy, broad smile. "Say hi to Iris, everyone!"

The crowd beams at me, "Hi, Iris!"

"My young friend Iris here is a living example of the positive influence I am blessed to exert on young women. Iris came to me because she loved my book. Oh, don't be shy, sweetie. She's blushing! Honestly, you're so adorable. Now, Iris had been following my content for a long time, and she wanted to meet me and tell me the impact I'd had on her life." She drops her head. "That was so sweet. Thank you, Iris. I can't begin to tell you what that meant to me."

Funny, I think, because you have no problem telling everyone else right now.

"Since that day, and it wasn't that long ago, either! Was it Iris? Like a week? We have become friends, haven't we, sweetie? I think I can say that when I first met you, you were a shy mousy thing, remember?" She laughs. "Iris was so nervous she used to drop things all the time." Everyone laughs along. "But seriously, you know, sometimes the Lord brings you people who need your help. I decided to take Iris under my wing, on impulse. And look at her. A self-assured young woman."

The room erupts in applause. And I'm thinking, well played. I'll give her that. The fact that she brought up my name a hundred times (Iris!) has not gone unnoticed. I know what she's doing. This is the setup phase. By the time she posts my confession to her fans, the shock of the betrayal will be so great, so total, her fame will be assured. Also, they'll probably hunt me down to the end of the earth.

Once the applause has died down, Veronica asks if there are any more questions before we wrap up.

A young woman with a beret shoots up her hand. "I was wondering, why did you call it *Diary of an Octopus?*"

"That is an excellent question. Thank you." But instead of answering, Emily taps one finger on her chin and looks up. "I think it was because of … the mermaid? Or was it a siren?" Everyone looks at her, and for an excruciating moment—to Emily I mean—it seems that she doesn't remember.

And I am absolutely here for it.

She flaps a hand. "I'm in the middle of a different project, a podcast. Very interesting, but consuming. My brain can't hold that much information all at once!" And she laughs in a way that says, *You all know I'm just being very modest, right? Of course my brain can do anything.* "But Iris here, my lovely friend will know. You know my book by heart, don't you, Iris? Would you like to tell the audience why I called it *Diary of an Octopus?*"

Again, the room cranes its collective neck to look at me.

I wait for a moment, smirking at Emily, enjoying her discomfort. Because it's there. I can see it.

"Iris, sweetie?"

"It's because of the Kraken," I say.

"Oh, that's right. It's because of the Kraken," Emily says.

"What's a Kraken?" woman in beret asks.

Emily raises her eyebrows at me.

Still smirking somewhat, I tell them about the time Mr. B. read Tennyson's poem about the Kraken to the class. *In roaring she shall rise and on the surface die.* How he'd explained the Kraken was an octopus that terrorized men and angels, and then he quipped, "Not unlike Am—Emily, here," and everybody laughed. Emily asked him afterward why he'd said that, and he put his hand on the back of her neck and whispered that she too was terrifying, that she too had a strange hold on men and angels. Emily looked up that poem later and was surprised to find in the original, it's a he, not a she.

"And that's when Emily decided to call her diary *Diary of an Octopus*," I say.

Everyone stares at me blankly.

A different woman raises her hand. Addressing me, she says, "I don't remember that passage in the book."

It happens slowly, the blood draining from my face. I read Emily's version from start to finish, and I'm wracking my brain to remember if she included it, and I can't. I gaze at her across the room. She's smiling at me, smug and triumphant. And I realize then that for some reason, she left out that passage. Which means I have just outed myself as the real author of the diary in front of twenty-odd eagle-eyed readers.

Blood is roaring in my ears. Another woman frowns at me. "So is it in the book or not?"

I smile like a lunatic at her, like I've just returned from the dentist and they forgot to take out the rubber mouth opener.

"I thought it was," I say. I touch my own hair, the way Emily does. I'm going insane, I can tell. Soon I'll start laughing manically while taking all my clothes off and running through the crowd. It's only a matter of time.

"Or maybe Emily told me about it. Maybe that's how I know," I say. I turn to Emily, my eyes pleading.

And Emily, still with that smug expression on her face, takes a decade or so to think about it.

Then, finally, she says, "That's right, Iris. I told you that story, remember?" She turns to her audience. "I decided to cut it out of the final book because it felt a little academic. But I kept the title anyway because I liked it."

And I don't know if I'm imagining it, but I can feel the tension in the room release slowly, like a dying party balloon.

I close my eyes. I tell myself never to underestimate Emily again. She can oust me as Charlene Bellamy's cold-hearted murderer with a click of her fingers.

And if I'm not careful, she will.

CHAPTER 33

Killing Charlene would be easy. Chet would strangle her, plain and simple. He'd enjoy every minute of it too. And since she was always drunk, she wouldn't fight back. A child could do it. In fact, a child *would* do it. Or that's what it would look like by the time he was done.

But that was some way off. There was a lot of work to be done before he got to that point.

Step One: Exercise total control over Rose. She had to believe that Chet loved her, and she had to trust him more than any other adult in her life. Over the next few weeks, he would pay much attention to Rose. He would encourage her to drop by his office whenever she had a new poem to show him. Not every teacher had an office in this shabby, pathetic excuse for a school. There had only ever been one office available, and Chet had insisted he should have it. As the sole English teacher, he needed to have more concentrated time with the students. Who needed geography and history anyway? And math? Nobody from this school would ever excel at math, and everyone knew it. English was the students' only chance to make even a modest success of their lives, and Chet needed the office.

"How are you, Rose?" he'd ask, his face a picture of concern. "If you want to talk, I'm always here for you." And talk, she would. She'd tell him how her mother was sad all the time. He'd nod gravely. "It's because she's jealous of you," he'd say. "Because you are so talented. It's very threatening to her." Other times he'd tell her, "You are destined for great things, Rose Dunmore. But there are always people who'll try to take you down because of it. Take Lola, for instance." And Rose would be shocked at hearing her little friend accused like that, but Rose had to be isolated; therefore, Lola had to get lost. "I've noticed Lola is very jealous of you," he'd said. "I can see it every day. It's getting worse."

Rose would shake her head violently. "No! Lola is nice! Lola is my friend!"

"If you say so." He'd sigh, returning to his marking.

Meanwhile, she'd tell him about her dreams (lately her dream was to build a rocket and go into space). Chet would listen, his fingers steepled together against his chin, and ask questions to show he was interested. (When you say into space, where in space exactly?) It was excruciatingly boring, but Chet was a professional. The work had to be done. It was that simple.

And it was going brilliantly.

Step Two: Make Rose doubt herself. She had to question her own judgment, come to distrust her own version of the facts, and rely on him for guidance. For this crucial step, Chet dusted off some of his old college psychology texts. When Charlene was asleep, he would study how to screw with a child's mind to the point where they could no longer tell the difference between what was real and what wasn't.

The following week, Rose walked into Chet's office with some short story about a chemistry lab accident that kills all the teachers in the school, leaving the children to roam free for the rest of the year without the parents realizing. "Do you think I should send it to that writing competition?" she asked.

While she waited for him to read her masterpiece, she fiddled with objects on his desk. She always did that. It was a disgusting habit, but one he would use now, and again later. Today it was a small bronze bust of Charles Dickens, small enough to slip into a pocket. Rose turned it over in her fingers without really seeing it. She was staring at him, waiting for his feedback.

"Terrific!" he said finally. "You have a uniquely wonderful way with language, Rose." Her eyes snapped open wide, not at the compliment—although that too—but at the realization that *she'd imagined him saying exactly that only a few days before!*

Later, after everyone had left, Chet put the bronze statuette in Rose's locker. The next morning, he asked her about it. "I can't find it. I saw you play with it yesterday."

"I didn't take it!"

He laughed. Making sure no one was watching, he brushed her cheek softly. "I know you didn't. I was only asking because it's gone."

An hour later, dutiful, honest, weirdly principled Rose went to see him, looking sheepish. She pulled out the small bust from her pocket. "I'm sorry. I didn't realize I took it, I swear!"

"That's all right, Rose. I understand. It's your honesty that matters. Admitting to your mistakes is the most important thing."

He would make a point of complimenting her on her looks. "You look very pretty today," he'd whisper, before winking at her. Then he'd welcome her to his office to discuss her story, her grades, whatever, and later hide whatever object she'd been playing with—a letter opener, a paper-weight in the shape of a globe—in her locker. She was always remorseful, confused, and he was always kind and understanding.

Until he wasn't.

"You really hurt my feelings, Rose. Do you *want* to hurt my feelings? Is that what this is about?"

Tears. "No!"

"Have I not been kind to you, Rose? Because I think I have been, but clearly, you don't think so."

"That's not true!"

"I wish you were more responsible for your actions, Rose," he'd say, shaking his head. "Then we could work on your behavior."

He reinforced that concept often. "Personal responsibility is what's important, Rose."

He'd show her a scratch on the front of his desk, where she always fidgeted.

"What I'd like to know is, why did you scratch my desk? It looks deliberate. Was it deliberate?"

"I don't…"

"Personal responsibility, Rose. Don't lie to me, please. Why did you do it?"

She'd bow her head. "I don't remember doing it."

"You don't remember? Or you don't want to remember?"

"I don't remember."

"Do you think you block these things out? Because you don't *want* to remember?"

She looked up. "No?"

"Ah, but that would make sense, wouldn't it? Because if I ask you, why did you do it? It's because I *know* you did it. I know you did, Rose."

Her face would fall. Her chin would wobble.

"Just say you're sorry, and we can put it behind us. Okay?"

She'd nod.

"Are you sorry, Rose?"

"Yes."

"Let me hear you say it."

"I'm sorry."

"Why are you sorry, Rose?"

"Because I scratched your desk?"

"That's right. Now off you go."

Then he'd switch tack again. He would be the wonderful teacher again, her special friend who made her feel understood, appreciated, and loved. Meanwhile, Rose's relationship with her mother was disintegrating to rubble. He knew this because she'd complain to him pretty much daily about some slight her mother had done, and every time Chet would tell her, "Your mother is cold, Rose. I can tell. I'm very good at reading people, and your mother is cold, as well as insanely jealous of you."

Everything was proceeding like clockwork. The only downside was Amy. She was his dream girl. Sweet, shy, adoring, and unbelievably good in bed.

But he couldn't spend much time with her at the moment. Not while he was working on his relationship with Charlene. At home, he was the nice, fun husband, and Charlene loved it. With Amy, he was pleading. "I love you, baby. I love you so much. There's no one else I want to be with more than you."

But Amy would pout prettily. "You say you love me, so why won't you leave Charlene? Or put her in care? Because

I'm beginning to think you're lying to me, Chet!" She would stomp her little foot.

He would kiss her delicate little hands. "Please don't say that. I swear I love you. You have to trust me."

It was time for Step Three.

CHAPTER 34

I'm doing my very best to play nice with Emily. Mostly because I am absolutely terrified of her, but also because I need some time to figure out what the hell Chet Bellamy was up to, and I only have a few hours to do that. Because something is very wrong about this syncing thing. About the fact that he was reading my diary. And I know, I just know, deep down that there's more to it than some salacious impulse on his part. He was manipulating me. I just know it. And I have to figure out why, before Emily makes me record my confession.

"You were great," I say when we're in the car on the way home.

"You think so?"

"Sure." She studies my face. "Don't give me that look," I say. "I'm just saying you were great."

"Okay, well, thank you." She smiles. "So were you."

I sigh. "Thanks for bailing me out."

"Oh, sweetie. You're welcome. It was very amusing, watching your face and all that."

"I'm sure it was," I say.

That night we watch some interminable true crime series on Netflix. At least she doesn't bring up *my confession*, and I use the time to go mentally through all the things Mr. Bellamy said, and all the things he made me say, and all the things he said I did. I'm like an obsessed historian, a crazy time traveler. Turns out, keeping a diary solidifies events in your mind. I go through every detail in the right order without skipping a day, but still, nothing makes sense. Come to think of it, nothing made sense back then, but it didn't matter, because he was there, explaining it all to me. *You're having blackouts, Rose. You steal things, Rose. You need help, Rose.*

And why would he put his hand on my knee, my elbow, grazing my neck when no one was watching? He knew how I felt about him. I used to watch like a hawk if he behaved that way with the other students, but he never did. Just me.

That's not true. Me, and Miss Amy.

I have a sudden, visceral memory of sitting at the back of the class. I spent entire classes practicing telepathy on her: *Mr. Bellamy loves me. He's just feeling sorry for you 'cause you're new here.* I'd considered writing an anonymous letter to Mrs. Morales, the school principal, to say that students were aware Miss Amy and Mr. Bellamy were in a secret relationship, and that the trauma inflicted on our young minds would lead to a pathological fear of learning. Therefore, it would be best if Miss Amy were transferred to Alaska.

But I didn't. I figured Mrs. Morales would know it came from me because of the heart I carved and because, as far as I knew, I was the only fully fledged nutcase in the school. Except for the goths. They'd heard about little Pauly—everyone had heard about Little Pauly—and they would pass me notes asking if I wanted to go to a satanic ritual that involved boiling bats or something. I told them to leave the bats alone, that bats had never done anything to them, and if I heard of one of them touching a single hair on a bat's head, I'd make them pay. That was the positive side of being Scary Crazy Rose. I was so far down the human likability scale, I couldn't go any lower. It made me feared and fearless in equal parts.

I became consumed by the need to know about him and Miss Amy. I imagined the worst, obviously. Secret lovers' trysts, a furtive brush of fingers against skin, maybe a curtain flowing in the breeze. It was as excruciating a vision as anything I might have drummed up later, when I had more specific carnal knowledge.

I had to know. And if there was something sweet and romantic blooming between them, I would find a way to make it wither and die. So I spent the next few days watching Miss Amy like she was a rare specimen and I was a field scientist. I took note of what she wore, the color of her lipstick, whether her hair was up or loose. I'd pass her in a corridor and bare my teeth at her, just for a second, just for fun, and she'd hurry on, hugging her books to her chest. I took note of the times she went to see him, with that little smile on her face like she had a secret. She'd slip into his office like a thief and close the door while I lurked in dark corners, biting my cuticles until they bled. If teachers asked what I was doing, I'd say I'd been summoned to the principal's office, and honestly, nobody ever blinked twice.

I started to follow her home after school. She lived in an apartment on the other side of the river that she shared with another woman, a nurse at the hospital. The apartment was on the ground floor, and it had its own private entrance on the side of the building. I'd watch Miss Amy through the window to the living room, through the sheer curtains. I'd watch her talk on the phone, laughing, her pretty head back. I'd watch her fluff the cushions on the couch and settle in to watch TV with her roommate. I'd watch her buff her fingernails, and I'd watch her eat a bowl of something that looked like cornflakes, but I didn't think it was cornflakes.

Then one day I saw the roommate go out with her boyfriend who came to pick her up in his truck. Minutes later, Mr. Bellamy's Chevrolet drove up. I crouched behind a parked car so fast my elbow caught on the side mirror which left a bruise for days. I watched him go inside while I stayed in the shadows, and I watched as he took her in his arms and kissed her hard on the lips. By the time she closed the drapes, I was already running home.

It's fair to say that I was beyond crushed. For days afterward I walked around in a daze. I stopped bringing Mr. Bellamy poems or short stories, which seemed to make him even more attentive. It was thrilling but also confusing. Did he love me? Or did he love Miss Amy?

And of course now, from the vantage point of my twenty-two-year-old self, it's not thrilling. It's creepy as hell. And now that I know he was reading my diary, I can see this behavior was designed to encourage me in my obsession with him. And not because he had designs on me. He didn't. Not those ones, anyway.

And then, something comes to me. A memory. It makes my heart race and my breath quicken.

Emily turns to me, frowning. "You okay?"

I nod. "Just thinking about tomorrow," I say.

She smiles. "It'll be fine, sweetie. It will be over in half an hour, and you'll have your money. Think of it this way. After tomorrow, it will all be over."

I nod, stand up. "I think I'll go to bed," I say. Because I have to think.

And I have to talk to Lola.

CHAPTER 35

The following Monday after class, Chet walked into the classroom, sat at Rose's desk with a ballpoint pen, and carefully drew a large heart. Inside the heart, he scratched *Rose + Mr. B. 4ever* in Rose's rounded, girlish writing, making sure to copy the way Rose did a little upward tick at the end of her Rs, and the little loop at the end of the V. He traced over the letters, over and over, pressing on the pen hard enough to make groves in the wood. Kids scratched the top of their desks all the time. Nobody bothered to clean them anymore. It was a complete waste of time. When he looked up from his task, he thought he saw movement through the small window in the door. Had someone been watching? He walked to the door and opened it. There were a few students shuffling around their lockers, but no one gave him a second look.

Chet grabbed his things and went home.

The next morning, Chet stood at the front of the class like he always did, watching the students file in, loud and boisterous, dropping bags on the floor and shouting to each other. Rose would be one of the last ones to arrive, because on Tuesdays it was her turn to get food for the hamster from the canteen's kitchen. Chet strolled idly between the desks while the students got settled. He ambled past Rose's desk where he did a double take, took a theatrical step back, and bent down to look closer.

"What the—" He tapped on the heart. "Rose, Rose, Rose…" he muttered. "This is ridiculous!" He turned to Jonah, who sat on the other side of the aisle.

"You saw Rose do that yesterday," Chet said, like he was merely stating a fact. Don't ask if the subject has witnessed the accident, suggest that he has and take it from here. Then he added, "I know Rose spends a lot of her time doodling away, but I never…" He shook his head. "Unbelievable."

Jonah, a little shit who sported a permanent sneer on his pimply face, craned his neck to see and made a little gasping sound. Then he looked at Chet as if to check what the correct answer was. Chet raised his eyebrows. "You saw her. Yesterday. Do this." He flicked his pen over the heart. Jonah nodded once.

"I knew it," Chet said. And Jonah nodded again. He wasn't going to contradict Chet. Also, all the students liked Chet because he was the cool teacher, the one who wasn't afraid to kick a ball with them or high-five them in corridors or keep his door open if they wanted to chat about an assignment. And it wasn't exactly a stretch. Rose was always scribbling away, always drawing something in her notebook when she wasn't looking at him from under her hooded eyes.

By the time Rose came in with her little cardboard box full of limp lettuce, everyone had seen what she'd done and were giggling behind their hands.

· · ·

"This is childish, immature, and outrageous!" Chet bellowed. "I walked in this morning, and I couldn't believe it. I could not believe what I was seeing."

Rose was sobbing. He'd waited until the very end of the day to confront her about it. They were alone in the class-room—with the door open, of course—open door policy at all times—and he was letting her know in no uncertain terms how shocked and disappointed he was.

"Do you think I would have spent time with you, tutoring you, counseling you, encouraging you, for Christ's sake? If I'd known you had a stupid schoolgirl crush on me?"

"It's not like that!" she wailed.

"Not to mention damaging school property! Did you want everyone to know? What's wrong with you? You're not supposed to have a crush on your teacher! We're too old for you! What the hell are you thinking? What are you trying to do, Rose?"

"I don't know!" More wails.

"Because I am very disappointed. *Very* disappointed."

She nodded.

"Why would you do such a thing?" he asked sternly, arms crossed.

"But I didn't!" she whined.

He raised his hands and let them fall. "Everyone saw you do it, Rose. *I* saw you do it. And look! That's your writing, Rose. You can't deny that. See the way you wrote the R?"

"But I didn't!"

"Rose. Please don't lie. Liars go to hell. Do you want to go to hell?"

"No!"

Chet waited a few minutes then crouched next to her. "Come on. Don't get upset." He brushed her cheek softly with the back of his hand then wiped it off on his shirt, careful to hide his disgust. "I think I know what's happened here."

"Wh...at?"

"It's like the things you steal from me and have no memory of doing. I believe this is the same phenomenon."

"The same...what?"

"Rose. I think you have blackouts."

"What?"

"You go into a dissociative state where you do things you don't remember."

She wiped her nose with her sleeve cuff.

"I do?"

He nodded. "I'm sorry I've been so hard on you, Rose. I see what the problem is now. It's not uncommon in young girls and usually goes away by itself, so it's probably nothing to worry about. No need to mention it to anyone at this stage. If it gets more serious, then I'll talk to Mrs. Morales. But we'll just wait and see, okay?"

"Okay!" she hiccupped.

Chet gave her knee a gentle squeeze because what the hell, then stood up. "Come on. Dry your tears, and let's not speak of it again."

She pushed her chair back and left the room, her head bowed, her shoulders hunched, her little body still convulsing with sobs.

Now, Chet could have simply left it at that, then killed Charlene and placed Rose at the scene of the crime, but Chet was smarter than that. While Rose was well and truly questioning herself and her own choices, she would still deny killing Charlene until she was blue in the face. While it would be easy to stack the evidence against her, the police would undoubtedly investigate Chet. Therefore, Chet's alibi had to be unassailable, and Rose's guilt had to be undeniable. And most importantly, Rose had to believe it.

But she wasn't ready. There was still work to do.

Chet needed everyone to see that Rose was changing. She was no longer the happy-go-lucky kid she used to be. She was going to the dark side. Changing her looks would help. So, Chet began to tell her things like, "Young women poets should always embrace their feminine side. Poetry is about love, and art, and feelings. There's nothing more unattractive than a young female poet dressing like a tomboy." And sure enough, she'd swap her baggy jeans for skirts and her sweat-shirts for tight-fitting tops.

But it wasn't enough. All the girls were changing at that age. He needed something *dramatic*.

One day in his office, he told her about Cleopatra's bewitching beauty. "Let me show you," he said, opening a browser window. And Rose would rest her elbows on his desk and her chin in her hands, while he showed her images of Elizabeth Taylor as Cleopatra, gushing about her beautiful kohl-rimmed eyes. "And look at the blue eyeshadow!" he marveled. He sat back and sighed with admiration. "Those eyes are something else. What a beautiful woman."

He sensed Rose stiffen next to him. He turned to her. "You should try it. You would look a lot prettier than you do now." He smiled and touched her cheek with the back of his hand.

Sure enough, the next day, Rose showed up at school looking like a cross between a ring-tailed lemur and a silent film star. He winked at her as she left class, and later, passing her in the corridor, he mouthed, *Beautiful*. Then he went to his office and laughed so hard he had to lock the door while he recovered himself.

And sure, some of these events would make their way into her diary, but Chet wasn't worried. The whole thing read like she was on crystal meth anyway. Maybe he should procure some and get her addicted to it. He'd have to think about that one.

One day, Chet made a necklace of dead grasshoppers and left it on the floor by her desk. When she showed it to him later, shocked, he said, "You've been making that necklace for ages. I've been watching you. I was wondering what these were. Dead grasshoppers! You didn't kill them, did you?" Then he confiscated it and showed it to his colleagues. "I sure hope she didn't kill them," he said gravely.

"Oh, dear. I think she did," Amy replied, biting her bottom lip.

Obviously, by then teachers were openly talking about Rose's state of mind and what could be done.

"Nothing," Chet would say gravely. "It's just a phase, that's all. She'll grow out of it."

"I'm very worried about her," Penny said. "She's changing before our eyes."

"Don't be. The worst thing you can do is bring attention to it."

And they clicked their collective tongues at him in appreciation for his patience and his kindness. He was a benevolent teacher striving to help an emotionally troubled student. They were lucky to have him in their midst.

Really, it was going swimmingly. Couldn't be better.

It was time to take things up a notch.

CHAPTER 36

Upstairs I close my door and sit on the bed, my back to the headboard. I pull out my phone. I must find a way to talk to Lola. I don't have her number anymore, but I know she's on Instagram because she's been messaging Emily. *Your book reminded me of Rose Dunmore...*

I open the Instagram app. I haven't checked it for ages. I've never posted anything. All I've used it for was to check out Emily. I search for Lola and find her immediately. I bite on a fingernail, try to think how to approach her. I just have to be upfront, that's all, and hope she'll get back to me.

I shoot her a direct message.

Hi Lola, it's Rose Dunmore. Long time, I know, but I need to ask you something. It's really urgent. This is my phone number. Thanks.

My phone rings immediately. I stare at it. I don't recognize the number and I'm tempted to let it go to voicemail, but what if it's Lola already? I pick it up. "Hello?"

"Rose! Hi! I got your message. My God, it's been so long! How are you?"

"Lola!" My heart is thumping in my chest. If I'd known she'd call so soon, I would have prepared myself. Braced myself, even, for the judgment in her voice, the silent resentment. But she sounds nothing like that.

"Thanks for calling me so quickly. It has been a long time. I'm okay," I say. Also a total liar. "And how are you?"

"I'm good. Really good. Wow, Rose, it's so good to hear your voice. I've been trying to call you, too! I've been looking for you everywhere! I looked for your mom…"

"She remarried," I say. "She goes by a different name these days."

"Oh, right, that explains it."

She's so much more friendly than I'd expected, and certainly more friendly than I deserve. I basically dumped her as my friend back then, with the kind of cruel disregard for her feelings you'd expect from a budding psychopath.

"Are you still in Pike Creek?" I ask, picturing her the way she used to be, climbing up a tree, her dark curls bouncing, reaching for a fruit or a branch to sit on with a book to read.

"*Diary of an Octopus*," she says. "I read it. I'm…stunned, Rose. I mean, it's you, isn't it? Emily Harper, I mean. Is it you?"

I rub my forehead. "No…"

"Oh. Really? I thought… I mean, there was so much that reminded me of you… I guess you must have told her. I mean, it's pretty much your story."

"I know. It's complicated. But listen. I'm so glad you called me back. I won't keep you—"

"No, sorry. And yes, I'm still in Pike Creek. Is that bad, do you think? It is, isn't it. What can I say? It's home. And I'm doing my apprenticeship with a new hair salon in town. I'm going to be a hairstylist. Come and visit! Get a haircut! I'll give you a discount! Sorry, I'm rambling. I'm a bit nervous. I don't know why!" She giggles.

"No, I get it. Me too."

"It's just been so long! So what about? Where are you these days?"

"Oh, you know, here and there. Listen, I wanted to ask you something about Mr. Bellamy. Is he still in Pike Creek?"

"Huh, now there's a blast from the past. I haven't seen him in ages. He and Miss Amy got married, but they broke up about a year ago, I think. She moved away, and not long after, he moved away. Or maybe it was the other way around. Why do you ask?"

"I've been thinking about the last year I was at school…" I let the sentence trail. *When I went crazy…*

"Yeah. That was a tough year. But you're all good now, yeah? You sound good."

"Thanks, yes, all good." And still a total liar.

"So what about Mr. Bellamy?" she asks.

I take a breath, close my eyes. "I've remembered some things, and I…" I pause. This is so hard. My head is spinning. I feel like I'm floating, and not in a good way. I don't understand what's happening to me exactly, but I think it's the memories. Like my brain doesn't want to think about all that stuff, but they're coming anyway. And they're not what I expected.

"Go on," Lola says softly.

I take a breath. "You remember the day we found Pauly in my locker?"

"God, Rose. Yes. Of course."

"And you remember the night before, we walked home together. You wanted to hang out, but I wanted to go home. Remember?"

"Yes. We argued about fishing or something—"

"Bike riding," I correct. "You were pissed at me. And you had every right to be, by the way. You accused me of being in love with Mr. Bellamy."

"Yes, well…"

"I know. Then the next day, I waited for you at the crossing like I always did, but you didn't show up."

"I remember. I was angry. I went ahead without you."

"I get it," I say. "And this will sound really trivial, but it's really important to me. Because here's the thing. We left school together that day, and Pauly was totally fine in his cage. Then the next morning, I got there late because I'd waited for you, and by the time I arrived at school, Pauly was dead, strangled, in my locker. So my point is, how could it have been me? It wasn't physically possible. I never thought of it at the time because, well, I was confused about everything back then, and I didn't know which way was up. But now I'm thinking, there's no way I could have done it. And it's not like I went back there in the middle of the night to kill Pauly. Remember our school? They had CCTV everywhere."

There's a pause that goes on for a while. I'm about to pull the phone away from my ear to check that she's still there, when she blurts, "Oh God, Rose. I'm so sorry!" She sounds like she's about to cry. "There's something I have to tell you."

CHAPTER 37

Everything Chet had put in place so far was for this moment. After today, Rose would believe, without a shadow of doubt, that (a) she was inherently evil and (b) capable of murder.

Chet picked up the hamster from its cage and twisted its little neck in one quick motion. The creature died instantly and without so much as a murmur. Then he carefully placed the dead hamster in Rose's locker.

The following morning, word quickly spread that the hamster was missing from its cage, and over twenty children in various states of shock and despair stared at the little paw that had slipped under the door of Rose's locker.

Rose was late. Perfect. "Did any of you see Rose with little Pauly?" Chet asked. He crossed his arms over his chest. "Did anyone see Rose yesterday near her locker?"

He scanned the faces. After a moment's hesitation, Bonnie, a shy girl with bangs and glasses, put her hand up. But Bonnie was too obvious. She was always vying to be the star student, always looking for his approval. Nobody would take what Bonnie said seriously.

Chet looked around, and his gaze landed on Lola. Perfect.

"Lola. You're Rose's friend, aren't you?"

Lola said nothing. Excellent.

"Can I talk to you for a second?" Then he dropped his voice. "I don't want to discuss this in front of everyone, for Rose's sake. Let's talk over here."

They moved a few feet away. He went down on his haunches. He didn't have much time before Rose arrived, but he couldn't rush things either. "I really need your help here, okay, Lola?" Then, leaning a little closer, in a conspiratorial tone, he said, "I know you're always looking out for Rose. Even when she does bad things. Like the grasshopper necklace."

A pause, then, a tiny nod.

"Good. Good. But you can't protect her anymore. Not when she does things like this, you understand? And Rose has not been a good friend to you lately, has she."

It was not a question. Lola hesitated then shook her head.

"Good. Rose hasn't been a good friend, and now, Rose has done something very bad, and she needs to be punished."

Something in Lola's eyes lit up, and she gave a tiny nod.

Excellent. He'd planted the seed that by punishing Rose for hurting little Pauly, she was also punishing Rose for not being a good friend. He glanced over his shoulder. Still no sign of Rose.

"You're a good girl, Lola. Now, close your eyes. That's it. Now picture Rose taking little Pauly out of the cage. Can you see that? Yes? Good girl. Now, picture Pauly's little bow tie around its little neck. Rose is tightening the little bow tie and squeezing little Pauly's neck. It's all right. No need to cry now. It's just a memory, that's all. Just picture it. Now Rose is hiding little Pauly under her sweatshirt. She's walking to her locker. She opens the locker and puts little Pauly in there. She shuts her locker and scuttles away. You saw it all, didn't you."

Lola opened her eyes but didn't respond.

He put his hand on her shoulder. "Rose has been bad, and Rose needs to face the consequences. Rose needs to be punished."

A tiny nod.

He gave her shoulder a firm squeeze as he stood up. "You've been very helpful, Lola. You're a good girl. You did the right thing."

Chet took Lola to Mrs. Morales's office, where Lola—with Chet's prompting—described how Rose had killed little Pauly. As Chet said, things had gone too far, and he could no longer stand by and be silent.

By then, Rose had arrived at school, and word had spread that she'd strangled the hamster and hid him in her locker. There were witnesses.

Chet could barely contain his grin as he watched Rose from a distance opening the door of her locker, two dozen children in a semicircle around her.

Little Pauly flopped to the floor. Children screamed, and Rose burst into tears.

Chet wiped the grin off his face and rearranged his features to make himself look shocked, appalled, and horrified.

Then he called out to her. "Come here, Rose."

She followed him, sobbing, as he guided her into an

empty classroom. He sat her down at a desk while he stood with his arms crossed. "Why did you do it?"

"I don't know, I didn't!" she wailed.

He shook his head with disappointment. Of course, she would say that. But this wasn't good enough anymore. They'd already been through all that many times, but this was much more serious.

"It's highly possible that you are a psychopath, Rose. You kill small insects. You killed Pauly. You hurt people. You destroy the things I love. You steal things. You should reflect on that."

"But I—"

"Come on, Rose. Why did you do it?"

"I don't know! I didn't!"

He scratched the back of his neck. "Okay. Maybe I've got it wrong. I was hoping it wouldn't be the case…"

"What? What case?"

"It looks like you had another blackout."

"Does it?"

"Yes. I'm afraid so. It's all right, Rose."

Chet told Rose it wasn't completely her fault. It was those darned blackouts again. When she asked between sobs if it were possible she hadn't done it, that somebody else put dead little Pauly in her locker, he explained that she had been seen by half a dozen students, including Lola.

"Lola saw me?" She dropped her voice to a whisper. "Hurt Pauly?"

Chet nodded sadly. "Yes. She's very upset, as you can imagine, but let's not dwell on that. All that matters now is poor Pauly."

Rose put her hands over her face and wailed. "Poor Pauly! I'm sorry! I'm so sorry, Pauly! I didn't mean to do it!"

And just like that, Rose believed that she wasn't only weird, but also not above killing small innocent animals.

But Rose wanted to go home, and Rose wanted her *mommy*, and Chet didn't want that to happen. He'd met Mrs. Dunmore a couple of times, and he got the sense she didn't take any nonsense from anyone. He could just see her march to the school and demand to talk to Chet, which would be fine, and Lola, which would not. Lola would crack, and he needed to keep Rose isolated. He needed to reinforce the idea that she'd done it, and while she didn't *remember* doing it, she *believed* she did it.

"Hey, listen." He put his arm around her shoulders. He'd never done this before, and he felt her move ever so slightly toward him. He knew that if he put just a little pressure, she would lean against his chest.

He shuddered.

"Hey, wouldn't it be better if you stayed at school for the rest of the day? What will you do at home? You'll just be lonely and upset. Here, you've got your friends." *Who all hate you*, he didn't say. "I'll talk to Mrs. Morales. I'll explain that you had a blackout and that it's not your fault. She'll understand. Then we'll say no more about it. How does that sound?"

Rose still had her hands over her face. She was still sobbing, still saying Pauly's name over and over, still apologizing to the hamster for killing it. "I loved little Pauly," she whimpered.

"I'm sure you did. We all did. We'll all miss him terribly."

"Me too! I will miss him so much!" she wailed.

"Exactly. So in honor of little Pauly's memory, wouldn't it be better if you stayed at school today? Braved the consequences of your actions?"

She gave a crying shudder and nodded. Chet guided her back to her class (geography) and went to see Janice Morales again, this time to explain that Rose was experiencing what's known as dissociative fugue states—Chet had a double major, he reminded Mrs. Morales, in both English and psychology—and that in his educated view it was best not to make a big deal out of it. It happened sometimes at the onset of puberty, particularly in girls (that, he made up), and usually disappeared after a year or two.

"I've asked Rose if she wanted us to call her mother to pick her up, and she said no. She doesn't want to go home. She wants to stay at school with her friends." He stood up. "I'll just keep an eye on things at my end."

But without warning, Janice Morales picked up the phone and called Rose's mother. Chet stood and listened, his hands on the back of the chair he'd just vacated. He was gripping it so hard his knuckles were white. He didn't go through all this for Janice Fucking Morales to blow it out of the water. It was critical that *nobody* interfere with Rose's beliefs right now, and for as long as possible.

Janice left a message for Mrs. Dunmore asking her to come in for a chat at the end of the day, and she could take Rose home then. Chet asked to be present. Janice Morales agreed.

Chet spent the day formulating what he would say, how he could convince Rose's mother that there was something wrong with Rose, but not so wrong that Rose would need psychiatric help.

In the end, it was fine. Chet could tell Rose's mother had difficulties reaching her daughter. Rose just cried, snot pouring out of her nose. She couldn't talk, so Chet talked for her. She and her mother didn't understand each other, anyway. You could tell that a mile away. Maybe she was a cold bitch after all. Meanwhile, he acted as a go-between, and by the time they left, Mrs. Dunmore's pointy head was filled with words like *fugues*, and *dissociative states*, and *blackouts*, and in spite of appearances, it was nothing to worry about.

"I know that your mom was very disappointed in you

after you killed little Pauly," Chet said to Rose not long after the meeting. "I tried to explain about the blackouts, but she seemed to think it was about your character. What was it she said? Ah yes. Rose always had a black heart. Just like her father." He clicked his tongue sadly and watched with satisfaction as Rose's face fell with misery.

"Oh, you didn't know? Don't mention it to her, then. It must have been a slip of the tongue on her part."

Honestly, he was having so much fun, he almost didn't want it to end.

And then Chet made another mistake.

Amy was beginning to openly question Chet's commitment to her. "I am not the girl who you think I am," she said once, her little chin defiantly up. "I would never have slept with you if you hadn't assured me that you and Charlene were over."

"And we are over!" he said, pleading. "But you know what a tricky situation this is, with Charlene's health! I'm working on it, baby. I promise you!"

"But you say that all the time!" Amy said, her little chin now wobbling.

He was on his knees, kissing her hands. "Please, Amy. You have to trust me. I just need a little more time, that's all."

"How much more time?" she'd cried. "Are you asking me to wait until she *dies*?"

Well, yes, essentially, Chet thought to himself.

Also, Amy didn't like that Chet was spending so much time helping Rose with her mental health problems—which is how he justified the attention he was giving her.

"She's obsessed with you. Frankly, it's a little disturbing."

"Yes," he'd say gravely. "You're right. And I'm aware of that. I just don't want to give up on her quite yet. Someone has to try and *do* something. Otherwise, Rose could spiral into dangerous territory. You saw what she did to little Pauly. Who knows what else that disturbed child is capable of?"

And Chet patted himself on the back for reinforcing these facts about Rose. In fact, whenever he and Amy were alone, he made sure to bring up Rose's obsession with him, her violent tendencies, and her dissociative disorder. By the time Rose quote-killed-unquote Charlene, Amy would be a star witness for the prosecution.

And for that reason, he had to watch himself in front of their colleagues so as not to betray his passion for Amy. But Chet was only a man, and he was growing careless.

They had been seen, and by Rose of all people. He'd found Amy alone in the staff room reading the previous day's *Star* and went to sit with her, pretending to be interested in the article she was reading. He wasn't looking at the words. He simply wanted to spend one more minute beside her. He gazed at her cheek, at the perfect shape of her ear, and without thinking, he gently brushed away a strand of hair and tucked it behind her ear. Then suddenly, from the corner of his eye, he saw movement at the door.

Rose.

She was rushing off by the time he'd looked up, but he would have bet his crappy house that she'd seen them. He had the urge to go after her, yank her by the hair, and slam her face against the wall.

But that wouldn't help anything. He took it as a signal. It was time to shake himself out of his complacency. He had to move fast. He had to activate the final step of the plan.

He had to act now.

CHAPTER 38

I'm sitting there, my head spinning, while Lola talks a million miles a minute, telling me how guilty she's felt for years, that she meant to tell me the truth but she couldn't find me. I was like I'd disappeared.

"I never saw you kill Pauly," she says. "Mr. Bellamy wanted me to say that I did. He kept asking me not to lie. He said I was trying to protect you, but that I would be making the situation much worse if I didn't say I'd seen you. I'm so sorry." Her voice cracks on the last words.

"Believe me, I know exactly what he was like." Blood is rushing in my ears. She tells me how he confused her, and I'd been acting so weird anyway. I'd changed. He was so convincing. Then she says something that is so brutally honest, it takes my breath away.

"I was angry with you because you weren't the same as before, and you weren't my friend anymore. I can't tell you how sorry I am. I knew you hadn't killed Pauly. I was angry with you, and I lied, and I'm sorry."

I'm silent for a moment, processing what she is telling me. *I knew you didn't kill Pauly.*

"I can't tell you how sorry I am. I literally have been looking for you for years to tell you. I felt so bad!"

"It's not your fault, Lola. It's that…creep. Mr. Bellamy."

"So who killed Pauly?" she asks. "And who put him in your locker?"

My head is throbbing. I press my temples with my thumb and index finger of my free hand. "I think he did," I say finally.

"Mr. Bellamy?"

"Who else?"

I explain to her about the laptop he gave me, how it was syncing to the cloud. How I only just found out he was reading my diary. He was toying with me. He knew I had a crush on him, and he was playing a cruel game, enacting the same gestures of affection I was dreaming about.

I spew it all out like lava, bits of volcanic rocks burning my throat. Like all the times he made me believe I was stealing things from him but didn't remember, how he made me doubt everything about myself. And yet sometimes he was almost tender, often very encouraging, complimentary. He'd insist I was special, talented. I was not like other girls. Then he'd tell me I was bad, I was a liar, I was deliberately trying to hurt him. I was desperate. I couldn't understand why I was doing those things, but I wanted to be special again. I tried so hard, and then he would switch. I was special. I was talented. I wasn't like other girls. It was nuts, like being trapped on some crazy roller coaster going round and round the same bends over and over. The way he berated me after I killed—or thought I killed—Pauly… *You know what you are, Rose? You're a psychopath. You kill things. You destroy the things I love. You steal things.*

Then I tell Lola about Emily Harper, how she found my laptop at the airport and published my diary, although she changed it to make it look like my fantasies actually happened, while at the same time claiming it's all fiction.

The floorboards creak outside my door. I pause. "Hang on," I whisper into the phone, then I slip under the covers just as my door flings open.

"Jesus, Emily! Don't you ever knock?"

"Who are you talking to?" she asks sternly.

"Nobody. I'm trying to sleep. What do you care?"

"With the light on and your clothes on?"

"I'm afraid of the dark. Get out of my room, Emily."

She touches her hair. "Well. Technically, it's not your room. And I'm sure I heard you talk in here."

"I was rehearsing for tomorrow."

Her eyes light up. God that woman is an idiot. "Oh! Of course! That's a wonderful idea. I can't wait to hear it." She tilts her head.

"Tomorrow, Emily."

"I could help!"

"Tomorrow, Emily."

"Fine. I'll leave you to it then. Good night, Rose."

"Who the hell was that?" Lola says when I get back on the phone.

"Emily. She's insane," I whisper. "She's got me holed up in her apartment, and she wants my confession so she can say publishing my diary was some kind of sting to draw me out. In exchange, she'll give me ten thousand dollars and two days to run away."

"Sorry," Lola says. "What confession? What for?"

"For killing Charlene Bellamy," I blurt, like it goes without saying.

Which goes to show I'm not thinking straight. I was dragging an armchair in front of the door, my phone wedged in the crook of my neck, which is why I got distracted. I've shocked her into silence. Finally, in a voice that sounds like it's coming from the North Pole, she says, "You killed Charlene Bellamy?"

"Truly? I don't know," I say, sitting down on the bed again. "I thought I did."

CHAPTER 39

Chet woke up with a song in his heart and butterflies in his stomach.

Today was the day.

Today, Charlene would die.

Today, Chet would be free.

And Rose was ready.

Chet chose this day because of the baseball game. It was an exciting game because Coach believed that if they could win this one, they had a shot at participating in the playoffs, which had never happened before. Chet had offered to help, and Coach had accepted, which meant that Chet would be in the dugout for the duration of the game.

Chet's plan was simple. He'd bought Charlene a gift the day before but hadn't given it to her yet. It was a turquoise gemstone pendant on a braided leather lariat, the kind you pull to tighten, like a noose.

Before leaving school, he would leave it on his desk and ask Rose to come in. Then Rose would pick up the necklace and play with it absentmindedly, because she always picked up whatever shiny new thing was on his desk. DNA on the murder weapon? Check.

Then Chet would go home for an hour or so before the game. He would give Charlene her present, make sure she was wearing it, then feed her a handful of Valium.

Then, as he was getting ready to leave, he would ask her to walk him to the door. Outside, he would call out to old Doris and have a neighborly conversation. He'd make sure Doris saw Charlene on the porch, call out to her if necessary. (Charlene! You want me to bring anything home for dinner?) Then he'd get in his car, drive around the corner, park on the edge of the golf course where the trees provided a hiding place, and wait a few minutes. He'd slip on a dark hoodie, quickly walk back, down the side of his house opposite to Mrs. Garcia's where she had no line of sight, and reenter through the back door. He already knew he'd find Charlene back in bed, watching TV, and that's where he'd strangle her, using the very necklace he gifted her earlier. All he had to do was put on a pair of gloves and pull.

A child could do it.

Of course, Chet had to as place Rose in the house while he was at the game, loudly boosting the players' morale. And honestly, that was the easiest step of all.

The last class had finished, and a few minutes later, Rose knocked on his opened door.

"Come in!" he said wearily.

He didn't even look at Rose as she closed the door after her. *Open door policy, remember, cretin?* He didn't call her out on it. He was pinching the bridge of his nose, his eyes closed, the phone against his ear, listening to a dial tone.

"Charlene. Please. Let's discuss it later... Yes, I know. I

know you do." He made sure to look like he was in pain, like talking to Charlene was bordering on unbearable. That was something he'd started to do since he'd come up with the plan. Whenever Rose came into his office, he would enact a variation of that same conversation. *Let's talk about it later... Please, I don't want to have this conversation right now.* He'd wanted Rose to be crystal clear about the state of his marriage: Chet was miserable, he was shackled to a miserable harpy, and no matter how patient or how kind or how willing Chet was, Charlene was intent on making his life a misery.

All accurate, in fact.

"I have to go." He hung up and brought his hands together as if in prayer. "I've had enough of this. I can't take it anymore."

Then he opened his eyes.

"Rose. There you are. We haven't spoken in a couple days. How are you?"

God, she looked awful. Her eyes were so sunken, it was impossible to tell if the dark circles were makeup or bruises. Her hair was matted on one side, like she'd stopped combing it altogether.

"Is your wife mean to you?" Rose asked, ignoring his question. At least she was predictable.

He nodded in a heavy way, like he was tired of pretending.

"Then why don't you leave her?" she said with a shrug. Like she knew what she was talking about. Like they were having a perfectly reasonable, adult conversation. "People separate all the time."

"You really want to know?"

She nodded once, but violently.

He put his pen down and leaned back in his chair. "Charlene is lonely. She's unhappy, deeply so. She thinks she's in love with me, but she isn't. She's merely clinging to her idea of a happy marriage. We're not happy. We haven't been for a long time. Whenever I suggest that we go our separate ways, she breaks down in tears and begs me to change my mind. She's decided the problem is this town, Pike Creek. She hates it here, and she wants us to move. And since Charlene always gets her way, we're moving."

Rose's jaw dropped. "What?"

He shrugged. "That's the way it is."

"Move? Where? When?"

"She wants to go back East. That's where her parents are. She's very close to them."

"When?"

"I don't know, Rose. It's not up to me."

"But you can't!"

He gave her a sad smile, his eyes full of love for her. "I'm going to tell you a secret, okay?'

She nodded.

He leaned forward. "If Charlene found out I was in love with someone else, she would leave me."

She gazed at the desk, finally noticing the necklace. Her hand hovered over it. He willed her to pick it up.

"If she found out about Miss Amy?" she said, looking up at him and pulling her hand away. "I saw you go to her house the other night."

Chet's chest rose with anger. He swallowed his shock. "What were you doing there?"

She shrugged. "Just walking."

Liar. For a second he almost panicked. He couldn't abort the mission now. He only had one shot at this. He pushed his chair back and came around to her side, perched himself on the corner of his desk, and took Rose's hand in his, turned it so that her palm was facing up, and softly rubbed his thumb in the center. He had never touched her quite so deliberately, so intimately, before. Rose turned pink all the way to her ears and started to shake. He pretended not to notice.

"Sometimes, appearances are not what they seem, Rose. Sometimes, the best way to stop people from suspecting you of feeling something...that you shouldn't be feeling..." he paused for a moment and stared into her eyes. "Is to throw them off the scent." He focused on her hand. "What I was going to say before is that the only way my wife would leave me is if she found out I was in love with you."

Rose gasped out loud. "Me?"

He nodded, took a deep breath, then proceeded to reel off all the stupid things Rose had been writing for months. *I think about you all the time. It's you. It's always been you. If you could find it in your heart to consider an old man like me. We'd have to wait a long time, but if you would give it some thought, you would make this old fool so very happy. I could talk to your father, ask for your hand in marriage. You'll be eighteen in five years. It's not so long. I can't stop thinking about you. I've never felt this way before. Of course, we wouldn't do anything intimate at all. Not until you were old enough and we were married. You are so precious to me.*

"I don't want to leave Pike Creek," Chet said. "I don't want to leave you. And if you went to talk to Charlene—I mean, if you wanted to—and if you explained about...how we feel about each other, she would listen to you. You have a wonderful way with words, Rose. If you explained, she would set me free."

"Me?" she asked again, eyes big and round.

Now come on, Rose, he thought. *This is your dream come true. Stop asking and get on with it.*

He nodded and smiled at her like he couldn't hide the joy, the hope, any longer. "You could go there later while I'm at the game."

He told her his address. She already knew where he lived, of course. She'd followed him once and put that stupid scarf around the tree outside his house. "Say around six fifteen? She'll be alone. If she doesn't hear you knock, it's probably because she has the TV on too loud. Just go in. The door will be open." And before she had a chance to reply, he bent down, and very, very softly, he whispered, "It's you, Rose Dunmore. It's always been you."

He stood up and put his hand on her shoulder. "Also, don't put any of what we've discussed today in your diary. Do you understand? Not a single word."

She nodded. She would assume he referred to some vague diary, a pink notebook with a red ribbon around it. It was he who'd suggested she keep a journal, after all. *To practice your writing.* And how very lucky did that suggestion turn out to be?

He opened the door, let her through first, watched her walk away, unsteady on her legs, then went the opposite to the teachers' lounge, where his colleagues were having cake for Penny's birthday.

"I thought you were going to miss my party!" Penny beamed.

"Never!" he replied, kissing her on the cheek. "Happy birthday to you. How old are you again? Twenty-one?"

She laughed, tapping his shoulder lightly before cutting him a slice of the cake Amy had made especially for her birthday.

"You're going to the game later?" he asked Rob.

"You bet!" Rob said before belching.

"Absolutely!" Penny cooed. "I wouldn't want to miss it for the world!"

Amy just smiled and wiped crumbs off the counter.

Chet jerked his thumb over his shoulder. "Did any of you see Rose just now? I asked her if she was going to the game, and she said she wasn't in the mood and had better things to do. She was very odd. Almost aggressive."

"Nothing new there," Rob mumbled.

Penny clicked her tongue. "I'm very worried about that child."

"She's not even going to the game?" Amy asked.

"Nope," Chet replied.

Amy dropped the crumbs in the trashcan and brushed her hands. "I'm surprised. You let her follow you around like a puppy, I would have thought she'd be the first one there."

Chet ignored the gentle barb. The attention he gave Rose was still a point of contention between them. He was dying to pull her to him, bite her slender neck, and whisper, *Don't worry, my perfect sweet girl. Rose is a means to an end, that's all.*

"I think we'll need to talk to her mother next week," he said gravely. "I'll suggest to her she refers Rose to a psychiatrist. I think it's time."

"You tried your best, Chet," Penny said. The three of them mumbled in agreement, then looked at him like they felt sad for him. Because he'd tried his best.

But he couldn't stop seeing Rose's face in his mind's eye. The awed, innocent, gullible quality of it. And it was only at that moment that he remembered she never picked up the necklace.

He felt his jaw set. And the necklace was still on his desk. Chet would pick it up on the way out, but he felt a strange sense of foreboding.

He cheered himself up by picturing Charlene's bulging eyes when he strangled her. And while it was unfortunate Rose hadn't touched the necklace, she would still leave her grubby prints everywhere while Charlene lay there, dead.

CHAPTER 40

"Do you actually remember killing her?" Lola asks.

"No! And she was alive when I went there," I say. "She was in bed. She was pretty out of it, but she spoke to me."

"I don't get it. Why do you think you killed her?"

"Because I had blackouts, I did things I didn't remember. Oh God, Lola, I don't know! He told me there was something wrong with me. I killed Pauly—"

"You didn't."

"But he told me that I did, but I didn't remember because I was disassociating. Just like I didn't remember carving that heart on my desk."

"Wait," she says. "I saw him. The day before."

"Who?"

"Mr. Bellamy. I'd left my water bottle behind the day before, and I went back to get it but the door was closed. But I saw him through the small window. He was sitting at your desk."

"You're kidding!"

"Then the next morning the heart was there."

My heart is thumping in my chest. "But you never said anything."

"Yeah, well, we weren't really talking by then. I assumed you'd done it the day before and that's what he was looking at."

"Except he told me he'd walked in that morning and was shocked to see it."

"He did it," she says. "He carved that heart on your desk."

I am speechless for a moment.

"You didn't strangle Charlene Bellamy, Rose," she says. "Honestly. You had your problems, but you wouldn't kill anyone."

I'm crying again. I wipe my nose with the back of my hand. "You think so?"

"Yes. Just like you didn't kill Pauly." After a pause she says, "Tell me everything, Rose. Tell me what happened that day."

And so, I do. I tell her about the conversation I had with Mr. Bellamy that day in his office, how he told me he loved me, and I'm embarrassed even to say it out loud. Because frankly it sounds way too far-fetched be true.

It never happened, Rose. It's all in your head.

Except it did happen. I know it did.

"Then I went home," I say. "I helped my mother with the laundry. Then you stopped by on your bike…"

"I remember. I thought we'd go to the game together."

"And for obvious reasons, I didn't want to go. You got angry with me, understandably You grabbed my bike and shoved it to the ground."

"Yep. I was crushed," she says. "I couldn't believe you

didn't want to go with me. We hadn't spoken for ages, and I missed you so much. That's why I came to see you. I wanted to make things better between us. I thought you were ditching me for Mr. Bellamy, and you didn't even want to be seen with me at the game."

"Hey," I say softly. "I know. I'm sorry for all of it."

"So what happened then?" she asks.

I rub my forehead. "You took off on your bike at full speed. I told my mom I was going to the game, and I rode to Mr. Bellamy's house."

I tell her what happened next as best as I can remember, and it occurs to me that I can remember it just fine.

There was the knitted scarf I'd wrapped around the oak tree weeks ago outside his house. I leaned my bike against the tree and went up the three concrete steps to the porch and knocked on the door. She didn't answer. I heard canned laughter from the TV. I cupped my hands around my face and looked through the small glass pane in the front door.

I could see part of the living room, the end of a couch. A lamp was on. I could see straight through to the kitchen and farther to the back door. I knocked again, but she didn't answer, so I did what he told me to do. The door was open, and I went inside. I called her name. "Mrs. Bellamy? Hello?" The living room was empty, and the TV was coming from another room. I went in there. It was their bedroom.

She was in bed, propped up against the pillow, looking right at me, but in a weird unfocused way, and immediately I thought of the movie Jane Eyre, and crazy Mrs. Rochester locked up in the attic, and I thought, that's why we never see her. She's insane. That's why he can't leave her.

"Mrs. Bellamy?" I came closer, and I noticed the green pendant around her neck because it was the one I'd seen earlier on Mr. Bellamy's desk.

"Who are you?" she said. She was slurring her words, like

her mouth didn't work properly. I got scared, my legs were like jelly. I walked backward and ran out the way I came, grabbed my bike, and barreled home.

"That's it," I say. "In my mind, I was there for like three minutes. I was inconsolable that I hadn't been able to do what he'd asked me. The next day was a Friday. I went back to school early so I could talk to him. And I was on my way to his office to apologize, and I overheard other students talking about it. Mrs. Bellamy was dead. Someone had gone in and strangled her with the necklace she was wearing while Mr. Bellamy was at the game. He found her when he got home."

I take a breath. "And that's when I realized what I'd done. Or what I thought I'd done. I figured I'd had another blackout. I mean, what else would I think? I'd done the same thing to Mrs. Bellamy that I'd done to Pauly. I ran home and hid in my room. I was freaking out. I opened my laptop and typed the last entry I'd ever write in my diary. Three short sentences. *I did it again. I'm a monster. I'm going to hell.* He would have read them. He would have known I thought I did it."

I grit my teeth, make myself breathe. "That's it. That's the end," I say.

"I wish you'd told me."

"So do I. He set me up, Lola. I know he did. Everything about that year was to make me look like I was nuts enough to kill his wife."

"So why didn't you get arrested? Why did he never say anything?"

"I think he tried because the police came to my house to talk to my mother. I was hiding. I heard the chief say that Mr. Bellamy had told them about me. I think the only reason the police didn't pursue it is because my mother gave me an alibi."

"And they said it was those robbers or something."

"Exactly."

"And all these years you thought you killed her."

"Not exactly. I was afraid that I had."

"My God, Rose. That's horrible."

"I got used to it," I say.

"What do you want to do now?" Lola asks.

"I don't know yet. I want to make some calls. I'll talk to every single student in that year. I'll talk to the teachers. I'll talk to the neighbors. I need to figure out how he did it. I'll take the laptop to the cops and show them that he was reading my diary. I'll tell them everything. I'll get them to look at her death again. I want that investigation reopened. If it turns out that I killed Charlene Bellamy, then I'll face it, Lola. But I don't think I did."

I'm breathing hard. Lola doesn't say anything.

"I have to figure this out before Emily turns me in," I say. "That's my main problem. She's got my laptop, and she's threatening to tell everyone that I stalked her." I pause. "I mean, I did."

"I'm coming to New York," Lola blurts.

"No! You don't have to do that."

"Damn right I do. I'm owed some leave from work anyway. I'm getting on the first plane in the morning. I'll find a cheap hotel, so don't worry about that. We're going to war-game this thing, Rose. We're going to set Emily Harper straight, and we're going to go to the police and have her arrested for blackmail. I'm going to put together a list of all the students and the teachers from back then, the ones I know are still in Pike Creek, and we're going to make some calls together, okay? Because somebody must have seen or heard something. Somebody will back us up. Then you're coming back with me to Pike Creek, and we're going to the cops. We'll tell them to reopen the case, and we're going to prove what Chet Bellamy did to you and to his wife, and he's going to jail for a very long time."

"Thank you," I say, my voice cracking.

"You bet. I've got your back, okay?"

CHAPTER 41

Chet opened the door to his house with a spring in his step. "Hey, babe! I'm home!"

"Hi, hon!" Charlene called out from the bedroom. She met him in the living room, wearing an old tracksuit and a sleeveless top that had a stain on the front. She had a half-empty glass of wine in her hand, and her hair looked like it hadn't been washed in a month. Chet could barely hide his disgust, forgetting for a moment that he was the one who'd gotten her addicted to pills and alcohol in the first place.

"I got you a present," he said then pulled out the necklace.

She tried to focus. "Oh Chet! That's beautiful!" She stood on her toes to kiss him. For once he didn't recoil. He could do it. Heck, it was almost over.

He helped her slip the necklace over her head, then said something about getting a drink. In the kitchen, Chet pulled out a bottle of Valium from his pocket, mixed half a dozen pills in whatever was left of Charlene's boxed wine, returned to the living room, and refilled her glass.

"I'm just going to get changed, babe," he said and took his drink to the bedroom.

Fifteen minutes later, Chet was ready to leave. He turned on the TV in the bedroom then went to the kitchen, where he found Charlene fiddling with the microwave.

"I'm putting this in the car," he said, holding up his sports bag.

"Okay, hon," she replied without looking up.

Outside, Chet's neighbor Doris was tending to her roses. Perfect.

"You're going to the game tonight, Doris?" he asked, putting his bag in the back seat of his car.

"Oh, Lord, no. I'm sure it's all very exciting but not for me," she said.

"That's too bad. It'd be nice to have you down there cheering on the boys. I bet they'd love it."

She made a polite attempt at a laugh, but her heart wasn't in it. Chet could tell Doris didn't like him. He didn't care. The feeling was mutual.

"Hey, Charlene!" Chet called out. Nothing. The door was open, and he could hear the TV.

"Charlene?" he called out again, louder.

"She can't hear you with the TV, Chet. Why don't you just go in," Doris said.

And why don't you mind your own business, you old hag. "You're right," he said with a tight smile. He bounced up the few steps to the house and found Charlene heating instant nachos. "Hey, babe, didn't you hear me call?"

"Oh, sorry, hon. You have fun, okay?"

He wrapped his arms around her waist from behind and kissed the back of her head. "Come out to the porch and wave goodbye to your husband. It's for good luck."

She giggled but didn't move. Chet glanced at his watch. He needed to hurry. "Come on, babe. I gotta go. Come and say goodbye on the porch like a good wifey."

The microwaved pinged. She took out the dish. "Don't be silly!" she said. "You go, Chet, and have fun, okay?"

"Please, baby!" he whined. "It's for good luck, babe. If we lose, it will be your fault!"

She giggled again, and for a moment he wondered what it was going to take. Should he drag her by the hair? Put her neck in an armlock? But to his relief, she put her plate on the counter and put her hands on his chest.

"All right. Go on. Out you go."

"You're the best."

She was swaying so much he had to guide her by the elbow. So he overdid it with the pills. Never mind. It would only make his task easier.

He positioned her just outside the door, kissed her cheek and bounced down the steps again. Doris was still in her yard.

"See you, babe! And you, Doris!" Chet said.

"Bye, Chet. Good luck," Doris said without looking away from her roses.

At the car, he blew a kiss to his wife. "You want me to bring something back for dinner?" he asked loudly.

"That's okay, hon. I've got my nachos."

"Okay, baby, you have a good night, okay? I'll see you later!" He glanced one last time toward Doris. She'd stopped with the roses and was staring right at Charlene.

Chet opened the car door, then behind him, he heard Doris.

"Are you all right, Charlene?"

He turned around. Charlene hadn't gone far. She hadn't even closed the front door yet. She had one hand against the

244

wall to steady herself, and she was looking down at something on the ground.

"Charlene?" Doris asked again.

"Oh, hi, Doris!" Charlene slurred.

"She's fine," Chet said with a tight smile. "She's just tired. Aren't you honey? You go to bed, babe."

"Let me help," Doris said. She put her shears down on a plastic chair. Her hands were shaking like crazy. He didn't think she'd managed to cut a single rose yet, the old fool. That's how weak and old she was.

"Oh yeah! Come on in, Doris," Charlene said. "I was just going to have some wine."

"I think you should go to bed!" Chet yelled out through a strained smile, his hand still on the car door.

"Don't be silly, Chet," Charlene said. "It's not late!"

That never stopped you before, Chet thought.

"I'll make you some tea, Charlene," Doris said. "You just look a little under the weather, my dear."

Doris had walked out the front of her yard and was about to turn into Chet's when he put his hand on her shoulder. "She's fine. She just needs to lie down, that's all."

She looked down at his hand. He had gripped her harder than he'd intended. She was so weak. Like a dried-up old tree. He let go of her shoulder.

"It's no trouble," she said. "I'll make her some tea and settle her in. She looks a bit unwell to me."

And before he had time to stop her, Doris was going up the porch steps.

Chet watched his wife let herself be guided by motherly Doris. Then Doris closed the door without even a second look at him.

Chet got in his car and slammed the steering wheel with the flat of his hand. He stared at the front door for a full minute, his jaw so tight it hurt. He drove off and parked around the corner. He had to gather himself. He couldn't go back now. He couldn't kill them both, and God knows he was tempted.

Chet checked his watch. Meddling Doris would be there a while, and Chet was due at the game in five minutes. He vaguely considered going to Rose's house to tell her not to go and see Charlene, but her mother would probably be there, and he could hardly ask to speak to Rose in private.

He gripped the steering wheel until his knuckles turned white then relaxed his hands and took some deep breaths.

He'd have to come back later. That's all. He would park his car a little away from the baseball field. There would be a short break. He could do it then. It was not ideal, and he'd have to be quick, but he could do it.

He had to do it. He had no choice.

CHAPTER 42

It's after midnight when Lola and I say goodbye.

My head is spinning. I can't stop thinking of what Lola said. *I never saw you kill Pauly.* I think of my mother. I have a sudden urge to tell her, right now. Also, I have questions only she can answer.

She lives in Maplewood, a small town in New Jersey. It takes a train and two buses and about forty-five minutes to get there, which I've done precisely twice, both times for Christmas. When I see her now, I hardly recognize her. She used to be brittle and bony, her elbows protruding like door-knobs. She had an attractive face, but it was obscured by the big glasses, and she'd stopped smiling a long time ago, although even back then she still wore her bold red lipstick. Like she still had hope.

These days, her edges have softened. Her black hair is streaked with gray; she still wears glasses but with bright-red frames so that they, too, seem lighter and happier. She's happy with Albert, a retired banker with a comb-over, an aquiline nose, and small blue eyes that crinkle and sparkle like he's always about to tell you a really good joke.

I don't care what the time is. I call my mother on her cell. She picks up after three rings.

"Rose? What's wrong?"

"Did I used to have blackouts?"

"What?"

"Did I ever have blackouts? Fugue states. Doing things without realizing I'm doing them. Like I'm in a trance. Maybe passing out, too?"

"What are you talking about? Of course not."

"Are you sure?"

"Of course I'm sure. You're my daughter. You've never had a blackout or fainted or anything like that as long as you lived under the same roof as me. What's going on? Are you all right?"

"Do you remember that incident with the hamster at my old school?"

She takes a sharp intake of air. "Of course I remember."

"I don't think I did it."

I meant to sound triumphant, and honestly, I would have settled for petulant, but instead I sound miserable, my voice thick with it. A globule of resentment bubbles up my chest. *All this time,* I want to say. *All this time you were disappointed in me, and now it turns out I didn't even do it.*

"I know that," my mother says softly.

"Oh, come on, Mom," I scoff. "You thought I killed him. What was it you said? I had a black heart, remember? I was such a disappointment?"

The back of my eyes are stinging with tears. Honestly, for someone who hasn't cried in almost ten years, I'm sure catching up on lost time. I rub them with my knuckles. "Anyway, let's just say new information has come to light. It looks like I didn't kill Pauly. Just saying."

She is silent for a moment. Then, she says, "I know you didn't hurt that hamster. I know you, Rose. I know you would never hurt an animal. I tried to explain that to Mrs. Morales, but *he* wouldn't let me get a word in. He wouldn't let anyone speak but himself. He thought he could impress me with his big words, like he knew you better than I did. I tried to explain, but everyone looked up to him. You, Mrs. Morales…like he walked on water. Like he was some fricking authority on my own daughter."

I stare at the wall in front of me, shocked into momentary silence. "Why didn't you say anything before?"

"I tried, Rose. I really tried. But I couldn't reach you. You hated me. It wasn't your fault, with your dad and all—you were so young—but you hated me. And for the record, I have never, ever been disappointed in you."

And I'm thinking, so why did I think she was? Why did I think she believed I had a black heart? And then I remember. Because *he* told me. Repeatedly.

"What did you mean before, when you said you had new information?" she asks.

"I spoke to Lola. Remember Lola?"

A pause. "Yes… of course."

"She was the one who told Mrs. Morales that I'd done it."

"I remember."

"I just spoke to her. She says she never saw me strangle Pauly, but Mr. Bellamy made her say that she did. I thought I'd done it because he kept telling me I had these blackouts and I couldn't remember the bad things I did."

She takes a few seconds to speak, and when she does, her voice is low and angry. "I always thought there was something not right about that man. He came to see me, you know? The day after that, a policeman came to ask about you."

"Mr. Bellamy came to see you?"

"It was you he wanted to talk to, but you weren't there.

He asked straight up where you were the night Mrs. Bellamy died."

"What?"

"The gall of the man," she mutters. "Then he said there was something wrong with you. He reminded me that you'd harmed the school pet. He didn't like that I'd told the police you were with me all night. He accused me of lying."

My heart is thumping. I knew it. Mr. Bellamy killed his wife, and he wanted to make it look like I did it. And the only person who got in the way was my mother.

"Why did you lie to the police about where I was that night?" I ask.

"You were in trouble, Rose. The police come to my house and ask where my daughter was the night her teacher's wife was murdered. He wasn't there for milk and cookies. I was protecting you. I don't know where you went that night, but I know with God as my witness that you never hurt that poor woman. And no policeman is going to come to my house and suggest otherwise, and no Mr. Bellamy either, for that matter. I don't care what you were up to that night, but I know it wasn't that. You were only gone for ten minutes, maybe fifteen at the most. I didn't think that counted."

I think of Mr. Bellamy coming to me under the mulberry tree. It would have been after he'd gone to see my mom. He didn't find me accidentally. He'd been reading about my secret place for weeks.

Did you do something bad, Rose?

He wasn't guessing. He already knew. *Tell the police, tell your mother, tell somebody, Rose! Tell them what you did!*

"Thanks, Mom," I say. "For doing that, for vouching for me back then."

"You're my daughter. I love you." And I honestly cannot remember my mother saying those words to me before. I realize I should be pleased, but honestly, my first thought it, *Is something wrong? Is she dying? Am I dying?*

"What brought all that up, anyway?" she asks. "Is it because you spoke to Lola?"

"Yes," I lie.

"I didn't know you were still in touch."

"We weren't. We just hooked up again on social media."

"Oh."

Something about the way she said it. *Oh.* "You seem surprised."

"How is Lola?" she says, not actually answering my question.

"She's fine."

"And her lovely sister Kimberlee? How is she?" And honestly, she sounds so much nicer when she asks about Kimberlee than when she asks about Lola.

"I don't know, Mom. Her name didn't come up."

"No. I suppose it wouldn't," she says lightly. "They weren't close, from memory."

Well, no, they weren't. I think back to all the things Lola used to say about Kimberlee. *She cut her favorite dress then said I did. She broke her own money box and accused me of doing it.*

"I should let you go," I say. "You're probably tired. You should go back to bed."

"All right." Then, before we say goodbye, she says, "I'm glad we talked, Rose."

"Me too," I say.

CHAPTER 43

Chet stood in the dugout with his arms crossed, his jaw set, watching the play and not seeing a thing. He was imagining Rose knocking on the door of his house. If only he'd had the presence of mind to tell old Doris to stay put and wait until he got home. Then Rose would have showed up, turned around, and gone home. Surely even crazy Rose wouldn't declare her undying love for Chet in front of the neighbors.

But it wouldn't happen this way. Of that, he was certain. Rose was going to show up when Charlene was alone, and all hell would break loose.

He'd taken his eye off the ball. That was the problem. He hadn't planned for contingencies. But Chet would fix it. He just needed a break, that's all. A moment to get away, unseen.

Except he never got a break. Every time the opportunity came up for Chet to get away, Coach Dave would come to him to discuss strategies or get his opinion on substitutions. He was starting to panic. He closed his fists as he imagined the conversation that was taking place, maybe even at this very minute.

"Mr. Bellamy, your husband and I are in love. You have to let him go. It's me. It's always been me."

Chet felt sick. He wanted to kick himself and everyone else for having screwed his perfect plan so royally. What was Charlene doing now? Was she asking Doris for a ride so she could go and retrieve the phone that had the evidence that could put Chet in prison for a decade?

He just needed a break.

In the last possible moment before the next top inning, he made excuses (nature calling) and slipped away. On the way out, he saw Amy waving at him from the stands. She was wearing that cute summer dress he liked, with the straps and the little flowers throughout. It gave him strength. *My perfect girl.* He waved back. He was already jogging to the exit when Janice Morales came to stand in front of him, barring his way.

"Chet! How are you? I was looking for you."

He gritted his teeth then forced a smile. "Janice. If you could give me a sec—"

She moved closer, conspiratorially. "It's going well, isn't it? You must be thrilled. You and Coach have done wonders for those boys."

"Thank you." He jerked his thumb behind him. "I have to—"

She puts her hand on his arm. "If I could ask a favor, the Johnson brothers, they'll need a ride home after the game. Trevor Johnson, their father—got a call from the hospital. Oh no! Nothing serious. I just saw from your face you thought someone got hurt!" She laughed. Needless to say, Chet thought no such thing.

"No!" she continued. "Mr. Johnson is a doctor, if you remember. And he's on call tonight." She sighed. "Anyway, you live that way, don't you? Near the golf course? You don't mind giving the boys a ride home?"

"No! Totally fine. I'll just—"

"Thank you, Chet," she said, patting his shoulder. "I knew I could count on you. They'll meet you in the parking lot. And how's Charlene? I haven't seen her in months. Is she here?"

"No... She wasn't feeling too well. She decided to stay home. Now if I could—"

But on and on she went, and no matter how hard he tried, he couldn't get rid of her.

And then, to his horror, he heard the whistle that signaled the start of the next inning.

"Oh! That's you, isn't it?" she said. "You're going this way?" She pointed in the direction he had just come from.

And Chet's stomach churned like someone was twisting it with a pair of pliers. He almost made a run for it, but it was no use. It was too late.

"Yes," he said finally, resisting the urge to take her head in both hands and squeeze it until her brain exploded. "I'm going this way."

After the game, he met the Johnson brothers in the parking lot and took them home. He used the trip to formulate what he'd say to Charlene.

You must've dreamt it. Why would a kid say those things?

He parked outside, his heart thumping. He stared at his house. He wouldn't have been surprised if she'd burnt it down, but it looked the same as he'd left it. Through the front window, he could see the glow from the lamp in the living room.

He walked up the steps to the front door and slowly turned the handle. The door was unlocked.

"Charlene? Babe! We won!"

Nothing. The TV was on in the bedroom. Could it be she hadn't heard him? Of course not. She was probably waiting around a corner with a baseball bat.

"Honey?" he said softly.

Nothing.

He put his sports bag on the floor and grabbed an empty, grubby vase from the bookcase as a weapon. Just in case.

"Charlene?"

Nothing. He tiptoed into the bedroom. Charlene was sitting up in bed, her eyes closed. She was asleep.

He let out a long breath and put the vase on the dresser. Maybe he got lucky. Perhaps Rose had come in and found her comatose and left.

He turned off the TV and went to pick up the glass of wine and the dirty plate from the bedside table.

But something didn't feel right, and it took him a moment to figure out what it was. It was her head, the way it had lolled at a funny angle. And now that he looked at her closely, there was something about her color too.

He touched her shoulder with his fingertips. "Charlene?"

She slipped sideways, like a dead weight.

He jumped back like he'd been burnt. "Charlene?"

And that's when he saw it. The necklace wasn't around her neck; it was on her chest, broken off, and there was a thin purple mark around her throat.

He stared at her, wondering if he was dreaming. He wasn't. Charlene was dead. Strangled. And it took him a moment, through the haze of the shock, to understand that Rose had done it after all. Maybe they'd had an argument. Maybe Charlene had threatened her. Who cared? It was a miracle.

Rose had killed his wife.

He pressed his hand over his mouth and stood there, trying to control himself. But it was no use. He bent over and laughed, pressing his hand hard to stifle the sound.

Then, when he recovered sufficiently, he screamed for help.

CHAPTER 44

All I can think is, *He did it, not me.* It's on a loop in my brain. Chet Bellamy killed his wife and worked for months to set me up to take the fall.

I'm going to find him. One day, I'll make him pay.

I think of Ben, of all the things I said and the things he now believes about me. Sure, he said he didn't, but he must have thought about it. He must have decided I was telling the truth.

Suddenly it feels unbelievably important that I talk to him. I check my phone. It's twenty to one in the morning. It's his night off. I tell myself I should let him sleep.

And then I call him.

"I'm sorry," I whisper when he picks up. I put my hand over my eyes. I tell him everything, more or less. He listens in silence while I vomit my story. I tell him about the crush I had on my teacher that year, about the diary I wrote synced to his laptop. I try to explain what it was like. The encouragements, the special attention, the building of confidence, the tearing down of confidence, the gaslighting.

I tell him about Cleopatra. I was jealous of Cleopatra, I say, because he made such a big deal of her, of how beautiful she was. He wanted me to wear makeup to look like her, and that's what I did, and it made me look mad. I was barely thirteen years old, I say. I would have walked around with a tinfoil hat on my head if I thought he'd like me better that way. For a while there, I'd convinced myself he loved me too. Then I tell him about Pauly, and the despair I felt when I realized what I was capable of.

And then I tell him that all along, he had a plan, and as a result, for many years, I believed I'd killed his wife. Then I tell him, it's only now that I understand I didn't do these things. I couldn't have. I know I didn't kill Pauly because I wasn't there. I know I didn't kill his wife because I don't believe in blackouts anymore. Also I was only there for a few minutes.

I am not evil. I'm an idiot, but I am not evil.

Ben is deadly quiet, and my stomach slowly fills with wet cement. "You believe me, don't you? That I didn't kill her?"

"Of course I believe you," he says softly. "You're the savior of rats. Tell me what I can do."

He says that last part in a tone so thick with tenderness it makes my eyes water all over again. I tell him I'd like to move in with him while I figure it all out and prepare what I will say to the police. He says he'd love that.

"I'm supposed to go to Boston in the morning with Liam," he says. "We're closed for two days. It's for the new restaurant—"

"That's right. I remember. You told me."

"But I'll tell Liam I'm not going."

"No, don't do that," I say quickly. "It's important."

He insists, but I explain about Lola coming over in the

morning, and could she crash on his couch for a couple days?

"Sure. Your friend is welcome to stay here."

"You go to Boston with Liam," I say. "Truly. It will give Lola and me some time to catch up."

"If you're sure…"

"I'm sure." And then I add, "Oh, also, my parents didn't die in a car crash. My mother lives in New Jersey with her husband Albert, and I'm not sure where my father is these days, but I'm suspect he's alive. Sorry about that bit."

When I hang up, I see that Lola sent a text. She's booked on the first flight out of Kansas City, and she'll land in Newark at 9:58 a.m. I text back, tell her she can stay at Ben's and that I'll be there too, and send her the address.

I lie down, but I'm too wired to sleep.

I pick up my phone again and search for the murder of Charlene Bellamy. I click on the first article that comes up.

Pike Creek Shaken by Grisly Murder of Woman Found Strangled in Her Home

The tranquil community of Pike Creek was left in a state of shock following the murder of a local woman, identified as 37-year-old Charlene Bellamy.

Authorities were alerted to the crime when the victim's husband, local teacher Chet Bellamy, returned home to find Mrs. Bellamy's lifeless body in their bedroom. Preliminary investigations have determined that she was strangled with a leather necklace.

Mr. Bellamy was reportedly attending the local high school baseball game when the incident occurred, and his presence during that time was corroborated by multiple witnesses. So far, no charges have been filed, and Mr. Bellamy is cooperating fully with authorities. The Bellamy's next-door neighbor, Mrs. Garcia, spoke to the victim shortly after Mr. Bellamy left for the baseball game. "We talked for ten, maybe fifteen minutes. I can't believe she's gone," Mrs. Garcia said.

Authorities are urging anyone with information related to the case to come forward and assist in the ongoing investigation.

I remember reading that Mrs. Garcia was the last person to see Charlene Bellamy alive. Other than me, obviously, and Chet Bellamy.

I have to talk to her. She used to babysit me when I was a kid. I wonder if she remembers me.

I read more articles, gnawing on a fingernail. I try to figure out when he killed her. If it were me, I would have done it before I left, then pretend to be shocked when I got home. But she was alive when I went there, so he must have done it when he got home after the game. Would the authorities know if she'd only just died? How long before he called the police?

I put my phone away and stare at the ceiling. Something inside me feels like it's cracking open, but not in a bad way.

I think I know what it is.

I was a mess during my first year at Sacred Heart High School. I barely slept at all. I just couldn't stop thinking about what I'd done to Mrs. Bellamy. My roommate would tell me that when I did sleep, I'd cry out in the night that I was sorry. She thought I was homesick. Hardly. She also thought I was weird. Spot-on there, although that would also have been because I stretched a piece of string down the middle of our room, at ankle height, to trip me up in case I woke up with the urge to kill her. To be clear, she seemed like a very nice person, but that had never stopped me before.

We never got close. That should go without saying.

I emerged from another sleepless night one day, a year after Mrs. Bellamy died, and decided I couldn't take it anymore. The guilt was literally killing me. So I told myself, that's it. Either I keep going like this and end up in an asylum, or I stop thinking about it, accept that I'm a psychopath, and move on.

So that's what I did. I pushed it all down into the vault of my cold, steel heart, slammed the door shut, poured layers of concrete on top, then nailed sheets of titanium around it. I embraced my inner psychopath. I removed the word *remorse* from my internal vocabulary. I displayed a stunningly shallow range of emotions. I wore my lack of empathy like a badge of honor.

But cracks are appearing. Charlene Bellamy wants to speak out. I can feel it.

She wants to blow up the vault.

CHAPTER 45

I wake up early, feeling almost euphoric—even though I barely slept—which is a new experience for me. Usually, I wake up feeling absolutely nothing.

The first thought that popped into my head was, *I didn't do it!* Which was great. Then the second thought was that I was going to see Lola.

I can't wait. As I pack my bag I can't stop thinking about how much I've missed her. I just never allowed myself to think about that. Also I assumed she hated me, because... well, I was evil inside.

But everything is different now. And today, I'm breaking the spell. I'm leaving this place, I'm getting as far away from nut job Emily as I possibly can, and there's nothing she can do to stop me.

It's going to be awkward, for sure. Emily's entire redemption act is built upon the foundation that I'm an evil killer, and frankly, I was okay with that. I mean, up until now I would have gladly thrown her off the balcony. Now, it turns out I was just painfully naïve and innocent.

It's going to be a blow.

.   .   .

It's a beautiful warm day, and Emily has opened the doors to the terrace. She's leaning with her back against the door-jamb, a steaming cup of tea in her hands, tousled hair, bare-foot and draped in a silk robe. She looks like an ad for a luxury hotel. *Indulge yourself in a haven of tranquility…*

"Morning, sweetie! You're ready for your close-up?"

Honestly, there's a special place in hell for people who greet you every day with the same put-down joke. And you just know that if you call them out, they'll tell you they were only joking and can't you take a joke?

Today, I can take a joke. "Ha ha!" I say. "And good morning to you too." I make a beeline for the coffee machine. I need an intravenous shot of caffeine for this conversation, but short of that, I'll have an espresso. I take it to the couch.

She comes to sit next to me, puts her tea on the coffee table, then makes a square with her thumbs and index fingers, like she's looking at me through a camera. She still terrifies the hell out of me.

"I was thinking about your makeup," she says. "I have a look in mind for the video. Darker. More threatening. I could thicken your eyebrows and accentuate the rings under your eyes. Maybe highlight your cheekbones. What do you think?"

"About that," I say, putting down my cup and folding my hands on my lap. "There've been some new developments."

She smiles at me, but I can tell she doesn't like it. "What kind of developments?"

I raise my shoulders. "I didn't do it."

She scoffs, but with a smirk of condescension, like I just told a joke but it was a lame one. Then she frowns at me. "You okay?"

"Yes!" I'm doing that grinning thing again. My cheeks

are hurting. My top lip is stretched against the bottom of my nostrils.

"What's wrong with your face?"

"I don't know," I say. "I'm just happy."

"Is it hormonal?"

"No, it's because all this time, I thought I was a horrible person, a psychopath with no redeeming qualities whatsoever. Now I'm pretty sure I didn't kill Mrs. Bellamy."

She cocks her head. "I don't get it."

"It looks like I was framed."

Her eyes grow round and wide, a pantomime of dawning realization. "Ooh...." she says. "Framed! That's original."

"No, really!" I tell her in a rush of words that my teacher set me up for the murder of his wife. By now you'd think I'd be pretty apt at telling this story, but she keeps stopping me, asking questions, making me go back, go forward, contradicting me, so by the end, I'm confused too.

"But you did kill her," she says.

"No, that's the thing. I didn't. Chet Bellamy did. And everything else was a setup to frame me for his wife's murder."

"Okay," she sighs. "Assuming what you say is true—"

"It's—"

She raises a hand to shut me up. "Where does that leave me? I mean, I'm supposed to be the heroine here. The woman who put herself in the path of incredible danger at great peril to herself in order to avenge the life of a woman she never met." And you can absolutely tell she's workshopped that line. In fact, I'd put money on it that it's the pitch for her Netflix series. "How am I going to look now?" she asks.

I raise a finger. "I have an idea about that." To be clear, my idea is just a bunch of lies and false promises I cobbled together to soften the blow so I can get out of here. None of what I'm about to say is going to happen.

She frowns. "What?"

"Instead of going to the police, you go to the *New York Times* or *The Atlantic* or whatever. You tell them the same story as before. That you found the laptop, realized it held the key to a long-forgotten murder, et cetera. You published it to lure me, like you said, but then I came along and explained that the real murderer was in fact Chet Bellamy, not me. So you don't need a confession from me because I didn't do anything wrong. I don't think. Over the next few days, I'm going to get my ducks in a row and—"

"What ducks?"

"I have to talk to people in Pike Creek. I want to gather as much proof as possible that Mr. Bellamy killed his wife. I want to talk to his neighbors, to other students who were there then, I want to talk to teachers... Anyone who was around who can back me up. I'll take the laptop to the police, give them everything I've found out, and then..." I pretend to play a drum.

She frowns. "What are you doing?"

"Drum roll."

"I see. So what's the big idea?"

"We're going to write a book together."

"Excuse me?"

"You're so much better at writing than I am. What you did with *Diary of an Octopus*, I mean. Truly incredible. It would have been a flop if I'd published it as is. Not that I would have, but you know what I mean. You have real talent, Emily Harper."

She raises an eyebrow, twirls an earring. "Well..."

"I can't do this without you, Emily. So once the real killer is caught—Chet Bellamy, to be abundantly clear—you and me will get together and write a book about the whole saga. *Diary of an Octopus: The Sequel.* It's going to be amazing."

She nods slowly. "Okay…but so now…you're the heroine."

I roll my eyes. "It's not like that."

"It's exactly like that." She pats her hair. "You're Batman, and I'm Robin. That's what you're saying. You're Sherlock Holmes, and you solved the case, and I'm Dr. Watson chronicling your amazing powers of deduction for your posterity."

"Don't be silly! And hey, I'm happy to discuss how to approach it so you are front and center." Front and center of a firing squad, more like. "Also, I was wondering…" I scratch the back of my head. "Where's the laptop?"

"Why?"

"Because I—we—have to take it to the police. Not necessarily today, but soon. It has the evidence Mr. Bellamy was syncing and reading my diary the whole time. This is a key element of our book, Emily."

She nods slowly. "It's at Tiff's place. I'll call her later and ask her to drop it off."

"Do you want to call her now? So we can dot the i's and all that."

"I'll call her later."

I smile. "I understand." God, I hate her all over again. Not that I'd stopped, but I'd put it on hold for a minute there. Anyway, who cares? I can call Tiffany myself. I've got her number. I'll tell her it's evidence in a murder and it's not to be tampered with.

"Anyway… I just wanted to keep you in the loop," I say, my smile affixed to my mouth. I rummage through my bag and pull out my phone.

"What are you doing?"

"I'm going to stay with Ben. There's no point in me

being here now that I didn't kill anybody, so I'm going to call an Uber..."

And just like that, Emily has snatched the phone out of my hands, walked to the terrace, and tossed it over the railing. She didn't even *throw* it, she just tossed it. Like she couldn't be bothered.

I'm on my feet. "What the hell?"

She grabs me by the arm and pulls me back down, digging her sharp fingernails into my skin.

"Listen to me, Rose, and listen carefully. You thought you killed her, but now you don't think you did? You want to know what I think? I think you're in denial. I think you're experiencing killer's remorse because you're about to be found out, and I understand, I really do. But all this nonsense about suddenly realizing you haven't done anything wrong? That's just crazy talk. That's the kind of thing that happens in the movies, sweetie. I'm sorry. I know you're sad and all that, but what do you expect? That this mythical proof is going to fall in your lap just because you wish for it? Please. Grow up. The only proof you'll ever find is that you're a horrible person and you kill hamsters."

I jerk my arm away. "I know it doesn't suit your narrative—"

"Oh, it's nothing to do with my narrative, sweetie. I don't need another angle. I published this diary to lure a dangerous killer lurking in our midst. It was an act of great courage on my part."

"Right."

"Right nothing. I would be doing you a disservice. Because deep down, you know you did it. So for the love of God, confess! You'll feel better, you'll see. You'll thank me later."

She looks so desperate that I want to laugh. She rummages through the stuff on her table, looking for her camera that is right there, right under her nose. I go back upstairs. I don't even bother to run. I loop the strap of my purse over my shoulder, grab my duffel bag, and throw it down the steps. It misses her head by an inch, and she doesn't even notice.

"Okay, you're ready?" She's got the camera in her hand, pointed at me.

I ignore her. I make for the door. She falls on her knees, barring my way.

"Don't go. Please! What do you want? You want money? I can give you money! How much do you want? I have so much money! Thanks to you! A hundred thousand dollars? You want a hundred thousand dollars? I can make it two hundred! I can do it now, today. Just give me your confession, Rose!"

"You're insane." She grabs my ankle, and I kick her off. I'm about to open the door, but she's grabbed the door handle before I have the chance. She yanks the door open, shoving my head into it, hard, and I see stars.

CHAPTER 46

Honestly, I'm so over being bossed around. I want to hit her back. I want to break her nose, but I don't. This is the new me. I am unflappable. I wouldn't hurt a fly.

Emily has her back against the now closed front door, her arms out, her hair standing in every direction like she's just licked her finger and stuck it in the nearest power socket.

I stand up, one side of my face throbbing, and carefully brush myself down. Then I yank her away from the door by the arm as easily as if she were a rag doll. I hear something pop, which I suspect might have been her shoulder joint, and I won't lie, it sounds as exquisite as the ping of a wind chime in the breeze.

She cries out in pain, holding her arm, and I seize the moment to run down the stairs and out of the building.

I find my phone wedged in a flower box with barely a scratch. I'm almost maxed out on my credit card, but I take a taxi to Ben's place anyway.

. . .

"Rose!" Lola is already there, waiting outside. She throws her arms around me.

"Oh my God, I can't believe you came! I'm so happy to see you!" I cry. We stay like that for a minute, inhaling each other's hair. A kaleidoscope of memories flash by. The two of us laughing, jumping into lakes, climbing trees, running with the wind in our hair…

"I've missed you," I say.

"I've missed you too. I can't believe everything that's happening." She pulls away. "We're going to sort this out, okay? Whoa! What happened to your face?"

"It's nothing." I mean, it's not. It hurts like hell, a pulsating mass of pain on my cheekbone and my forehead. "A door ran into me." I try to laugh, but it hurts too much.

"Let go upstairs," I say.

I find an ice pack in the freezer and hold it to my cheek.

"You look great, by the way," I say. "You don't wear glasses anymore?"

"I had my eyes zapped."

"Suits you."

"Thanks, babe." She puts one arm around my shoulders and squeezes. "And you look terrible."

"Thanks, babe," I reply and pretend to punch her arm.

We sit on the couch. She holds my free hand. There's a lot of talking over each other, a lot of questions, especially about Emily. Or, as Lola refers to her, *that bitch Emily*, and sometimes *that bitch* for short. I try to answer them as best I can.

"By the time I left, she was offering two hundred thousand dollars and forty-eight hours grace before she took my confession to the cops."

"And you didn't take the money?" Lola asks, wide-eyed.

I laugh. "I should have. She whacked my face with a door."

She stands up abruptly. "Give me her address."

"Why?"

"I'm going to see her. I'm going to give her a piece of my mind."

"I doubt she'll let you in."

"I'll climb through a window."

I raise my hand, palm out. "Not so fast, Spider-Man. She's got the laptop. She knows about the SkyDrive. She's going to delete every trace of it. I just know she will. She needs me to be guilty, and she's going to do her darnedest to make sure I look that way. Forget about Emily. We don't have much time. There must be someone out there who saw something. Maybe Mr. Bellamy confessed to someone."

Lola makes a face. "Unlikely."

I sigh. "I know. But maybe someone saw him coming out of his house that day when he was supposed to be at the game?"

"Yes. You're right. And that's where we should start. I made a list of everyone I can remember who was in our class, and the teachers too. I've got a few phone numbers. We can start there."

I tell her about the article I read last night, and about Mrs. Garcia. Lola says Mrs. Garcia babysat her, too, when Lola was a kid. I guess she used to babysit half the town's children. Lola says she's still there, still in the same house.

"This is the part I don't understand," I say. "We know Mrs. Bellamy was alive when her husband left. I know that. Mrs. Garcia knows that. Then supposedly, he came home and she was dead. So when did he kill her?"

"When he got home," she says. "He strangled her then pretended he found her like that."

"That's what I thought, but I read a lot about the case last night, and he was never a suspect. I don't get it. You'd think the police would have considered the possibility. We have to call her. She might know something."

I search for her number in the Pike Creek white pages online and find it immediately. Lola goes to the kitchen to make coffee while I make the call.

She answers on the fourth ring.

"Mrs. Garcia? It's Rose Dunmore."

A pause. "Who?"

Poor Mrs. Garcia. She sounds about a hundred years old. "It's Rose Dunmore," I say again, louder this time. "I don't know if you remember me. You used to babysit me a long time ago. My mother's name was Donna Dunmore?"

A pause. "I remember you."

"I wanted to ask you about the day Mrs. Bellamy died. If that's all right with you."

"Did the police talk to you?"

"The police? No, why?"

"No reason. How is your mother, Rose?"

"She's well, Mrs. Garcia. Thank you for asking. She's remarried."

"Yes, I know."

"They're very happy."

"That's nice."

"Okay…well…erm… I was wondering, sorry to rack all this up again, but it's important. I understand you spent some time with Mrs. Bellamy just after her husband left for the game?"

A pause. "Why are you asking me this, Rose? What's it about? Because I told the police everything already. I told them everything when she died and when they came back last year."

"The police came back?"

"Yes, dear. And I told them the same thing I told them ten years ago. I don't have anything new to add."

"I understand. I'm sorry to ask this, but when Mr. Bellamy came home after the game, did he call the police right away? Do you know?"

"Of course he did. He walked in that door and screamed his heart out."

"How long was he home for, before he screamed?"

"Hardly any time at all," she says.

"But how do you know? Did you see him?"

"Only after he started screaming!"

"So how do you know it was hardly any time between when he came home and when he started screaming?"

"Oh dear, the police were all over that. He gave a ride home to two students who live a block away. Literally one minute later he walked inside his house and started screaming. I was watching TV and I ran outside. He yelled for me to call 911, and I did. And before you ask, the police say he couldn't have done it. Poor Charlene had been dead quite a while by the time the paramedics arrived, and he was at the game at that time." She pauses. "I didn't like him one bit, Rose. I didn't like the way he treated his wife. I didn't like how he encouraged her to drink all the time, even when she was trying to cut down. I found his smoothness irritating. But he didn't come home and strangle his wife. If that's what you're asking. And I didn't kill her either, in case you're wondering."

"I wasn't—"

"I've had arthritis for years. Even back then, I could barely prune my roses. And whoever strangled Charlene used a lot of force. That's what the police said."

"I wasn't suggesting, Mrs. Garcia." Lola puts two mugs down on the coffee table and sits opposite me.

"Is it possible he came back halfway through the game,

only for a short while?" I bite on my fingernail. It's such a loaded question. But who else can I ask? She's the only person who might have seen something that night. And I need *somebody* to tell me *something* that will place him back at the house with enough time to kill his wife.

A pause. "Not that I know of. Why don't you talk to Amy?"

"Amy? Miss Amy? Sure! I'd love to talk to Amy."

"She might have something to say about it. She lived with him next door, you know. They lived there after his wife was murdered in that house. He was waiting for the insurance money from Charlene's death to buy another house, but they dragged their feet because the murderer wasn't caught. Or that's what he told me. Amy hated living there, but she stayed. One day they had a big fight, and she left. That was a few days before the accident."

"What accident?"

"When he got hit by that car."

"When was that?"

"A year ago this August."

"So he still lives next door?"

"No, no. He's in a nursing home in Wichita now. He can't speak or feed himself anymore. The accident left him in a terrible way."

Well, at least that's good news. I mean, sure, I would have preferred to hear that he was dead, eaten alive by African driver ants, but heck, being stuck in a nursing home unable to speak or feed yourself must be the next best thing. I hope he lives until he's a hundred.

"And Amy moved to New York City," she says.

"Really? That's where I am!"

"Do you want me to call Amy and pass on your number?"

"Thank you, Mrs. Garcia. I'd love to talk to Amy. And if

she could call me as soon as possible. It's really urgent." I give her my number.

But I am crushed. I won't lie. I was hoping to solve this case with a couple of phone calls. Now I wonder if he hired someone to kill his wife while he was out, and it seems so obvious I don't know why I didn't think of it before.

"Why are you so curious about that night, Rose?" Mrs. Garcia asks.

Well, at least she hasn't read the book. "It's a long story, Mrs. Garcia. Can I ask you one last question?"

"Yes."

"Did you see anyone else near the house that night? Anyone else at all?" And honestly, I don't know what's wrong with me. It's like my mouth is running two steps ahead of my brain. Also, I'm an idiot.

"Yes," she says slowly. "I saw someone else come to the house that evening. A schoolgirl. On her bike. She had the green school jersey on." Then in a low voice, she adds, "I didn't think much of it at the time, Rose. I never mentioned it to the police. I didn't think it was important. But you and I both know who I'm talking about."

CHAPTER 47

When I end the conversation with Mrs. Garcia, I see that I have a missed call from my mother.

"She saw me," I say to Lola as my finger hovers over the icon for my voicemail.

"What are you talking about?"

"Mrs. Garcia. She saw me. That night."

"She saw you?"

I nod. "She saw a schoolgirl. She described what I was wearing, and then she said, 'We both know who I'm talking about.'"

I put my hand over my eyes. "I can't believe I just did that. The police are on the case again, and I've just reminded Mrs. Garcia that the only person who came by that evening was me. I am literally building a case against myself."

I press the voicemail button, bring the phone to my ear and listen to my mother's message.

"Call me the moment you get this, Rose!"

Oh, God.

. . .

"The police were here! Just now!" she shrieks in my ear.

I'm on my feet. "What? Why?"

"One detective from Pike Creek and another one! They said they went to your address—"

I pace the room, pulling at my hair with my free hand. "What address?"

"Oh... I don't remember, an address on Ninth Avenue—"

Oh my God. Emily's address.

"But that's not your address, is it? I told them you live in Brooklyn! Was that all right? They said not to contact you, but what am I supposed to do? What's going on? Why are they looking for you?"

"Did you say one of them is from Pike Creek? What did he want?"

"They want to talk to you about Mrs. Bellamy's murder! Why, Rose? Why would they say that?"

I rest my forehead against the wall and close my eyes. "She told them," I say. My voice sounds like it's coming from far away.

"Who? Who told them what?"

A wave of vertigo overcomes me. If police from Pike Creek are here, and they already went to Emily's house, then that means she must have called them yesterday. Or maybe even earlier. That's why she was so insistent about getting my confession this morning. *Now, it's tomorrow, Rose. Tomorrow morning.* She had it all set up. She was never going to give me the money, or two days' grace. She was going to get my confession, then the police would arrive to arrest me. That's why she was so desperate to keep me there. That's why she smashed my face into the door. But I left anyway, and now she doesn't know where I am. And on all my official paperwork, I list my mother's address as my residence, which is why they went looking for me there.

"What did you tell them, Mom?"

"I told them the truth, that I don't know *where* you are."

"Do they have my phone number?"

"Well, yes! I gave it to them! What was I supposed to do? Albert says he's going to get you a lawyer. Do you need a lawyer, Rose?"

"Sorry, Mom, I have to go."

"But Ro——"

I hang up. I have to turn my phone off. "The cops are looking for me," I say to Lola.

"I got that."

She looks as pale as I feel. I try to shut my phone off completely but it's not happening. My hands are shaking too much, and right now I don't remember which buttons to press. "Emily told them," I say.

"I'm sorry, Rose, but you have to see this."

I look up. Lola is standing in front of me, staring at her cell phone. Whatever it is, it's bad. I can tell from the look on her face. I can't do any more bad. I'm so scared I'm going to vomit. I'm going to faint. I'm going to scream.

Lola lifts her phone to show me.

Frozen on the screen, is Emily. She looks small and vulnerable, her lips swollen, pearls of tears delicately hanging on eyelashes, one arm in a sling. It's the kind of look that makes grown men drop whatever they're doing and set off in long strides to climb up some tower somewhere.

I want to grab the phone and bite it.

Lola presses the play button.

"My dear friends, my fans. Something terrible has happened to me——" Emily's voice breaks. She looks away, and a delicate tear rolls down her porcelain cheek. She brushes it softly with her fingertips, takes a courageous breath, and turns back to the camera.

"A little over a week ago, a young woman came into my life. She called herself Iris. I met Iris at a book signing. She seemed so young, so innocent, and so very lost. And I can relate to that."

I'm biting my fingernails so hard I'm probably down to my knuckles already.

"Iris needed a place to stay for a few days. I told her she could stay here while she got back on her feet. Now, I know —" She raises a hand to shut us all up. "I'm too trusting. I know that. My friends warned me not to do it. But I believed Iris needed saving."

Emily flaps a hand in front of her face, air-drying the glistening tears. "Then, this morning, I went out early. I came home and found her in my room, going through my personal belongings. I confronted her. I told her that her behavior was unacceptable. She assaulted me." She raises her arm slowly, gingerly, like a war wounded, her little chin wobbling. "I tried to defend myself as best I could, but she ran off. She left her bag of belongings behind, and I went through it for a clue of where to find her, and you know what I found?"

She bends down then holds up the glass pyramid *Best Emerging Influencer* Award. "She was stealing from me."

I can feel Lola's gaze on me.

I scratch my head. "I might have," I mutter. "Only because I hate her."

Lola nods in my peripheral vision. "I totally get that."

Emily holds up various things in turn. The box inlaid with mother of pearl, the brass candle holder I should have used to hit her on the head, the gold ring with the blue stone, and even things I *didn't* steal. Like a picture of Emily in a silver frame I've never seen before, like I'd want *that*. That's how much of a megalomaniac she is. She actually put her framed photo of herself among the things I looted from her place.

"And then I found this." She holds up the receipt from the restaurant. *TO ROSE: ½ lobster mornay with staff discount: $20.*

I close my eyes briefly.

"I don't think her name was Iris," Emily says. She puts the receipt away.

"I thought Iris—sorry, I mean Rose—was shy because she *acted* shy. But you tell me, does this look shy to you?" She flicks through her phone then holds it toward the camera.

It's one of the selfies she took at Jack's Bar. She's front and center, and I'm in the corner of the shot, my face half obscured by my hair. I have one hand raised, cupping the side of my head.

"I don't think this is shyness," she says. "I think this is someone who has something to hide." She puts the phone down and comes close to the camera. "And I know what that is. That's why you assaulted me just now, Rose. Because I know too much." She shakes her head sadly. "Rose, sweetie, if you're watching this, I know who you are and the terrible thing you've done. Remember the four Rs? It's time for restoration, sweetie. Turn yourself in, Rose. It's better this way."

She turns off the camera.

I fold in two, wrap my arms around myself. "I'm dead."

Lola puts her phone down. "It gets worse."

"Oh, come on!"

"Hashtag *turnyourselfinRose* is trending."

"Really?" My heart is thumping. "That's quite a mouthful." I press my fingers against my eyelids. "I'm so dead. Oh God. Ben."

"What about Ben?" Lola asks.

"Emily met Ben, and she has the receipt from the restaurant. She knows where I work. They're closed for a couple days, but she must have passed on the information to the police." I sit down and text Ben with shaking fingers.

If the police contact you, you ,don't know where I am.

I'm about to turn it off, or I'm still trying anyway, when it rings.

I drop it like I've been burnt. It spins slowly on the coffee table, still ringing.

It's the police. I know it is. I reach for it, my hand shaking. I'm not picking up the call. I'm going to turn off my phone then I'm going to zap it in the microwave.

But Lola has already answered on speakerphone. "Hello?"

"Is this Rose?"

I look at Lola and shake my head. *No.*

"Who is this?" Lola asks.

"It's Amy Palmer."

I jump in. "Amy. It's Rose here. Can we talk? In person? Now?"

"Err… Yes," she says. She doesn't sound convinced. "Doris called me. We need to talk. I have some time tomorrow…"

"No, no. I can't wait that long. I need to talk to you now." I tell her where Ben's apartment is and suggest she come here. "And Lola is here too."

"Lola?" she blurts.

"Yes. It's imperative we speak to you, Amy."

"It's just that I—"

"I'm in trouble, Amy. It's about Charlene Bellamy."

A beat. "I understand. And yes, I can help you." And for a moment, I think I misheard. I stare at Lola. She raises her eyebrows.

"There's a Starbucks on Columbus Circle. I could meet you there in ten minutes. Alone, okay? Without Lola."

I look at Lola again. She looks surprised. Then she raises a hand. *It's fine.*

"I'll be right there," I say.

Finally, I manage to turn off my phone.

"You don't mind?" I ask Lola. "She says she can help me."

"No, it's fine. You go."

"Okay." I disappear into Ben's bedroom. I find a pair of aviator sunglasses and a Yankees cap. I shove my hair into it and pull it low over my eyes.

"I don't know why she wants to meet alone," I say when I return. But she's not there. I don't know where she is.

I walk out of the apartment.

CHAPTER 48

I walk quickly with my fists deep in my pockets and my cap low over my eyes. Amy is already seated when I get to Starbucks, spooning sugar into a cup. There's a small pot of tea in front of her along with a piece of cake with frosting on top.

I quickly slide on the chair opposite her. "Thanks for agreeing to see me," I say in a low voice.

She jumps, a look of horror on her face. I get it. Half my face is red and puffy. I'm wearing mirrored aviators and a baseball cap. I look like someone on the run from the authorities. Someone who comes with a "don't approach" warning. I slide my sunglasses to the top of my head. "Sorry. It's been a rough day."

"Hello, Rose."

She has the same straight blond hair in a high ponytail, bangs that come down to her blue eyes. She looks healthy, her cheeks glowing like red apples.

She asks how I am. I cross my arm on the table and lean forward. "I don't have time for niceties. I wanted to talk to you about Chet and Charlene Bellamy."

She nods. "Okay."

"Remember that last year I was at Pike Creek High? Yes? Some things happened. There are things you don't know, and I'll start there, okay?"

By now I've got the hang of telling my story. It's like telling someone the plot of a movie you've watched a hundred times.

I go through the major plot points. *Crush on teacher, teacher reads diary, teacher gaslights student, kills hamster, kills wife. Psycho Influencer finds diary, publishes book, blackmail.*

"I read it your book," she says. "*Diary of an Octopus.*"

I groan. "It's not my book. I mean, not really. Emily stole it from me and then changed it." Kind of.

Amy nods. She searches for something on her phone and holds out the screen. "This her?"

I wince. It's the video of Emily, the one she posted earlier.

"That's her."

"I thought Emily Harper was a pseudonym and that it was you."

"You're not the only one."

"I even wrote a comment on her Instagram, asking if she was you. It didn't make any sense. I could clearly see she wasn't you, but I thought, I don't know… that you had an arrangement or something."

I nod. I remember the comment I deleted in a panic. *Is this you, Rose?*

"I have to talk to you about Chet Bellamy," I say. "I'm sorry, truly. I know he was your husband—"

"Things got complicated."

"But the truth is, he did it. Chet Bellamy killed his wife and set me up to take the rap."

She bites her bottom lip. "He always maintained that you killed her but he couldn't prove it. He thought the chief of police was an idiot for suggesting the murder was tied to a robbery that never happened in the first place. He went to great lengths to convince Chief Craine. I think he even went to talk to your mother, but you had an alibi."

"I didn't do it, Amy. I swear to God. On my life."

She nods.

"But the police are looking for me." I grab her hands. "I'm desperate here. If I don't find anything to prove I didn't do it, then I have no choice but to go to the police voluntarily. Emily still has Mr. Bellamy's laptop, and there's a slim chance she hasn't deleted the SkyDrive yet. That's my only proof he was reading my diary. Also, I never touched Mrs. Bellamy. My DNA is not on the necklace that was used to strangle her. That means something, doesn't it? The problem is, I don't know if it's enough."

I bite the inside of my cheek. Who am I kidding? Of course, it's not enough.

Amy looks scared of me. I glance at her hands, realizing how tightly I'm squeezing her fingers.

"Sorry." I let go, rub my hands over my face. "Emily is telling everyone, as you can see," I jerk my chin at her phone, "that I attacked her. She's lying. She didn't stumble upon my real name. She always knew who I was. She's the psycho, not me. She drugged me with sleeping pills she keeps in her bathroom cabinet. She keeps a gun in her bedside drawer. She's nuts. I could have killed her a hundred times over if I wanted. And when you think about it, if I was truly guilty of killing Mrs. Bellamy and Emily had the goods on me as she claims…" I lower my voice. "Why pull her arm and leave her to tell her story? Surely I would have killed her, then disappeared, don't you think?"

She doesn't reply. She just stares at me. I sit back. "You said you could help me. Can you?"

She fidgets, looks around. "I'm sorry. I have to go to the

bathroom. I'm pregnant and it's making me pee every five minutes."

"You're pregnant?"

She stands, puts her hand on her belly. "Four months." She looks to the counter. "Did you want to order something?"

"No…but, not…" I let the question hang.

"Rose, please. Chet is in a home and can't even lift a spoon. Also, we're divorced."

"Sorry. Of course. Congratulations." I almost say, *on the divorce*, then stop myself just in time.

"Thank you. I'll be right back. Please wait for me."

Not that I have much choice. I glance around the room. I have a horrible feeling people are looking at me. Are they looking at me? Maybe it's the state of my face. I pull my cap lower and put my glasses back on, which probably makes me look even more suspicious. I wait, drumming my fingers on the table. Finally, Amy returns.

"Sorry," she says, taking her seat.

I glance around. The vibe I had before, about being watched, is gone. People are enjoying their coffee and chatting to each other.

I let out a breath. "Okay. What were you going to say?"

"The police reopened the case last year," she says.

"Mrs. Garcia told me. Do you know why?"

"Because of me. I found a letter from Charlene's mother to Chet. It was stuck on the bottom of one of his psychology books. She was extremely angry in that letter. She said she and her husband knew Chet had treated Charlene very badly. They knew he had affairs. They wanted Charlene to leave Chet, but she kept putting it off, hoping things would get better. And now she was dead. Helen—that's her name— wanted to know why Chet wouldn't get involved in the campaign they were running to find their daughter's killer. I don't think it was the first letter she wrote to him. I called her. She told me lots of things, terrible things. Like Charlene wasn't sick at all. And Helen and her husband hired a private investigator after their daughter died because they thought Chet's behavior was suspicious. They found out the life insurance Chet had taken out on his wife's life was recent, and a few weeks before her death, he'd been going to different doctors and getting a script for sleeping tablets at least twice a week. She told me, outright, her and her husband suspected Chet of killing their daughter. I told them what he'd said about you—"

"Thanks a lot."

"But she dismissed me. She said anything that came out of Chet's mouth was a lie. But you know…" She leans forward.

I hold my breath. "What?"

"I found empty bottles of Temazepam in his toolbox, years ago. I asked him about it because it was so odd, and he got angry with me. He told me never to go through his things again. So after I spoke to Helen, I got suspicious. I went to the police and told them what she'd told me. There's a new chief of police there now. Chief Walker. He's very good. He told me he was surprised by how little work his predecessor had done on the case. He brought Chet in for an informal chat—without mentioning me—and let me tell you, when Chet got home, he went crazy. He was banging the walls, calling Chief Walker names."

"Wow. This is amazing information. Do you have a number for Helen?"

She nods. "I'll forward it to you."

"Thank you. That'd be great." I cross my arms on the table. "So what happened then?"

"Chet changed. He became paranoid. I got scared of him. He swore to me he didn't kill Charlene, but he knew who had, and he could prove it. He just had to tie a few loose ends."

She stares at me. I feel the blood drain from my face. "Did he mean he could prove it was me? Because it wasn't—"

"No."

"No?"

"I went to stay with my parents. Then one day I was contacted by the hospital. I was still listed as his next of kin. He'd got hit by a car." She leans forward. "I don't think it was an accident."

"What?"

"It happened when he was coming back from Longstaff one night. Hit and run. No one saw a thing. He's in a very bad way. He spent three weeks in the hospital then straight to the nursing home. The staff got in touch one day, not long after he got there. He'd asked for me."

"I thought he couldn't speak?"

"He can't. But he could still write a little, with great difficulty. I went to see him."

My heart is pounding. I hold my breath. I am hanging on her every word.

"He was holding a piece of paper. The handwriting is hard to read. It was very difficult for him to hold the pen."

She opens her purse and hands me the piece of paper, folded twice. It's a small torn-off scrap. I unfold it, my stomach clenched. The handwriting is shockingly bad, and in a couple of places the pen has pierced the paper, but it's legible enough.

My heart slams against my ribs.

I look up. "Lola?"

CHAPTER 49

I've stood up so fast I've knocked the chair behind me. "What the hell is this?" I'm still staring at the piece of paper in my hand, the words dancing in front of my eyes.

IT WAS LOLA

"That's what he wrote."

"When?"

"Months ago. September."

"But what does it mean? What the hell does Lola have to do with anything?"

She looks at me, head tilted. "Lola isn't the most stable girl, Rose."

"What are you talking about?"

"She has a very jealous streak. You must know that. She was horrible to her sister Kimberlee, to the point where Kimberlee had to move away."

"That's not true! It was the other way around. Kimberlee made up stories about Lola to make her look bad!"

"I'm sorry Rose, but that's not what happened."

"How would you know?"

"I taught at that school for seven years, remember? I

know Lola's mother. I taught Lola and Kimberlee. I'm telling you, Lola was insanely jealous of Kimberlee to the point where Kimberlee moved away the moment she turned eighteen. I know it's hard to hear—"

"Even if what you say is true, and it's not, by the way, but even if it was, what does it have to do with Charlene Bellamy?"

"I don't know. But I know that Lola was very upset with you around that time. Am I wrong?"

"She had every right to be. I was a bad friend to her."

She cocks her head at me. "Why is she here, Rose?"

"She's helping me."

"How?"

"We're making calls. We're looking for proof. She's already been really helpful. She told me that she lied about me killing Pauly."

"Pauly?"

"The hamster. The class pet."

"Oh, sorry. That's right. I remember. She accused you of doing it. So that was a lie?"

"Yes, but she apologized. And it's not her fault. Mr. Bellamy made her do it."

"Or maybe she wanted you to get punished because she was angry with you."

"She admitted to that."

"She wanted to hurt you for being in love with Chet."

"What are you saying, Amy?"

"Where was Lola when Charlene died, do you know?"

"She was at the game! The whole time!"

"But how do you know?"

"She told me."

Amy looks at me like I'm an idiot. "She came to see you that day, before the game, didn't she? You wrote about it in your diary."

"So?"

"What if she followed you? What if she saw you go inside the house? Maybe she waited until you left and went in after you. Maybe she just wanted to know what you'd been doing there. She finds Charlene. Charlene isn't very well. She's in bed. I know this for a fact. I spoke to Doris at length about that night. Say Lola found her that way."

"So what?" I shout. People are looking at me now. Great.

"She lied about the school pet so you'd get the blame, Rose."

"And?"

"Don't you see? She killed Charlene to make it look like you did it. So you'd be punished. Really punished this time. She hated you, Rose."

"Okay. I'm done." I grab my purse, loop it over my shoulder.

"It's the only explanation," she says. "You know Chet didn't do it because a dozen people interacted with him at the game, myself included. Every minute of his time is accounted for. But somehow he found out who did it, and he wrote her name on that piece of paper. Lola did it, Rose. Lola killed her, so you would go to prison for a very long time."

"I don't believe you."

"Go home, Rose. Right now. Tell Lola to go back to Pike Creek. Trust me, she's not here for the right reasons. Once she's gone, let me know. I'll go to the police with you. I'll tell them everything I just told you."

She says other things, but I've stopped listening.

It's raining. I sit at a bus stop a block away, try to collect myself. I can't breathe. I rest my elbows on my knees and press my fingers against my temples, hard enough to stem the pulse of blood that feels like it's drowning my brain. I try to picture Lola strangling Charlene Bellamy, but I can't do it. It's too much. So I sit there and cry. A guy in a hoodie sitting next to me tells me to smile and that it's not that bad. I stand abruptly and kick him in the shin. He cries out, calls me a psycho, and hops away. I shout at him to smile. It's not that bad, I shout.

I walk back to Ben's apartment in the rain, my fists shoved deep in my pockets. I'm going to ask Lola, point-blank. And she'll laugh. I know she will. And I'll laugh too. We're going to laugh till we've got tears running down our faces because this is the stupidest thing anyone has ever said.

Lola is back when I open the front door. She's in the living room, scribbling in a notebook.

"How did it go?" she asks. "I talked with Bonnie. Remember Bonnie? She's totally on board. She had lots to say about Mr. Bell— what's wrong?"

I stand there, unable to move. I can feel the corners of my mouth pull down. Honestly, I don't know when I have ever felt so sad.

Lola has stood up. "What did she say? Is because of Emily's video? The second one?"

I blink away tears. "There's a second one?" I say. I'm confused now. I pull out my phone slowly, before remembering I've turned it off.

"Rose? What is it?" She's come right up to me. Then she notices something on the floor. "You dropped something…"

It's the piece of paper Amy gave me. It must have fallen out when I retrieved my phone. She picks it up.

"What is it?" she says, looking at me. I can't speak. She looks down at it. It's all scrunched up, and she opens it.

"It's a restaurant check," she says. She's looking at the

wrong side. I reach for it. I want to turn it around, to show her. My hand is shaking.

"Why are you so upset?" She frowns at the piece of paper. "Buffalo wings… nachos… potato salad… what is it? It's from yesterday." She looks at me again. "I don't get it."

I'm about to take it from her, to show her the other side, when the words finally reach my brain.

"From yesterday?" I snap, snatching the paper from her hand. I twist it around and stare at the date. My hand flies to my mouth.

And then I laugh. I laugh so much I can't speak. I'm crying. Lola's face relaxes, sort of.

"What the hell is going on? Tell me!"

"It's from yesterday!" I cry. I stab the top right corner of the torn-up restaurant check.

"I know! I said that. So what?"

I turn it around to show her.

Her eyes grow wide like saucers. "It was Lola? What the hell does that mean?"

I take off my cap and sit down, my heart clattering around my chest. I tell her exactly what happened with Amy. I relay every word of our conversation, explain how she went to the bathroom, and when she returned, she had this piece of paper upon which Chet Bellamy supposedly wrote *IT WAS LOLA*, with the last bit of strength he had in him. Months ago. Supposedly.

"She didn't need to use the bathroom. She went to write this on the first piece of paper she found in her purse! She tore off half a restaurant check! From yesterday!"

"But that's insane! Why would she do that?"

I press my fingers between my eyes. "She's protecting him. She lied about everything. She lied the whole time we were together. One minute she was saying Mr. Bellamy had accused me, and now suddenly it's you!"

"This is insane!" she says.

"I know."

She sits down too. "What's the last thing you said to her, before she went to the bathroom?"

I try to think. "That the police were looking for me. That Emily told them all this shit about me. That she's crazy, and if I truly wanted to shut her up, then why didn't I kill her? That—"

Lola raises a finger. "Wait. There's another video from Emily."

I frown. "Oh, right. You said that."

Lola loads it up on her phone.

"Okay, everyone," Emily says. She looks considerably more cheerful. "I have an update, but I can't say too much. It looks like something will happen very soon! I can't stay more right now… I wish I could!" She leans right up to the screen. "But see you soon, Rose. You're doing the right thing, sweetie."

"That's it?" I ask.

"That's it."

"What does it mean?"

"Something happened between the last video and this one," she says.

"Well, yes, I can see that, but what?"

"She thinks you're going over there."

My right leg starts to shake uncontrollably. "Amy didn't just use the time in the bathroom to write that note," I say.

"I think she called her," Lola says. "Does she have Emily's number?"

"I don't think so. But she could have messaged her on Instagram."

I hesitate, then pull out my phone and I turn it on again.

"What are you doing?" Lola asks. "I thought you didn't want to be contactable!"

"I've got Emily's Instagram login."

My phone pings with three missed calls and two messages. I ignore them. Literally. I avert my eyes. I just want to log in into Emily's Instagram account and check the direct messages.

And there it is.

Emily. My name is Amy. I used to teach Rose in high school. She wants to come and see you. She says she wants to do the confession and take the money. Call me on this number.

"Oh my God!" Lola shouts when I show her.

"I told Amy about the confession," I say. "I told her everything."

Lola stares at me. "What's the last thing you said before she went to the bathroom again?"

I blink. "That if I was truly guilty and Emily knew it, I wouldn't have just pulled her arm. I would have killed her."

Lola is on her feet. "She's gone to her apartment. Emily thinks she's bringing you, but she's not. She's gone to kill her."

"Oh my God!" My hand flies to my mouth. "That's great!"

She shakes my arm. "Rose! I know you hate her, but cut it out! She's gone to kill her and make it look like you did it! She's framing you!"

CHAPTER 50

We run. We run like we used to, faster than the wind with the rain on our faces. We run faster than anyone. We sure run faster than the traffic.

We slam ourselves against the door of Emily's building. I stab the code with my finger and we stumble inside. We walk up the stairs two by two, because I'm afraid of the noise the elevator might make. And only when we get to her door do I think, *What the hell are we supposed to do now?*

I still have Emily's key. Slowly, gently, I open the door, just enough to stick my head in.

Silence. There's no one here. Something catches my eye on the corner of the kitchen counter. A dead cat? Jesus. And then I hear footsteps upstairs. It must be Emily.

That's good, I guess.

I turn to Lola and whisper in her ear to have her phone ready to call the police, just in case. She nods, retrieves her phone. Then I tell to her to stay where she is, just outside the door.

I tiptoe inside, leaving the door ajar, and touch the

maybe dead cat. Except it's not a dead cat. It's a wig. A black wig, shaggy hair, not unlike my own, in fact.

"Emily?"

The footsteps upstairs stop abruptly. I freeze.

"Emily? Are you there?"

I look up the crazy floating steps just as her feet appear on the upper landing.

Except it's not Emily.

It's Amy.

And she has a gun. Emily's little pink-and-white gun.

And she's pointing it at me. She's shaking like a bird. The gun is shaking, too, which doesn't inspire confidence.

"You're not supposed to be here!" she says, her voice high and nervous. "Why are you here?"

"Where's Emily?"

"She's fine. She's having a nap."

I hear something behind me. Very subtle. A soft foot scraping the floor. I look over my shoulder. The gap through the front door is wider than before. I catch sight of Lola. She's got her phone facing out. She's still on the phone with the police. They're listening in.

"You left me no choice, Rose. It's all your fault," Amy says. "You kept asking me! How did he do it? How did he do it? I had to say something, so I said Lola did it." She purses her lips together, her fingers at her throat. "I had to do something to stop you two making calls like you did to Mrs. Garcia and stirring things up."

"I know you contacted Emily on Instagram and said you'd bring me to confess." I actually say all this for the benefit of the police on the call, so everyone is crystal clear. "You lied."

"Oh, who cares, Rose? When did you become Miss Goody-Goody?"

"What's the wig for?" I ask.

"I stopped at a drugstore on the way and got a cheap dark wig in case any CCTVs picked me up. I want it to look like it was you who came in here. I took it off in the elevator."

"What did you do to Emily?"

She blinks, her arm shaking. "Nothing yet. I asked to use the bathroom upstairs—she was giving me a tour of the place—and took her sleeping pills from the cabinet. You told me where they were, Rose. She offered me a glass of Prosecco, and I dropped the pills in hers when she wasn't looking. She's only just gone up. She's fast asleep."

"But why would you do this?"

"Because you! Rose! Should have been arrested for the murder of Charlene Bellamy. You were crazy enough to have done it, but your mother gave you an alibi, and everybody thought she was Saint Donna, so they didn't question it. Now you're stirring things up? You leave me no choice."

"You're going to kill Emily?" I shriek.

"No… You're going to kill Emily. You're going to strangle her. Just like you strangled Charlene."

"But I didn't!" I shout.

"Oh, I know that. I'm going to use this. I found it earlier. Is it yours? I hope it's yours." She holds up the belt of the dressing gown that was hanging behind the door of my bedroom. While it's not mine, I did wear it.

My heart is bouncing around my chest. "Did you hurt her?"

"Not yet. I was about to, but then you showed up."

"But why? Why are you doing this? Why are you protecting him?" I shout. "He killed his wife! Not me! You know that! You told me you went to the police with the letter from Helen! You told me that it was thanks to you that the case had been reopened!"

"I didn't go to the police. Helen did. Yes, there is a new

chief of police, that's true. And thanks to Helen, they are looking at Charlene's death again. It's why they brought Chet in for a chat." She sighs. She looks like she's going to cry. "It's unfortunate you've come, Rose…"

God, I wish the police were here already. But they're not, and I need to keep her talking.

"How did he do it?" I ask. "How did he kill her?"

She cocks her and looks at me like I'm an idiot, and it's like the air has been sucked out of the room. Time stands still for a moment, and the strangest thing happens. Charlene Bellamy's face pops into my head. Not the way she looked that day I went to her house—gaunt and sad and confused— but young and happy, hopeful, pretty. She cups her hand around her mouth and whispers in my ear, *Close the door.* And in that split second, I know what Amy is going to say. I swivel on my heels and slam the door in Lola's face.

"I just realized I'd left the door open," I blurt back at Amy. "You probably don't want that." And I am praying that Lola doesn't freak out and ring the doorbell. "What were you going to say?"

Amy blinks, confused, her arm outstretched and shaking. For a moment I think she's going to shoot me, but then she says, "Chet didn't kill Charlene, Rose. I did."

"Oh, God."

"I was very much in love with Chet. I still am. And he was very much in love with me too. But he would not leave his wife, and it was very confusing. I'd threaten to end things, and he would ask me to be patient, but you know… I think that's something some men do, to have their cake and eat it too. I was very young. And you know what I thought?" She narrows her eyes at me suddenly. "I thought he was in love with you. You with your big black eyes and your funny hair. And you were following him around everywhere like a duckling … but you were mad. You know that, don't you? You're

299

mad, Rose. You're insane. Everybody knew it except Chet. And you killed that hamster... I was so tired of waiting and being made a fool of. I thought maybe Charlene had money, and maybe that's why he wasn't leaving her."

She scratches her head.

"What did you do?" I ask.

"The night of the game I went to his house. I was going to talk to her, I swear to God, but then I saw you come out. Everything I told her earlier about Lola? About the scenario that might have happened? It was true. But it wasn't Lola, it was me. I saw you come out, and I waited a minute. Then I crouched down the side of the house and went in the back door so I wouldn't be seen.

"She was sitting in bed, asleep. She looked awful. The TV was on. She woke up when she saw me. She said something like, what's going on? Why is everyone in my house? She was wearing a leather braided lasso-style necklace around her neck. I thought of the hamster, how you strangled it with its bow tie—"

"I didn't—"

"And that's when I got the idea." She brushes a lock of hair out of the way. "I strangled her with it. Just like you did with the hamster—"

"I didn't!"

"But I pulled too hard. She made a gurgling sound and the necklace broke. She had her hand on her throat, like she was choking. I had to finish her off with my hands. I pressed my thumbs down on her windpipe. I'd never killed someone before. It's harder than it looks... Anyway. She was dead. I snuck back to the game, and that was that. Nobody questioned me. Why would I go and kill his wife? I'm a nice girl. A good girl. Unlike you, Rose, who everybody knew was a bad girl. An evil girl."

"You're the one who's evil!" I cry.

"That's not true. I did everyone a favor. I really believed she was sick because that's what Chet was telling me. I was helping, I was making things right for everyone. But your mother swore you were with her the whole time, and she was a well-respected member of the congregation, I'm told. And so it looked like nobody was going to solve the case. After a while, Chet stopped caring. I didn't care much either. But then Charlene's mother meddled, and the police opened the case again. And you know what Chet said when he came home after the chief of police spoke to him? He poured himself a bourbon and then he said, 'They're going to reanalyze everything. They have the necklace. They'll test it for DNA. They'll check the prints again. It's about time, Amy. It's about fucking time. They'll finally get Rose for this.' I panicked. I was young and foolish, and I didn't even think to wear gloves. I told Chet the truth. I said to him, 'You can't let them test for anything. And I won't give them my prints. You have to help me, Chet. We'll say Rose did it, and there's no need for DNA or anything! Rose did it!' And he looked at me, and you know what he said? This man I'd loved for so many years? He said, 'You can sort it out with the police yourself, Amy. I'm not getting involved. I didn't kill anyone.'"

There are tears streaming down her face. She wipes them with her free hand.

"He loved me. He really did. I was the love of his life! I was his perfect girl! I did it for him! For us! And now, after all these years, he was prepared to feed me to the wolves. I wasn't going to let him. He never saw the car. He didn't even know it was me. I was hoping to kill him, but somehow, I missed. He can't talk, but he can write. Very badly, but still. And if the police come too close to him, he will absolutely give them my name." She rubs her eyes with the back of her hand. "I did it for love, and look where that got me. You can't trust men. You really can't. And now, this!"

She sweeps her arm around. "You had to lose your diary, and Emily had to publish it. They'll talk to Chet. He'll give them my name. He'll write it down. They'll find my DNA… I'm not going to get caught for a little mistake I made ten years ago." She wipes her tears again, sniffles. "I can fix it now. It's unfortunate that you're here. That's going to complicate things." She sighs, looks at the gun. "You'll have no choice but to kill yourself after you strangle her, I guess. Maybe it's better this way. Either way, the case will be closed, and I can breathe easy."

A siren in the distance. Oh, thank you, God. Finally. My eyes don't leave hers. I'm about to say something else to keep her talking when something moves behind her.

On the upper landing, sneaking up behind Amy, a hand, crawling on the floor. The edge of a sleeve, a tuft of blond hair. Fingers moving, locking themselves around Amy's ankle, like a vise.

"Don't!" I shout. "They're coming!"

But it's too late. Emily has yanked Amy's ankle with all the strength she can manage on half a dozen Restorils. And when the gun goes off, for a second I think Amy shot me.

I'm shaking, my hands over my ears. There's the sound of fists pounding the door behind me. When I open my eyes, Amy is no longer on the top of those crazy stairs. She's on the floor, her head at a funny angle. It's a long way down, longer than it looks, but it's not enough to kill you. But hitting your head on the sharp corner of the coffee table on the way down, is.

I can't stop staring at the blood that's gushing all over the rug. Even when it reaches my toes, I don't move.

CHAPTER 51

People in uniform swarm the building. They wrap Lola and me in silver blankets and talk to us in the stairwell while officers go in and out of Emily's apartment. Emily has been taken away in an ambulance, but they assure us she will be fine. As if that's a good thing.

Amy, however, won't be fine. By the time the police arrived, she was already dead. Her body is still up there while detectives take our statement. It's going to take a long time to tell my story, but they got a chunk of it thanks to Lola's quick thinking keeping them on the phone all that time. That was the chunk before I slammed the door shut. Which I said must have happened because of a draft.

"So her husband, Chet, our English teacher, killed his first wife, and told Amy," I say. Lola doesn't even blink. She didn't hear that part. Emily did, but Emily was so out of it, I figured she didn't fully register who killed whom when and who gave an alibi to whom. I mean, at this point, even the police are confused.

"So yes," I say. "Amy said Mr. Bellamy strangled his wife. He told her later. He went there at half-inning, I think it was.

He told her he strangled his wife with the very necklace he'd given her, but it broke and he had to finish her off with his hands. His thumbs on her windpipe. That's what she said. Then he went back to the game. It's undeniable. He told her everything."

Under the blanket, Lola's knee presses against mine. I'm overdoing it. Got it. I scratch the back of my head. "Anyway," I say, "that's what Amy said. That Mr. Bellamy killed his wife."

The woman detective turns to Lola. "Did you hear Amy say this too?"

"The door slammed," I say quickly.

But Lola has already started to reply. "Yes. I had my ear against the door. I heard everything." She repeats pretty much everything I just said. "She said Mr. Bellamy killed his wife. He strangled her with the necklace he bought her, but it broke, and he finished her off by pressing his thumbs on her windpipe."

I gently press my knee against hers. *Thank you. I love you.*

Lola didn't know why I'd slammed the door before Amy had a chance to reveal who had killed Charlene Bellamy, but she knew I had my reasons.

The moment Amy opened her mouth to say *how he did it*, I understood, instinctively, that *she* had done it. I knew what Amy was going to say before she said it. *He didn't kill her. I did.* Which meant Chet Bellamy would get away with everything. Reading a student's diary is not against the law. He never touched me inappropriately. The worst thing I might have pinned on him was that he killed a hamster, and even then, I couldn't prove it.

I couldn't let that happen. Chet Bellamy deserved to go to hell. Charlene Bellamy deserved nothing less.

. . .

I've never been inside a prison, and when the heavy doors are drawn shut behind me, I get a whiff of what might have been. It could have been me. It was *almost* me. And I can tell already I wouldn't have liked it much.

And this isn't even a real prison. I mean, it is, but it's not where the general population is incarcerated. It's a kind of prison for people who can't feed themselves, let's say.

I walk into the visitors' area. It smells of male sweat and bleach. I sit at a booth and wait. Five minutes later, the door opens on the other side of the glass and Chet Bellamy gets wheeled in by a prison guard.

I burst out laughing. He looked pretty bad during the trial, but this is next-level. He looks about a hundred and three, hunched over in his crappy wheelchair that looks like it's being held together with duct tape. Whatever hair he has left is plastered down on his skull in greasy clumps. His face is gaunt, his green eyes are dull and bloodshot. He is a hollow man. A husk.

I send a prayer of gratitude toward Amy that she didn't kill him when she ran him down. Because this man looks like he's in hell.

The prison guard picks up the phone, wedges it in the crook of Chet's neck, roughly pushes Chet's head sideways to secure the phone against his ear, and leaves. And only then does Chet look at me.

"How are you, Mr. Bellamy?" I say. "You look good! Orange is totally your color. It makes your skin look pallid! I like it!"

There's a glint in his eyes. Like an awakening, a glimmer of hope. As if I've come to make things right. As if I'm still in love with him and would do anything for him. And I'm thinking, wow, you're even more far gone than I thought. I was a witness for the prosecution at his trial. I'm the one who said Amy told me that he'd admitted to strangling his first wife, and how. And Lola backed me up.

And here's the clincher. Actually, there are two clinchers. The first one is that by the time the trial rolled on, Chet Bellamy could no longer write anything. Amy literally went through all this trouble for nothing. She should have waited. But here we are.

But the *other* clincher, the most beautiful clincher of all, is that normally, whatever Amy said shouldn't have been admissible. You can't go around saying so-and-so told me that so-and-so killed his wife and expect justice to be served.

Except Amy said one thing that nobody knew, other than the police, and they hadn't told anyone. Whoever killed Charlene Bellamy first used the necklace, and then strangled her with their hands. Only the killer would know that. Everybody else had been led to believe that Charlene had been killed with the necklace. And that one detail was enough to overcome the objection to *hearsay*. It's got a technical name, too. *Sufficient indicia something.* Or something. I've got a technical name for it too:

Thank you, Miss Amy. Now crawl back to hell.

Sure, there was some argument that Amy knew that particular detail because she killed Charlene herself, but the jury didn't buy it. Lola and I testified as to what Amy had said, and we were considered reliable witnesses. Go figure. Then there were the testimonies of Charlene's parents, and the detective they'd hired, and my mother, and a bunch of people who had not nice things to say about Chet Bellamy, including about how he'd treated me.

And then there was Chet's supposedly ironclad alibi. But part of that alibi had relied on Janice Morales, the then school principal, because Chet Bellamy had gone missing for a little while. He was talking to Mrs. Morales near the exit.

Mrs. Morales had since retired to Florida, but she returned for the trial. She said she could tell that as they were talking, Chet Bellamy was itching to get away. She described him as fidgety and impatient. She'd met him right at the beginning of the break, but now she wasn't so sure. Could it have been later? Had he gone out, and back again? That was possible, she said with a shrug. She couldn't remember. She couldn't tell at the time either, but later Mr. Bellamy had told her what to say. And he could be so convincing…

And then, finally, there was Doris Garcia. I went to see her before the trial to tell her everything that had happened. She's almost blind now. It was the strangest thing, sitting in that house, next door to where Mrs. Bellamy died.

Mrs. Garcia listened to my story as we drank tea and ate cookies she'd baked, and I was pretty sure she'd accidentally swapped the sugar for salt, but I ate them anyway.

This will come as a surprise to anyone who knows me, but I don't like lying for no reason. Not anymore, anyway. I told Mrs. Garcia that Amy had said Chet Bellamy had killed his wife, and how, but the way she squinted at me, I could tell she knew something was amiss.

She patted my hand. "I never liked him. Everybody else did, but I never did. I could smell the devil on that man. And I didn't like the way he treated Charlene."

She narrowed her eyes at me. "You know, I never told anyone this, because I was very scared of him." She said this in the tone of someone who is scared of nothing and nobody. "But I'm pretty sure I saw him come back that night, even though he was supposed to be at the game. Only for a few minutes. I didn't want to say anything at the time. I'm just an old woman… But he's not going to hurt me now, so I can speak up."

My eyes watered, and she winked at me. We hugged for a long time, and then we toasted our tea to Charlene Bellamy.

Doris Garcia was a star witness for the prosecution.

I have to laugh again as I stare at Chet Bellamy's eager face, if that face could ever be called eager. Still, you can taste the excitement trying to come through behind those eyes. He thinks he can get to me. He thinks it's everybody else who put him there. He thinks I'm going to save him.

He opens his mouth, an effort that clearly costs him. I gaze idly around the room, drumming my fingers on the ledge while he makes a superhuman effort to form the word. *Aaammmmyyyy*.

"You're trying to say something? Sorry, I can't hear you. Is this thing on?" I bang my phone on the ledge. He winces at the noise in his ear, so I do it again. "You want to write something down? Oh wait, that's right. You can't."

Chet takes another shot. *Aaammmmyyyy*.

"Oh!" I slap my hand on the ledge. "I know what you're trying to say! Amy. You want to tell me something about Amy!"

He blinks a million times.

"You want to tell me…it was Amy…" *blinkblinkblinkblink*, "who…killed…" *blinkblinkblinkblink*, "Charlene! I think I got it! Amy killed Charlene, not you! Did I get it? Is that it?"

blinkblinkblinkblink.

"Ohhh! So she lied to me when she said you did it! That's what you want to tell me!"

blinkblinkblinkblink.

"Huh, that's too bad. And now you're in here." I look around the room again then put the phone down and lean forward.

"She didn't lie," I mouth slowly. Hey, I've seen the movies. I know they record everything on those phones. I know all the tricks. "She told me," I mouth . "I know."

His face falls—or would, if it could—with the dawning realization that it's not a mistake that he's in prison for a murder he didn't commit.

It was deliberate.

"Anyway, I just came to say hi." I get up. "And this one's for Charlene." I raise the phone for a toast, then I let it drop and walk out.

CHAPTER 52

I rarely read my horoscope anymore, but I did this morning.

It said, *The past is a nice place to visit, but don't go buying real estate there. It's overrated. The future is better.*

I like that. I think of it as I stand outside Barnes & Nobles on Fourteenth Street, my legs a little shaky, my heart a little racy.

"That looks amazing, Rose," Ben says behind me. I smile at him then put my hand on the window like I could touch my book. Not the old one. *Diary of an Octopus* is no longer for sale, thank God. Sure, you can pick up a secondhand copy somewhere, and people do. That used to bother me. I wanted every existing copy to be pulped to dust because it was never *my* book. It was Chet's version of my life, in a way, and then Emily's.

But I'm over that now. I've got my own book. *Good Seeds*, it's called. My publisher wanted to call it *Bad Seeds*, but I told him to get lost.

It tells a different story. And that story shows how easy it is to make children believe they are evil. And trust me on this: once children believe they are bad, they'll *become* bad. This stuff is self-fulfilling.

My mother, with whom I have become close again, tells me I once was a kind and happy child. Then she'll add, *before*. That's how we refer to our lives now. *Before*, and *after*. We don't need to say anything else. We know what we're talking about. For a long time, I had no memory of being either happy or kind. Everything *before* had taken on a murky, distant quality and held no interest to me.

Shortly after I found out I was pregnant, Ben and I went to visit my mother and Arthur for the weekend to tell them the news. They were over the moon. It was a truly wonderful day. Later, over dinner, my mother casually asked what we might want to do while we were here. Then she did what she always does when she's excited: she asked questions and answered them in the next breath. Would we like to go to the Burgdorff Performing Arts Center? There's always something fabulous on. What is she saying? Of course *I'd* like that. I've always loved theater and music. Always. Such a pity I didn't pursue it. I had such talent.

Ben was grinning at me, one eyebrow raised, and I was thinking, do I have a sibling I've forgotten about? Because I had no idea who she was talking about.

But then a twinkle of something. A sliver of light, like a tiny shaft through the bottom-dwelling dark recesses of my memory. Then an image, blurry and sepia-faded: little me dressing up for a Christmas pageant spectacular that I'd designed and scripted, which I put on in our living room, complete with cardboard judges who unanimously awarded me first place in every category. Me, at the Tiny Tot Theater Club, clutching a bouquet of paper flowers to my chest and smiling sweetly through my fifth curtain call to the dismay of my teachers trying to get me off the stage. Me again, dressed up like a pirate and refusing to remove my eyepatch for a week.

I'm getting to know that *before* version of myself again. And I like her. I could say I like her more than I like the *after* version of me, but that would be a lie. There's a lot I don't like about *after* Rose, but I'm also a little in awe of her spirit. And sure, I lost ten years of my life through circumstances that weren't entirely out of my control, but I'm happy now. I'm so happy I could burst. Some days I feel like an inflatable balloon, one of those marketing ones, custom-made to look like the company's mascot. Some days I feel like if I was any happier, I'd have to be tethered or I'd float away. Everything in my life is joy. Ben and I are getting married next spring. Our son Sam was born four months ago, and he's perfect.

And hey, I'm one of the good girls now. Watch me grin! I'm doing it again! That grinning thing! I get to pick out babies' names and nursery wallpaper and vacation destinations, and I would never, *ever*, take the money.

I turn around and smile at Ben again. Sam is asleep on his chest in a sling. I kiss his little cheek.

"It looks good, doesn't it?" I say.

He beams proudly. "It looks great, babe."

I wrote *Good Seeds* when I became pregnant with Sam. I thought he might want to know, one day, why his mother thought she was a murderer. I figured it was time to tell my story my way.

I did a lot of research to understand why I believed the things I did, why I was prepared to confess to crimes I never committed, and I was astonished to find I was far from unique. Most people are highly suggestible under the right conditions. It's not hard to plant false memories if you know what you're doing. I've read of experiments where volunteers thought they were recalling childhood events in vivid detail, like getting lost in a shopping mall and being returned to their parents by a security guard, or almost drowning, then were astounded to learn it never happened.

And today is my book launch in the same bookstore where I first came across *Diary of an Octopus*. Lola is coming with her boyfriend Derek—a fireman, hot—who clearly adores her. My mother and Arthur will be there, of course. Also, my mother realizes now that when it came to Lola and Kimberlee, she was relying on outdated intel. Since then Kimberlee has moved all over the country and got in trouble everywhere she went. There was even an old boyfriend who took out a protective order against her.

But Kimberlee is better now, or that's what she says. Still, nobody is under any illusion about her anymore. Also, everybody thinks Lola was an angel to put up with so much.

So that's nice.

Ben's parents are here, too, and his sister Joyce, Liam, and even Pip, who has become a good friend.

I haven't invited my father—we have barely communicated in ten years, so what would be the point—and Emily is unlikely to show up because she's in jail. Turns out that stealing someone else's book and passing it as your own is *not* a crime, but trying to get your confession in exchange for ten thousand dollars is extortion. Smashing a door in your face to stop you from leaving the house is assault and deprivation of liberty. She got the minimum sentence, so she'll be out soon. And the other day I read in a magazine that she is planning a podcast titled *Emily In Purgatory*, about all the bad things she did and how she's moving forward and forgiving herself. You've got to hand it to her for single-minded determination.

And when she comes out of prison, she is not to come within five hundred feet of me. Forever. (*Yes!*)

I said to Ben after her trial, "If I hadn't come when I did, she'd be dead by now. I spent over a week fantasizing about killing her, and in the end, I'm the one who saved her life."

"Yes, well," he'd said, drawing me to him and resting his chin on my head. "You're the savior of rats." But then he added, "And she saved your life, too…"

I looked up at him. "Oh, come on! Because Amy had the gun? Because she made her fall?"

"No. Because she burst the whole story open."

He had a point.

Lola has arrived. She throws her arms around me, then covers Sam's cheeks with kisses, then gushes at Ben, and I'm just beaming. I'm so happy I'm floating. I need to be tethered.

I take Ben's hand.

"You ready?" Ben asks.

"I'm ready," I say.

I'm so ready. I can't wait. Because once I've launched *Good Seeds*, I can let it all go. I just want to be Rose *after, after.*

Lola takes my other hand, and we walk into the bookstore. I think of my horoscope again—the short version.

The past is overrated. The future is better.

ACKNOWLEDGMENTS

Writing a book isn't necessarily the solitary pursuit you might think. Several people have contributed to making *Finders Keepers* the best book possible, and my first and loudest 'thank you' goes to my brilliant editor, Traci Finlay! Traci, I don't know how you do it, but you always manage to bring out the best in a story—and get rid of the worst. So, thank you again, from the bottom of my heart.

Thank you to Mark Freyberg for always being on hand to answer my legal questions. And Mark, thank you especially for suggesting a solution to my legal problem. Rose and I are very grateful for your help.

Thank you to veteran Police Detective Adam Richardson and the excellent people in the Writer's Detective Bureau Facebook group for answering my questions and for all your spot-on suggestions. I've relied on you all before so it's high time I include you in these pages.

My family and my wonderful friends, thank you for your never-ending enthusiasm. Thank you as always to my husband for keeping me fed and watered when I've got my head down, for reading my books and for saying all the right things. My wonderful friend and writing buddy Debra Lynch for being such an amazing and supportive person.

And thank you, dear reader! I'm thrilled you picked up *Finders Keepers*. It means the world.

Natalie

ALSO BY NATALIE BARELLI

Finders Keepers

Unforgivable

Unfaithful

The Housekeeper

The Accident

The Loyal Wife

Missing Molly

After He Killed Me (The Emma Fern Series Book 2)

Until I Met Her (The Emma Fern Series Book 1)